Dragon's Gate

GOLDEN MOUNTAIN
CHRONICLES: 1867

Outside, even at night, there is some kind of faint light from the stars. Light had never before entered this deep in the mountain, though. The walls seemed to suck up not only the heat but the light as well. If I paused, I felt almost as if the very darkness would swallow me up forever. The hardest thing to shake was the feeling that we shouldn't be there at all.

Shadowy men worked in the dim light, breath steaming from their mouths as they used hammers and chisels to smooth the walls. At the point where the tunnel began to narrow, men swung pickaxes to widen it chip by chip.

"This is like a battlefield," I said to Father.

"It's war," he grunted. "Because the mountain can kill you in a dozen different ways before you can blink an eye. And victory is twenty centimeters a shift."

Also by
Laurence Yep

The Dragon Prince
Dream Soul
The Imp That Ate My Homework
The Magic Paintbrush
The Rainbow People
The Star Fisher
Sweetwater
Tongues of Jade

Golden Mountain Chronicles
The Serpent's Children
Mountain Light
Dragon's Gate
A Newbery Honor Book
The Traitor
Coming soon
Dragonwings
A Newbery Honor Book
The Red Warrior
Coming soon
Child of the Owl
Sea Glass
Thief of Hearts

Chinatown Mysteries
The Case of the Goblin Pearls
Chinatown Mystery #1
The Case of the Lion Dance
Chinatown Mystery #2
The Case of the Firecrackers
Chinatown Mystery #3

Dragon of the Lost Sea Fantasies
Dragon of the Lost Sea
Dragon Steel
Dragon Cauldron
Dragon War

Edited by Laurence Yep
American Dragons
Twenty-Five Asian American Voices

LAURENCE YEP

Dragon's Gate

金山

GOLDEN MOUNTAIN
CHRONICLES: 1867

HarperTrophy®
An Imprint of HarperCollinsPublishers

Harper Trophy® is a registered trademark of
HarperCollins Publishers Inc.

Dragon's Gate

Library of Congress Cataloging-in-Publication Data
Yep, Laurence.
   Dragon's gate / Laurence Yep.
      p.   cm.
   Summary: When he accidentally kills a Manchu, a Chinese boy is sent
to America to join his father, an uncle, and other Chinese working to
build a tunnel for the transcontinental railroad through the Sierra
Nevada mountains in 1867.
   ISBN 0-06-022971-3 — ISBN 0-06-440489-7 (pbk.)
   I. Chinese—United States—Juvenile fiction.   2. Railroads—
History—Sierra Nevada Mountains—Juvenile fiction.   [I. Chinese—
United States—Fiction.   2. Railroads—History—Sierra Nevada
Mountains—Fiction.]   I. Title
PZ7.Y44Dqr   1993   92-43649
[Fic]–dc20   CIP
                                                                AC

Typography by Karin Paprocki
First Harper Trophy edition, 1995
❖
Visit us on the World Wide Web!
www.harperchildrens.com

14 15 16 CG/OPM 40 39 38 37 36 35 34 33

To Charlotte Zolotow,
who helped me
through my own gates

Thirty years ago, I began writing stories about one family, the Youngs of Three Willows Village, and their many friends. In those pages, I tried to chronicle their ongoing love affair with the Land of the Golden Mountain, or America—a love that has lasted over one hundred fifty years.

The first Youngs came to the Golden Mountain because they had no choice: It was the only way for their families in China to survive (*The Serpent's Children* and *Mountain Light*). However, their children realized that the Golden Mountain was—despite hardship and death—their destiny (*Dragon's Gate*). And so the third generation was actually born upon the Golden Mountain, sinking their roots inextricably into American soil—despite the attempts of hostile American mobs to tear up those roots (*The Traitor*).

The Youngs and their friends stayed even when the many rural Chinatowns that had once covered the West were destroyed and Chinese America itself had shrunk to a few small enclaves in cities like San Francisco. However, that didn't stop a new generation from immersing itself in American thought and technology in order to achieve its dreams (*Dragonwings*).

More than everything else, the Youngs and their friends were adaptable, even organizing their own professional basketball team to leave San Francisco's Chinatown and barnstorm across the country (*The Red Warrior*). However, some went too far and became so American that they lost track of the Chinese part of their identity and had to discover it again (*Child of the Owl*). And they changed once more when they discovered that the attitudes that had enabled them to survive over a hundred years of hardships and dangers no longer worked (*Sea Glass*).

Ultimately, the latest generation—which is only half-Chinese—faces the greatest challenge, for it has to redefine what it is to be a Chinese American (*Thief of Hearts*).

It has been my privilege to write about seven generations of the Young family and their friends, and how they have transformed the Golden Mountain and been transformed in turn. These books represent my version of Chinese America—in its tears and its laughter, its hungers and its fears, and in all its hopes and dreams.

☷☵

K'UN, the second hexagram of
the *Book of Changes*

"Thick ice comes; dragons struggle
in the wasteland."

PREFACE

By the summer of 1865, the North has finally defeated the South in the Civil War, and America works for even greater union. During the war, Abraham Lincoln set in motion a plan to build a transcontinental railroad that will effectively join the western half of America to the eastern half. In 1863, one railroad, the Union Pacific, has begun building westward from Omaha. In that same year, the Central Pacific has started eastward from California. However, in two years, it has only built thirty-one miles of track. By February 1865, the railroad is so desperate that it has begun experimenting with using Chinese crews.

At the same time, in China, the boy emperor has survived two more challenges to the rule of his people, the Manchus—a barbarian tribe that has controlled the kingdom for some two hundred years. His generals have crushed two different rebellions. One is the Taiping, or Great Peace, revolt, which has devastated wide areas of China. The other is the Red Turban uprising in southern China in Kwangtung Province, in which over a million people have died during the Manchu suppression.

Seeking revenge for the Manchu reprisals, the local clans in turn have started a genocidal war against an ethnic group known as the Strangers because it is believed the Strangers have provided information and aid to the Manchus. It is estimated that half of the three hundred thousand Strangers have died.

As a result of the turmoil, Chinese men have left Kwangtung in ever-increasing numbers for America.

CHAPTER | I

*The sixth month of the third year of
the era all in order, or July 1865.
Three Willows Village, Toishan County,
Kwangtung Province, China.*

"They're coming!" the servant cried from the pass. "They're coming!" The cry traveled up the valley faster than the stream.

"They're coming!" the sentry announced from the watchtower.

All over the village of Three Willows, doors and gates slammed as people tumbled into the street. It was a clear day between summer storms, and the sky was a bright blue.

In the schoolroom, I could hear the slap of their feet on the dirt. Though I was only fourteen, I sat in the back of the schoolroom with the older boys because I was ahead of my level. I rose eagerly from the school bench.

At the front, Uncle Blacky, our teacher, was lecturing about some ancient words that might occur in the government exams. The exams would qualify you for office.

He was a slender, middle-aged man in a scholar's robes. There were small black marks on his lips, for he had an absentminded habit of licking his brushes to a point. "Yes, Otter."

"Master, may I be excused?" I asked. "I think my father and uncle have arrived."

"Of course." What else was he going to say? Most of the subscription for his new school had come from my own family.

When I got ready to run excitedly, he looked at me sternly. "With dignity," he reminded me. That look was enough to intimidate my other classmates, but not me.

"I'm sorry, master." I started to walk away.

Behind me, I heard Stumpy laugh. He was the sixteen-year-old son of one of our tenants, and he was always trying to play the bully or to mock me when he thought it was safe.

When he wasn't playing one of his pranks, I almost felt sorry for him. His father, Stony, often needed Stumpy in the fields. As a result, Stumpy's schooling was sporadic;

but he was sharp enough to make up for the lost time.

Immediately, Uncle Blacky strode down the aisle and grabbed Stumpy's frayed collar. "You should thank Heaven for people like Foxfire and Squeaky. Without their sacrifices, we'd all be starving."

As he lifted Stumpy to his feet, his son, Cricket, brought him his bamboo rod. A young man in his twenties, Cricket acted as his father's assistant while he pretended to study for the government exams.

Uncle Blacky shook the boy as though he were a rat. "I'll teach you some manners, you little pig. Hold out your hand."

Reluctantly, Stumpy held out his hand, palm upward. There were two groups of boys in our school: those whose fathers had stayed here and those whose fathers had gone overseas to *America* to become guests of the Land of the Golden Mountain, as everyone called it. The difference was often between the poor and the rich. Since the guests paid for the school, their sons led a privileged life. The other boys, though, were fair game.

Determined to do the right thing, I turned. "It was my fault, Master. You should hit me."

"Why can't you be a gentleman like Otter?" Uncle Blacky asked. He gave Stumpy six of the best across his palm, even though I had been the insolent one.

As he sat down, I whispered, "I'm sorry."

Stumpy rested his hand on the table but would not look at me. "I'm used to it."

I felt bad because I could see some of the boys cringing—the ones whose fathers had stayed here. Uncle Blacky might give them six for not volunteering to answer a question; or even if they did, he might punish them if he judged their response a poor one.

What do you do when your family is so powerful that you lead a charmed life and even your teacher won't find fault with you? I tried to bring candy treats on different occasions for all my classmates. The poorer boys were lucky to get a bite of meat in an entire year, let alone taste sugar. And of course, on festivals, I used my allowance to buy toys and firecrackers for everyone. So I don't think they held it against me that Uncle Blacky treated me as his pet. The other guests' sons led just as protected a life.

Despite Uncle's bamboo rod, the school began to buzz with excitement behind me. When other guests came home, there were banquets and celebrations; but none of them could match one of Uncle Foxfire's homecomings. While Father and Uncle were home, life was one long festival of banquets and entertainments and fireworks displays.

I went out of the school into the little courtyard

where porcelain stools sat in the shade of a tree. The entire setting was also the result of my family's donations. My mother was generous with everyone but herself.

As I stepped into the village's main street, I met my mother, Cassia, striding along, too impatient to be carried along in a sedan chair as her sister-in-law wanted her to do. As the clan said, Mother still had mud between her toes.

Mother was tugging self-consciously at her jade necklace. It was her one piece of jewelry—and it had taken Father an entire evening of arguing to make her keep it. Her blouse and pants were clean but plain.

"Look at you." She frowned. "Dirty already." Seizing my arm, she made me stop in the middle of the street. Then, to my chagrin, she began brushing off my clothes as if I were still a child.

For the homecoming, the Lion Rock lady—Mother referred to her sister-in-law, Uncle Foxfire's wife, only as "that Lion Rock woman"—had insisted on new clothes for herself and her son, whom everyone called the Little Emperor. She had taken me along as well when we went to her hometown, Lion Rock, which was the market town for our area.

As we passed by the banquet hall, I saw that folks

were already sweeping off the wide porch. The tables and benches were all set out, and the columns and rafters had been freshly painted. The hall had been built five years ago for just such a purpose as this.

In fact, all of Three Willows had been spruced up, and anything that needed a new coat of paint had received one—and the bill was presented to Mother. With the smell of fresh paint tickling my nose, I had gone about pretending that the homecoming was for me.

As we merged with the excited clanspeople, I grinned at Mother. "Are you excited?"

She smiled back. "Are you?"

"Yes," I said, but I couldn't have told her how much. When I was small, I would ask Mother why she had adopted me. And she would stop whatever she was doing, put me on her lap and tell me, "The astrologers say you were born in the hour of fire on the day of fire in the month of fire, so you were bound to join my family, because we've been rebels and troublemakers for seven generations."

Some two centuries ago, a barbarian tribe called the Manchus came thundering down from the north to conquer the Middle Kingdom, or *China*, as it's called in the Land of the Golden Mountain. For two hundred years, our family has been trying to drive them off the dragon throne; and we have paid the price with our blood and our souls.

To hear my mother tell it, when we've carried out the Work, as she calls it, the Middle Kingdom will enter a new age. The universe will be balanced once more, and we will live in harmony and peace with one another.

By the time Mother was finished, I was convinced that once the Work was complete, rice would grow faster. Even the sky would be bluer. And she and I and Uncle and Father were put on this earth to carry out the Work.

As guests of the Golden Mountain, Father and Uncle earned the money that let us further the Work here. And they met with other rebels overseas to make all sorts of plans.

In fact, my Uncle Foxfire had been the first to leave Three Willows some ten years ago. He was famous in the clan not for what he had done for the Work but for his knack of finding gold in places where no one else could. The more superstitious believed that it was magic. They said he had found some object that turned stones into gold. Others thought he had developed some sixth sense that let him smell the nuggets. The more philosophical thought he had some special power of dreaming—that at night the gold would whisper to him and tell him where the various pieces were.

Mother said it was intelligence and not magic that had created his success. However, when she told that to the superstitious folk, they only thought she was covering something up.

I'm afraid that when I was small, I believed all the stories about him—and more because many of the other fairy tales I heard became entwined with his story. There were various times when I had believed he could: 1) fly, 2) kill tigers bare-handed and 3) call upon dragons as his friends.

And somehow I pictured that one day he would return from the Golden Mountain to finish the Work and drive out the Manchus. And when he did, Father and Mother and I would be right by his side.

In the meantime, the clan elders had collected by the gates. Uncle Pine, the oldest of the elders, was rehearsing his speech, his lips moving as he mumbled softly. Everyone was dressed in holiday finery. The actors and acrobats and even the man with the trained monkey were there as well to watch the spectacle.

Halfway up one side of the valley, Three Willows sat behind its ancient brick wall. To the left and right were orchards and terraced fields, while down below, on the valley floor, the rice fields gleamed among the dikes like bits of polished shell in a wooden lattice. And along the dirt dikes I saw a procession of people the size of ants.

The Lion Rock lady made quite an entrance in a sedan chair borne by servants. And when she stepped out of the chair, she wore an elegant robe embroidered with birds, and her hair had been wrapped around an elaborate wire frame. Bright semiprecious stones and pearls had been hung among her tresses. Her son, my cousin, tagged along behind like a miniature peacock.

"She looks like her head rammed a trellis," Mother whispered disapprovingly to me.

There was nothing wrong, though, with the hearing of that Lion Rock lady. Her plucked eyebrows formed an irritated wedge. "How splendid you look today, my dear. Why, you'd think you were selling your prize pig."

Bristling, Mother gathered herself for one of her lectures on waste, but Aunt Diligence shoved between them. "How happy you must be to be united with your husbands."

Both Mother and her sister-in-law remembered their manners. "Yes," Mother said.

"Quite," the Lion Rock lady agreed, and her features became as smooth and cold as those of a marble statue.

Over the gate, two men hastily unfurled a welcome banner, while above the gate, people lined the walls for a glimpse of the two fabled heroes. "They're here!" someone shouted.

I stood on my toes as if that would help me see better. I had been ten when they had last visited the village, and I remembered that their homecoming was worthy of kings. And they didn't disappoint me this time. The procession was led by musicians, in robes as brightly colored as parrots, who played horns in a triumphant air. Next came a pair of men staggering beneath the weight of a trunk hanging from a pole between them. And behind them stumbled more such pairs carrying more trunks and baskets. Finally came the chairs, gilded and lacquered and fit for an emperor.

When Father and Uncle climbed out of their chairs, I saw that beneath their elegant embroidered silk robes, they were wearing heavy western boots of leather rather than normal shoes. They were boots for storming the gates of Heaven. And as the roar went up from the village, they stood there, hands on their hips, mighty as lords.

CHAPTER | II

There were more lines on Father's face and his skin was as dark as leather, but he had the same easygoing smile. He swept off his hat and called to Mother. "Hey, old woman, who died?"

"Our fortune." Mother pointed at the new banner. "We paid for that thing." The neighbors, and my own parents, would have considered it unseemly to display affection in public.

"Really." The Lion Rock lady sniffed disapprovingly. She tottered forward on her bound feet, a maid on either side ready to give her support. "Welcome home, my gallant husband." She often spoke as if she were a character from the romance novels that a servant had to read to her—she herself could neither read nor write.

Uncle Foxfire nodded sheepishly to her. Then he and Father had to endure all the praise the elders lavished on them, using the flowery formal language reserved for such occasions. All the while, Father fidgeted along with Mother, eager to reach the privacy of our home so they could speak their true feelings.

However, that wasn't to be for a while, for they had to get back into their chairs so they could be carried up to Uncle Foxfire's mansion. Mother insisted on walking beside Father, and I kept pace beside her.

As they neared his house, Uncle leaned out of his chair to look back at Mother. "Did you ever think we'd own the Golden Cat's house?"

"Frankly"—she sniffed—"I always thought it was too flashy."

As Uncle laughed and his head disappeared inside once again, I asked Mother, "Who's the Golden Cat?"

"He used to be the richest man in the clan," Mother explained.

"He never had half of what we have," Father said proudly.

I folded my arms as I walked along. "What happened to him?"

Mother frowned at the house the way she always did. "He was a fossil who refused to send any of his family to the Golden Mountain. He thought he could keep one hop ahead of bad times; but no one's that nimble. His son, Stony, is one of our tenants."

I thought that explained why Stumpy was so hostile, and I decided to mull that one over when I had more time.

Father looked at Mother affectionately. "And the Cat didn't have your mother managing our money."

"Even I'm not that nimble," she grumbled.

"Don't rain on our homecoming," Father scolded her.

Mother chuckled. "You should be worried about the Lion Rock lady, not me. Did you see her expression when she saw your footwear?"

Father had a comical, rubbery face, so when he turned down the corners of his mouth, he looked as if he had drunk a gallon of vinegar. "These boots are comfortable."

Despite his wealth and reputation, Father had just as much mud between his toes as Mother, which made them a good match.

Mother crooked a finger at me. "Let's head off a scene with my sister-in-law. Fetch the pairs of shoes I made for your father and uncle."

As the procession entered the courtyard of the villa, I slipped down the street. In contrast to Uncle Foxfire, we still lived in the same little house where Mother and Uncle Foxfire had been born.

Mother could have lived in a villa like her brother's;

but she stayed on in the little cottage because she said she enjoyed its smell—the collected fragrances of decades of flowers and herbs drying from the ceiling rafters and the walls and even on the roof in the dry months.

Mother herself didn't give a leaf for anyone else's opinion. First, she'd married a Lau from Phoenix Village—which happens sometimes nowadays, since the Youngs and the Laus are cooperating on a number of economic projects, like the mill. However, back then, they were still feuding. As people in the county used to say, if a Lau met a Young in the road, only one of them was likely to walk on. The other would be lying in his own blood.

Not only had Mother done the unthinkable, but she compounded her weirdness by staying on in Three Willows with her husband, Squeaky, instead of moving to her husband's village as was the custom.

That was my mother. She lived by her own rules. When Aster, my birth mother, her best friend, had died during a riot in the village, she had defied the entire clan and adopted me, the child of Strangers, at a time when Strangers were being massacred all over the province. They still were.

The cloth shoes were on the table. On one pair, she had embroidered dragons so lifelike they looked as if they could fly. On the other, she had stitched tigers ready to leap at you. The one thing that the Lion Rock lady could not criticize was the quality of Mother's needlework.

As I stepped back into the narrow lane with the shoes, some of my classmates fell in step beside me. "Is your father going to just stay awhile or is he finally going to retire?" Stumpy asked.

In the lane some smaller children were playing a game of Hunt the Stranger and were arguing about who was going to be the dirty, stinking, greedy Stranger whom the others would hunt. Though it made me want to shiver, I hid my feelings as I always did when someone spoke of Strangers.

"I don't know," I said. "His letter didn't say."

"If he's going back, maybe I could go back with him," Stumpy suggested.

I stared at him in surprise. "You're only sixteen."

"Your uncle wasn't much older when he first went overseas," Stumpy grunted. "The agent says he'll give me passage if I promise to work five years over there."

"Or ten, or fifteen," Braid said. As had so many other rebels, Braid's father, Spider, had left for the Golden Mountain to save his neck.

Like Mother and so many others of the clan, Braid's father was involved in the Work of driving the Manchus out. Recently the British barbarians had invaded the Middle Kingdom a second time to force us to let them sell their drugs, their opium, here. As we had during the first opium war, we had cooperated with the Manchus against a common foe; but when the war had ended in disaster, rebellions had sprung up here and in other parts of the country. Though the Manchus had seemed helpless before the foreign barbarians, they were easily crushing the revolts now.

"My father wants me to join him," Braid added.

Sometimes it seemed as if all my classmates were talking about crossing the ocean. "Pretty soon, this village will be nothing but women, children and the old folks."

"If you ask me," Stumpy said, "now that this rebellion business is over with—"

"The Work is never finished," Braid snapped, "while there is one child of the T'ang left." The T'ang dynasty had its heyday some thousand years ago; its reign had been so glorious that everyone wanted to claim a connection to it.

"Well, it's over for a while anyway," Stumpy corrected him. "So we ought to get back to the real business of killing Strangers."

Braid made a point of clearing his throat noisily, but Stumpy didn't get the hint. "Wherever they go, they take over houses and land that isn't theirs."

I looked sharply at Stumpy. I knew he was trying to needle me; but I pretended I was only correcting his ignorance. "They've been in this area for two hundred years, ever since the Manchus forced them to leave the coast to keep them from helping the Ming admiral." The Ming dynasty had been the last native dynasty. Everyone involved in the Work wanted to restore the Mings to their throne; but among them our family stood out, for we had been carrying on the Work for generations.

Stumpy had a mind of iron. "And in two hundred years, they haven't learned our language or the customs."

Braid was practically gargling now.

"What's wrong with you?" Stumpy demanded.

"My biological parents were Strangers," I said. In fact, Mother had told me that it had been a mob led by Stumpy's father that had killed my birth mother.

Mother had also taught me a few fighting tricks, so I went into the White Crane stance.

As soon as I did, Stumpy realized he had overstepped himself. "Well, sure," he said hastily, "but you were raised just like us."

At times like these, I yearned to go someplace where it wouldn't matter what my birth parents had been.

Someplace like the Golden Mountain. I began to grow excited. If Braid could do it, why not me? The more I thought about the notion, the more excited I became. Why should I be the only boy who had to stay home? It would be heaven to be with my father and near my uncle, the living legend. Maybe a little of his glory would settle on me as well.

"Don't forget to ask if they're going back," Braid urged me.

"I won't," I promised, but it would be as much for myself as for him.

At that moment, a haggard woman stumbled into the lane. Her hair was a tangled bush and her clothes were dirty; and there were sores at the corners of her mouth. "There you are," she said to Stumpy.

"Go home, Mother," Stumpy said as the smaller children stopped their game and ran inside their houses.

She shuffled toward us. "Did you ask him?"

"I haven't had a chance yet." Embarrassed, Stumpy grabbed her shoulders and tried to turn her around so she could head back out of the lane.

However, his mother wrenched free with a shriek. "How dare you handle your mother this way!"

Braid drew away, but I knew there was no refuge for me, so I stood my ground. She extended a claw toward me. "You're a nice boy. Your father sits on a mountain all of gold, so you won't begrudge us a bowl of rice."

Behind her, Stumpy shook his head at me; but I already knew that she would take any cash and buy opium. "I'm sorry," I apologized. "I don't have any money on me, and I have to bring these to my father right away." I held up the cloth shoes as evidence.

Every muscle stood out taut on her bony body as she flew into a rage. "You're nothing but another one of those mean, spiteful Strangers. Real kin would help a clan member."

"That's enough, Mother." Stumpy got her in a bear hug. They were both about the same height, and she had starved her body so much in her addiction that she weighed hardly anything. When he lifted her up in the air, she kicked and screamed.

"Ingrate. Traitor." Twisting her head, she spat at me.

"Let's go home, Mother." Still carrying her, Stumpy stumped out of the lane.

Braid let out his breath. "That's another reason to leave here. You see more and more people taking the demon mud. Something has to be done."

"Everyone says that we have to do something about opium, but nothing happens." Still holding the shoes, I wiped at the spittle on my cheek with my sleeve.

For Braid, there was one answer that was the root of all our problems. "It's the Manchus. They're strong enough to keep us down, but not strong enough to stop the British from selling their mud."

In fact, the British had fought two wars to force us to let them sell their opium here. The first one had been some twenty-five years ago. My grandfather had fought against them and had been permanently lamed. The second one had taken place just five years ago; the British and their allies, the French, had pillaged and looted their way up the coast, and the Manchus, for all their boasting, were helpless to stop them.

I shook my head in puzzlement. "It's hard enough to understand one person hard-hearted enough to peddle opium, let alone a whole nation."

"And we have to pay the price. Does Stumpy's mother bother you much?" Braid asked sympathetically.

"She's one of the nicer ones, if you can believe it. Some of them try to break in and steal. Others try to scare us into giving them money. We're a target for every addict for twenty kilometers around. And every week there seems to be another one." I clutched the shoes against me. "It's like a poison spreading across the kingdom."

"Once we get rid of the Manchus, we won't let any

more drugs into the kingdom," Braid said, and held three fingers parallel to the ground. It was the symbol of the revolutionary brotherhood. "Banish the darkness."

"Restore the light," I answered, and hurried up to the villa before another addict could try to squeeze money out of me.

I knew something had to be done very soon for our poor country; and I wanted to be one of those who helped.

CHAPTER | III

Late that afternoon, the clan gathered at the banquet hall where Father and Uncle Foxfire held court like emperors and handed out treats to everyone—from exotic candies to bars of sweet-smelling soap to music boxes and odd western gadgets—and the rest of the clan fawned over them.

After the sumptuous banquet, the clan elders retreated to my uncle's mansion, where they began to drink western whiskey and discuss life overseas. The goldfields, which had once seemed inexhaustible, were now beginning to play out. The Golden Mountain, it seemed, was now only a poetical metaphor.

As always, Father made everyone laugh at his adventures; he had a talent for mimicry. To hear him talk, the Land of the Golden Mountain was one comic scene after another.

Father had almost finished when the doors suddenly flew open. In the dim lantern light, I thought the ragged group were beggars. "Help us," a voice rasped.

"If you go around to the kitchen in back of the hall, you can have a meal." Father pointed. "And don't worry. There's plenty for all."

"What good is that?" A woman laughed harshly. As she stumbled beneath the lantern, I saw that it was Stumpy's mother. "We need to fill our souls."

As the group shuffled forward, I recognized others in the clan. Uncle Pine was furious. He shot upright. "Get out, you scum." He looked over his shoulder.

"Why should you be the only one to get presents?" Lunging forward, Stumpy's mother seized the sleeve of the new robe Father and Uncle Foxfire had given him. "This should fetch a few cash." She tried to yank it off him.

"Somebody summon the Watch." As Uncle Pine struggled to pull away, he actually helped to undress himself. And beyond them, the other addicts looked as if they were gathering themselves up for a rush to loot what they could.

"Wait," Father called. "You shouldn't interrupt the entertainment." Seizing an empty plate, he tossed it into the air. Quickly he added a spoon and then a bowl, ignoring the gravy that spattered his robes. Among his other talents, he had learned to juggle from a friend called Ducky.

Enthralled, the addicts watched my father perform. By the time the Watch arrived, it was too late. The Watch quickly formed a wall before the tables and with their staffs began to drive the addicts away.

Neatly catching all his improvised juggling instruments, Father restored them to the table. "Wait," he said to the Watch.

As the addicts cowered, he spread out his arms. "Foxfire and I are going to fund projects that should benefit the entire clan. For one thing, we're going to repair the dam for the reservoir. That and other things will be our gifts to you. If we gave you money, it would just go right up your pipes."

"That for your dam." Stumpy's mother was again accurate with her spittle. "We don't want projects. We want opium."

"Get them out of here," Uncle Pine roared.

The Watch drove them out with hearty blows. Some of the addicts cursed. Others pleaded in a pitiful way. However, the Watch was relentless. It may sound heartless, but by now all of us had heard just about every pleading story possible from the addicts. Once the addicts had been evicted, the Watch stood guard against another invasion.

"The world is sliding into a cesspool," Uncle Pine complained as he shrugged back into his robe, "and it's opium that's greasing the way."

"It's a poison that's spreading through the whole kingdom," Father admitted somberly as he resumed his seat.

Uncle stood up then. "The only way to beat the British and stop the sale of opium is with *American* machines and weapons," he argued passionately. "If we could have a modern army, like those involved in the terrible civil war that just ended in the Land of the Golden Mountain, no one would dare invade us again."

If Father was a clown, Uncle Foxfire was a prophet. When everyone else had thought *America* was just a fanciful tale, he had believed; and time had only deepened his faith in it.

"If we had some weapons," Uncle Pine had to admit, "we would have stopped the British barbarians from peddling their opium here."

After the Manchus had proved so helpless in the last opium war, just about everyone was disgusted with them and sympathized with the rebellion.

"We could even drive out the Manchus," someone else growled.

Uncle Foxfire was careful to keep his sleeve out of the gravy on a plate. "And what do you think will happen when we've driven out the Manchus?"

"Why, we'll restore the Ming dynasty," Uncle Pine said.

"And then?" Uncle asked.

Uncle Pine rubbed his throat—which was a sign he was getting irritated. "Celebrate, I suppose."

Uncle Foxfire knew what was going on as well as any of us. "Whether it's Manchus or Mings on the throne, the Middle Kingdom is plunging toward disaster." He hooked his arm through his sister's. "Driving out the Manchus isn't enough anymore."

"Of course," Uncle Pine snapped. "We've just said that we have to stop the sale of opium."

Uncle shook his head. "It goes beyond stopping the British from selling their opium. We also have to be able to defend ourselves. You don't hear the news of the world like we do. The European countries are planning to carve up the Middle Kingdom. Britain and Portugal have already grabbed land. Russia's taking land from the north, and England and France are taking land from the south. They'll cut the Kingdom up into separate European colonies."

On this subject, Father and Uncle thought alike. (In

fact, they had spent more time together in America than they had with their wives here.) "Just like Africa," Father said, and went on to describe how the European powers were divvying up that continent.

I began to feel a chill that the warm summer air could not drive away, and Uncle's dark vision spread in my mind. "And the British can do what they like in their part—even sell more opium," I piped up from behind. I thought of a whole valley full of addicts like Stony or Stumpy's mother.

Uncle Pine glanced at me. "Your father and uncle could be wrong, boy."

Why couldn't he understand? It was so obvious. "But if they're right, there'll be nowhere to hide."

Uncle Foxfire nudged Uncle Pine. "You see? The boy knows. The Work must become the Great Work."

With a thrill, I realized that my own youthful impressions had not been that wrong. Here was someone who wanted to learn a real kind of magic that would save our kingdom. He was truly a living legend.

"How will you do that?" I asked, enthralled.

"We'll modernize. Three Willows, the whole Kingdom." He waved his arm in a sweep that included the entire valley. "In *America*, they have big engines now run by steam that can pump water anywhere." He clenched his fist and gestured excitedly. "One person might own a farm as big as ten of these valleys."

"And how would that person carry his vegetables to market?" Uncle Pine laughed. "It's ten whole kilometers."

Uncle Foxfire pumped his arm back and forth as if it were part of a machine. "In *America*, they have a fire wagon that has the strength of a thousand water buffalo. They call it a *locomotive*. It will pull all day and all night faster than any horse. If we had one here, you could get wine from the desert kingdoms thousands of kilometers to the west, and you could chill that wine in snow brought from thousands of kilometers to the north."

"It seems ironical to look to them for our salvation," Uncle Pine countered.

"In fact, they'll pay us while they teach us." Father poked a thumb at his chest. "We're going to go back and help the westerners build paths for a fire wagon."

"The roads are really rails, so they call it a *railroad*. Once the roads are built for that wagon," Uncle explained, "the west will be joined to the east."

"The true Great Work now," Uncle argued passionately, "is not only driving out the Manchus but saving the Kingdom from destruction."

Right then, I would have traveled overseas with him even if he had said we were going to have to walk across the ocean. A living legend could do anything. I understood why my father had followed him.

And as I listened to Uncle talk on and on, I wanted to help him and Father modernize the Kingdom and make our country strong and safe. Who wouldn't?

Afterward, when we had gone outside to watch the fireworks, I found Mother in the crowd. "Mother," I said eagerly, "may I go back with Father and Uncle?"

Mother's smile froze. "I've told you before. You're meant for better things. Someday you'll have to run all of the family enterprises."

In addition to contributing a tithe to the Work, Mother had invested the rest of my father's and uncle's money in a number of businesses as well as rich bottomland.

I screwed up my face in disgust. "I don't want to be a bookkeeper. I want to finish the Work with Father and Uncle."

"You'll do far more good helping me." Mother wagged her finger at me. "I'm teaching you how to defend what we have—from the bankers and the bandits as well as the Manchus. The Golden Cat is dead, but his son, Stony, is our tenant now. What happened to him could happen to us, too."

At that moment, one of the Lion Rock lady's

Muslim servants found us. She thought having Muslim servants from the north gave her household a kind of exotic elegance.

"Madame," said the turbaned servant with a thick accent, "the master sent me to bring you to the chairs where you can get the best view of the fireworks."

"Coming," Mother said. I saw her hand reach for me; but while her attention was momentarily distracted by the argument, I took the opportunity to slip away into the crowd to sulk.

I wanted people to point at me and say, "There goes Otter. He came back from the Golden Mountain to drive out the Manchus." And maybe I would even do something that would make small boys wonder if I could fly or kill monsters or hobnob with dragons. No one wonders that about bookkeepers.

Braid came over to me. "Did you hear?" His face was shining. "We were just talking about how something had to be done about the Manchus and the opium. And that's what your uncle's going to do."

"And you'll get to help." I tried my best, but a bit of envy crept into my voice.

Braid was growing impatient like the rest of the clan, waiting for the fireworks. "Will you be guesting too?"

At that moment, I would have cut off my left hand

if I could have accompanied my father overseas. "No, my mother needs me here," I explained.

"Of course," he said, but his eyes had a doubtful look. I realized he thought I was afraid.

"I'm not scared, but she really does need me," I insisted.

"Sure," he said, too quickly.

"Really."

When Braid gave me a polite little smile, I shoved him. "I'm not."

We exchanged one set of punches before a man next to us broke it up. "Shame on you. This boy's leaving on a dangerous voyage and you have to pick on him."

"I'd go if my mother let me," I said to both him and Braid.

From the side, another man smirked. "Sure, sonny. Mama needs you."

What was I to do? I couldn't pick a fight with the entire clan. I hid my indignation as best I could and apologized to Braid, who accepted my apology awkwardly. Fortunately the fireworks began then, distracting everyone.

Feeling even more miserable, I worked my way through the crowd over to my family. Father was sitting in a chair on the far right of the group.

Leaning over, I said in his ear, "Father, I want to go with you. You could order me to."

Father looked down from the fireworks to gaze at me. "I'd love to have you along, boy. But what about your mother? She works hard here. I couldn't take you without her permission."

Around us, the clan had begun to ooh and aah. "I want to help you and Uncle," I said. "Why won't mother let me go?"

He tugged my ear. "Because as funny as you look, she loves you."

"But she's letting you go back," I argued.

Father had to wait for a set of explosions to end before he could make himself heard. "Because as funny as I look, she loves me."

"I don't understand," I said.

The flash of the fireworks cast flickering, colored lights across his face. "I've spent too much time with Foxfire. He has me walking that same high road into the clouds. But you haven't, so she thinks she can keep you in one place."

"Then make her change her mind," I said in desperation.

Father sighed. "She won't listen to me, only to your uncle. I'll get him to help."

Uncle was on the far left of the group, and Mother was seated directly behind him. "How do you know if you don't try?" I asked in exasperation. "Why don't you step out from Uncle's shadow for once?"

Father refused to take offense—as if he had already considered and dismissed the subject. "Because your uncle casts such a long shadow, I would have to walk a long way to get out of it. And maybe the light's a little too harsh for someone like me."

I ducked instinctively as a rocket burst overhead. "What do you mean?"

Father had crouched when I did. "Some of us are born followers."

As I was, I thought; only I might have to follow Mother and not Uncle.

CHAPTER | IV

When I got up the next morning, Father was already in the main room, sniffing the air. "It hasn't changed." To my nose, it was a musty, dusty smell, but Father inhaled it as if it were perfume. He walked over to the wooden lattice that Mother's grandfather had carved to tell the story of their marshland clan. In bad times, the lattice had been sold, but Mother had managed to track it down and buy it back.

Father's index finger traced the curves of the intricate carving. The shadows cast by the lattice curled and snaked across his chest. "Now I know I'm home."

"You're looking a little peaked." Mother rummaged among the jars that stood on a shelf.

Father paled when he saw the bottle that Mother had taken down. "It was just the trip. I don't need your tonic."

Mother was already reaching for a spoon, though. "This will put the bounce back into your step."

Father looked at me, hurt. "You were supposed to break all the tonic bottles. I was depending on you."

Mother spoke up before I could defend myself. "If you want your son to do something, you shouldn't put it in a letter." When Mother opened the tonic, a foul smell spread through the house.

"That letter was addressed to the boy." Father backed away indignantly.

"Anything that comes into this house gets read to me," Mother said, and poured tonic into a spoon. "Now open." Holding the spoon steady, she stalked across the room after Father.

When the wall stopped him, Father gave in to the inevitable. Shutting his eyes, he opened his mouth. He made a face as he swallowed it. "Otter seems a little pale too," he said with malicious glee.

Betrayed, I stared at Father. "I didn't take any long trip," I protested.

"A spoonful of prevention is worth a basket of cures," Mother said, and poured out another spoonful of tonic for me.

As I took the dose, Father penitently put on some water for tea so we could wash the taste out of our mouths. "It feels good to be wearing plain cotton again." He was wearing an ordinary homespun shirt and trousers like everyone else.

"Did they give you the rental rate I asked for on the robes?" Mother called from the bedroom.

Father squatted before the square opening at the front of the stove and fed twigs to the fire. "Yes."

Disappointed, I asked, "You rented the robes?"

Father fanned the smoke away from his face. "Didn't you smell the camphor or whatever they put in to keep off the moths?"

"I thought that was your odor," I said, feeling foolish. However, even if the robes were rented, it only tarnished their image a little.

"It would be an improvement." Mother brought out a bundle of clothes, on top of which sat a battered felt hat. "May I burn these things?"

Father hustled over to save them. "I've just got them worked in. You don't expect me to go back in that rented monkey suit, do you?"

"At least they'll get a decent washing," Mother grumbled. "Otter, put these in the dirty-clothes basket."

The shirt and pants were of a rough denim material; and as I carried them, I smelled the sweat, the salt, the blood—and I knew that was his true scent; quite unlike the sweet, dusty scents of home. When I laid the clothes in the basket, they looked like discarded skins.

We had just poured hot cups of tea when Uncle knocked at our door. "Good morning," he said cheerfully. "Squeaky said we should examine Otter in English today."

Father and Uncle Foxfire had decided that I should learn that western tongue. Mother had agreed because that was the language they spoke in Hong Kong, and she wanted to investigate business opportunities there. The result was that I had daily lessons from a retired guest who had been a houseboy to a teacher in the Land of the Golden Mountain.

I glanced at Father, who winked at me. This was the help he had promised last night. Mother suspected something was up, though, and neatly inserted herself into our party. "Good, you can do that while I show you all the improvements to our holdings."

People called out greetings as we left the narrow lane for the village's main street. In the watchtower on the wall, the sentry, who was keeping watch in case of bandit raids, asked after his brother.

"He's getting fat and sassy in San Francisco," Uncle answered.

The path from the village zigzagged down the slope, because a straight road would have let all the clan's luck flow away. The valley floor itself was divided by a stream, next to which three willows grew in the center of the valley. They were supposed to be the three daughters of the First One, the founder of the village. The fields were reserved for rice in this season, and in the fall and winter for vegetables—which was part of the crop rotation. Beyond the ridgetop lay Phoenix Village, where the Lau clan lived. Though Father belonged to that clan, he had cut his ties with them long ago.

Mother and Uncle headed straight for one of our fields. It didn't have the best soil, but it was where their mother had died. They stood for a moment side by side. "We were so hungry in those days, remember?" Mother asked.

"That's why I went to guest on the Golden Mountain," Uncle said, touching her arm.

Next to us, the usual rattle of the water chain slowed to a low, ratcheting sound and then resumed again. A water chain was a narrow wooden trough through which a "chain" of wooden boards swept water along.

We turned to see Stony trying to irrigate the field. He was supposed to tread the foot pedals at an even pace as he held on to a bar; but even as we watched, he missed a step so that the chain slowed abruptly with another ratchety sound.

"I don't know what's wrong with me today. I keep stumbling," he called out with false cheerfulness.

"For starters, you could stop smoking opium," Mother said. It was impossible to have secrets in Three Willows. Everybody knew that all Stony's spare cash went right into his pipe.

"I don't touch the stuff," Stony swore nervously. He was afraid of being replaced. "I'm just a little tired today."

"We'll discuss this later," Mother said. She was determined not to spoil Father and Uncle's homecoming.

As we walked on, Father murmured sadly, "I thought he would have already smoked himself into an early grave."

"They say that it takes longer for opium to use up some folk." Mother slowed by the Three Willows. "It gets harder and harder to find dependable tenants. I could use some help supervising things here."

As we walked along the dikes dividing the fields, Uncle licked his lips as if he were undertaking a difficult task. *"How your schoolwork?"* he asked, struggling with each syllable.

"I'm doing very well," I answered carefully.

He glanced at Father and smiled, pleased that my English was so much better than his. Father nodded his approval. *"Good. You study hard."*

I had been looking forward to this moment and had even prepared a little speech; but I threw it all aside now. Something Uncle had said yesterday about the civil war in *America* had given me an opening. *"This war they fight in America. Why?"*

"Many, many reason," Father said, and licked his lips as he struggled to expand. *"They fight. Free slave."*

Nothing I heard about *America* should have seemed strange by now; but it did anyway. All my life I had been taught that if you're born poor or even a slave, you must have done something bad in your previous life. If you do something good, then you're rewarded by being born rich in the next. *"But it's fate if you're born a slave."*

Father glanced at Uncle for help, and Uncle plucked at his lip as he tried to find the right words in English. *"Everybody there, they free. Everybody, they equal."*

It was an even more radical notion than I had expected. I mean people aren't equal. Some grow up tall and some grow up short. And some are willing to take risks like Uncle, and some never leave the village.

Uncle said it as if it were indisputable. I realized that the differences between a guest and a clansman went beyond clothes and speech. They had been changed inside, too. I wasn't sure just how comfortable I was about being transformed. Even so, it wouldn't keep me from using such radical notions to my advantage.

"Well, then . . ." I hesitated, glancing at Mother who was hovering nearby. *"I should be free to go to America if I want."*

Uncle seemed pleased. *"You want go? You not like here?"*

I didn't dare look at Mother, or I might have lost my nerve. *"You said the world is changing. I want to see some of it. I want to be part of it."*

Uncle gave my shoulder a pat. *"Your mother know this?"*

"No, sir."

By now Mother was growing suspicious. "What are you two talking about?"

Father fussed with his sleeves. "Cassia, maybe it's time Otter left for overseas. The boy may be tired of living in a golden cage."

Mother stiffened like a hen when it sights a hawk hovering above its chicks. "And get the boy killed like Tiny? No. I absolutely forbid it." Tiny was my birth father; he had died within a week of joining Uncle Foxfire.

"Now, Cassia—" Father began.

Mother looked at him as if he were a traitor. "Shut up."

I couldn't believe Mother could be so shortsighted. This was to save the Kingdom. I looked at Uncle, who cleared his throat. "Supposing he wants to go."

"Everyone in the clan thinks I'm a coward," I argued.

Shocked and hurt, Mother had taken my shoulders and turned me around to face her. "You don't want to leave me, do you?"

She was asking me, in front of a living legend, if I wanted to scribble in ledgers all the rest of my life . . . and yet I couldn't have asked for a better mother. The memories of her dozens of daily kindnesses went rushing through my mind. I couldn't stand to hurt her.

I looked at Father, but he was too afraid of Mother to say anything. I turned to Uncle, but all he said was, *"On this you free. You can choose."* His tone made it clear what choice he thought a true hero would make.

By now, though, I was thinking not only of Mother but of what the clan would say. She had been right when she said I cared too much what other people thought. In my imagination, I could see them all shaking their heads and saying what an ungrateful wretch I was. Worse, they would shame my mother by telling her she was a fool to expect anything more from a Stranger child. I couldn't leave her to that. *"I don't want to go."*

Uncle Foxfire raised his eyebrows, and I looked away in shame. A hero had asked me to help him save the Kingdom. And I had chosen to stay a bookkeeper.

My shame deepened when he offered me a second chance. *"You sure, boy? If I listen your mother long ago, I never leave Three Willows."*

"It was just an exercise in English." I smiled feebly; but inside I felt miserable. I knew now that I wasn't made of the same heroic stuff as he was. I didn't deserve the freedom he spoke about.

"You can't let other people live your life for you," he warned me. I stared at him in puzzlement. Of course you could. Everybody did. You listened to your parents and your parents listened to the clan elders and the clan elders obeyed the wishes of the dead—as tradition required.

"Don't go filling the boy's head with your odd notions," Mother scolded her brother.

Uncle Foxfire opened and then shut his mouth, as if swallowing a retort. Then he looked back at me. "You can learn to change the world or go on being changed by it."

I didn't understand what he was trying to tell me right then, but I think Mother did. She poked her brother in the arm. "Enough, little brother!" she said. "You're still not so big that I can't box your ears the way I used to."

"But—" Father began.

Mother cut him off. "Otter will help me," she said.

"While you and Foxfire are bent on saving the Kingdom, he can help me preserve what we have."

"Now, Cassia—" Foxfire tried to coax her.

Mother clapped a hand over his mouth. "I won't have any more talk about that cursed land. It's bad enough you two keep walking in the clouds. My boy's feet stay firmly on the ground."

After that attempt, Father and Uncle did not raise the subject of my leaving.

During the rest of the time that they stayed in Three Willows, they did their best to play gentleman farmers. They sat with the elders and helped them settle disputes. Important people were always making their way to our obscure corner of the district to pay their respects to my father and uncle. And there wasn't a traveling troupe of actors, acrobats or puppeteers passing within twenty kilometers that didn't stop by to put on a show.

However, I could tell they were getting restless. They left on trips to visit their holdings and businesses around the district; and when they were back in Three Willows, Father and Uncle would receive visitors who came at night to our house, slipping over the walls and knocking at our door in secret codes.

When I asked Mother about it, she said that they

were involved in the Great Work and not to bother them with questions they could not answer. Of course, that made me eavesdrop all the more; and from bits and pieces, I gathered that they were discussing what kinds of machines they should investigate. Weapons were on the list, but so were machines like the fire wagon.

It only added to my shame that Braid was allowed to sit in on some of those sessions and I was not. He would act as their courier to his father, who had joined an exporting business. To my chagrin, he would not discuss it with me. He even managed to obtain a guest outfit like Father's that he wore around the village. The dark hat and denim clothes and outlandish boots made my school-mate look like an strange, exotic seabird blown off course by some freak wind.

When Father and Uncle finally left a few months later, it was Braid who went with them and not I. So I resigned myself to living out a dull, dreary humdrum life counting sweet potatoes in the Middle Kingdom.

CHAPTER | V

December 1866.
Dragon's Gate, Toishan County,
Hwangtung Province, China.

Over the next year I tried to put all that behind me—the way you try to forget a heartache. I tried to resign myself to the life of a young country gentleman. I would keep the family accounts and watch the family businesses and investments, and for my own amusement I would write poetry.

Every now and then, though, a letter from Braid made me ache to go overseas—as if the wounds had only been covered but not healed. At fifteen, I was like the toad that crawls into a jar and then grows so fat and comfortable that he cannot leave.

Strange how your life can turn around a single moment. I ask myself, What if I hadn't gone into that restaurant? What if I hadn't made the wish before that? What if I hadn't even gone to see the Dragon's Gate? What if . . . What if . . . On and on back to the creation of the world.

The sky was so blue that day. It was the bright, burning blue of a kingfisher as it twirled and darted under the sun. Though it was early winter, the weather had turned warm and balmy, so Cricket and I headed into the mountains to Dragon's Gate for the festival.

The more famous gate lies to the north; but we have one in the south, too. Ages ago, someone had erected a stone gate that stood astride the river just as it thundered out of a deep gorge and then thundered swiftly down the mountainside. It's said that if a fish can make the long, difficult swim upstream and through the gate, it will change into a dragon. If you want to wish good luck to someone sitting for the government exams, you give that person a picture of a fish swimming through the Dragon's Gate.

Over the centuries, inns had sprung up for all the tourists, so it had become a pleasant mountain resort with orchards of cinnamon trees scenting the air.

I remember that the day was pleasantly warm rather than boiling hot, and people had taken off their coats. Idly I wondered what Father and Uncle Foxfire were doing. In their last letter, they had said Uncle Foxfire had been made the headman of a railroad crew because of all his years laboring with a shovel and pick in the goldfields and mines. I wondered what it was like.

With the rest of the crowd, we stared dutifully at the old stone gate that stood astride the river. Time had worn away almost all but the faintest traces of the designs and words carved into the gate.

Curious, I leaned over close to see if I could make out any words that would let me identify the builder. At that moment, a man sidled up next to me. His head was shaved like a monk's and the sunlight bounced right off it. "Toss in a coin, young sir," he urged, "and then make a wish. You're sure to pass the test."

He had mistaken me for some young scholar about to sit for his exams. I straightened up. "I've been here several times, and this is the first I've heard about making a wish."

He wriggled his hand from side to side. "Doesn't every fish wish it could become a dragon?" His hand went flying into the air. "And isn't there some spirit in the gate that grants the wish of those hardy enough to pass through these portals?"

The water ran so swift and deep here that it was clear. It shot past down the mountainside in a series of falls. "And have you ever seen a fish pass through the gates?"

When he gave a little bow, the light reflected off his head again. "I've seen many strange things here."

I was finally catching on. He was a tour guide. "You mean, if we pay you."

He lifted his head and smiled pleasantly. "And well worth the price."

"Come on," Cricket said, and pulled at my sleeve.

I took out a cash and balanced the little round copper on my fingertip. "I wish," I said to myself, "that I could join Uncle Foxfire and help him build a better future." Then I flipped the coin into the air. It sailed right through the gate and splashed into the swift current.

"I'm hungry. Let's eat." Cricket had already started to head off.

As I started to follow, the tour guide stayed at my elbow. "I can recommend a good restaurant, young sirs."

"For which you'll get a generous kickback." Cricket came back and gave the tour guide a shove. "Leave us alone, you old turtle."

I expected a torrent of curses the equal of the river. Instead, the tour guide straightened his clothes and simply said, "Be careful what you wish, for it may come true." And with a theatrical bow and flourish of his arm, he returned to the gate to try to pry money out of some other tourist.

As he watched him leave, Cricket muttered to me, "He'll probably fish up any coins he can coax out of the tourists."

I looked at the cold river and shuddered. "He's earned it."

Cricket and I happened to go into a restaurant with a good view of the Gate. It was crowded, and we had to sit next to a drunk. His hair was scraggly, the crown of his head wasn't shaved at all and his shirt was open.

Before we could catch a waiter and give our order, he began singing into his bowl of noodles. At first, I thought it was an exterminator's song about hunting down lice and cockroaches.

"Let's go, Otter," Cricket said to me.

However, I was fifteen and the son of a prominent, wealthy house. So I asked myself what Uncle Foxfire would have done in a situation like this, and I acted accordingly. "Excuse me, would you mind not singing?"

He had trouble focusing on me. "Don't tell me you like rebels!"

It was only then that I realized that the vermin in the song were a thinly disguised reference to the local rebellion.

Suddenly all around us benches were scraping and people were hastily throwing money down and leaving. The singer leaned forward, his hand groping until he found what he wanted. When he straightened, we could see that he was holding an officer's cap with a long pheasant feather in it. "If you're a loyal subject of the emperor, you'll join me in 'How Blessed Are We.'" That was a traitorous song praising the Manchus.

It was the first time I had met a Manchu, and I can't say I thought much of the specimen. Even so, it might have been wiser to bow my head like everyone else; but Mother, school and the clan had made me believe I had a certain station in life as a young gentleman. Even if I hadn't come from seven generations of rebels, I wasn't about to bow my head to a drunken ruffian.

"I don't know the lyrics," I said, and started to get up from the bench.

Before I could get to my feet, though, the soldier planted a greasy hand on the back of my neck and squeezed until I winced. "I'll teach you."

"Not this way," I insisted, though the hand was squeezing even more painfully now.

The soldier slid a stiletto from the sleeve of his free hand. "Don't tell me I've caught me a rebel." He waved the sharp tip in front of my face.

"Of course not." Cricket began to sing in a quavery voice, "How blessed are we. . . ."

However, my mother had raised me to hate Manchus for what they had done to the Middle Kingdom. "Get that thing out of my face," I snapped, and raised a hand to shove it to the side.

The soldier thought I was trying to take his weapon. "Trying to kill me, huh?" He squinted as he tried to focus his eyes. "You *must* be a rebel."

The next thing I knew, I was struggling to keep my throat in one piece. My success wasn't due to any skill on my part, but to his drunken clumsiness. We wrestled for a moment, and suddenly I was looking down at the soldier on the floor. He had tripped over a bench and knocked himself out against a table leg.

"I'm sorry," I said, and tried to help him to his feet. His weight hung oddly in my arms; but I didn't comprehend the reason until I had rolled him over. It was then that I saw he had fallen on his own stiletto.

A half-dozen of his companions staggered to their feet. "Get the rebel!" As they capped their heads, a half-dozen plumes suddenly waved in the air.

"But it was an accident," I said, stunned.

Cricket caught me by my collar and started to drag me out of the restaurant. "Don't be as dumb as a Stranger!" He had forgotten who my birth parents were.

He flung me toward the door and then, pivoting, overturned a table to block the soldiers. They were so drunk that they tangled up with one another and fell over into a pile.

I made for the street, feeling as if I had done this before—perhaps in some series of forgotten nightmares. As my stomach turned somersaults, I wondered if the feeling went deeper.

My birth mother had died during a riot. Had she felt this way when the mob came for her? Or my birth father, when the gunman swung the gun barrel toward him?

The Manchu troopers began howling like dogs. It wouldn't have done any good to reason with them. I ran as my mother and my father had. The faces of the mob might change, but the results were always the same.

I was all for tearing down the street, but Cricket caught my arm and swung me toward a line of sedan chairs. The bearers squatted patiently, waiting for passengers. "We can't outrun them, so we'll have to outthink them."

The lead bearer rose. "Where to, young masters?"

"There'll be a big bonus if you let us hide in these chairs," Cricket promised him. Without even waiting to bargain, he shoved me into one chair and then hopped into a second. I barely had time to sit down in the chair and pull the curtain when I heard the boots of the Manchus thudding onto the street.

"You. Go that way. You that way," a voice ordered. It was still slightly slurred from wine. "I'll search the chairs."

"You don't want to look," the lead bearer grunted.

"I want to see who's in there," the voice insisted.

The bearer sounded properly self-righteous. "And if my lord finds that some dog has been gazing upon the faces of his wife and daughter, you'll lose your head."

I heard the Manchus muttering, but I couldn't make out what they were saying. I waited for them to inspect the chairs, but nothing happened.

After an eternity, the lead bearer whispered, "You're okay. They've gone."

"Thanks," I whispered back.

"Forget it," the lead bearer said. "Three years ago, the Manchus came into my village looking for rebels. They cut off the head of almost every male in my village and piled them in a pyramid. I was the only one who escaped. I wouldn't turn over a bug to them. So what did you do?"

"I killed one of them," I said.

"Good," the lead bearer declared with fierce satisfaction. "That's one less Manchu in the world."

CHAPTER | VI

Three Willows Village, Toishan County,
Hwangtung Province, China.

It was evening when we topped the pass that led into Three Willows. Once he had paid off the bearers, Cricket pointed to the pine-covered ridgetop that separated Three Willows Village from Phoenix Village. "Better go up to the cemetery. I'll tell Aunt Cassia to meet you there. You'll want plenty of room to run."

"Do you think she'll be very mad?" I asked.

"She'll be even madder at me for letting you get into trouble. By the time she gets done with me, her arm should be tired." Squaring his shoulders, he strode down to meet his fate.

With an encouraging wave of my hand, I began to angle up one side of the pass to the cemetery. It was a typical winter's day in Three Willows—cool enough to have to wear a shirt, the humidity low enough to be comfortable. Somewhere I heard parakeets squawking. We didn't get them wild like they did down in the hot, humid lowlands; but escaped pets could thrive and even breed up here.

I made my way through the bare-limbed orchard trees to the cemetery. I hadn't been up there in ages, and I found myself wandering among the stones and markers until I found my parents' graves. My birth mother had died here, and my birth father's bones had been shipped back from *America* so he could rest beside her.

Even now, in my dreams I saw my birth father, a big, dark shadow, smelling of smoke from his blacksmith's forge—with arms that could have tossed me up to heaven. And yet as strong as he was, he didn't last a week in *America*.

As I squatted by the graves, I felt guilty that I hadn't kept them clean. The markers were muddy from the rain and spotted with bird droppings; and with my sleeve I tried to tidy them. From the corner of my eye, I caught a splash of color, so I headed over there, high-stepping through the weeds, splashing the air with a thick, woodsy kind of smell each time I trampled a patch of weeds.

I found purple morning glories, the kind that mother

used for sore throats. Plucking a handful, I went back to the grave. A pair of eyes blinked up at me.

I stared down at the frog. Cricket, who despite all his education was as superstitious as they come, would have said it meant I was going to come into some money. To me, it just meant it was moist.

"Don't slouch, boy," Mother said.

She was a head shorter than me now, and thin as a rice stalk. Not that she was cheap—no beggar ever left our gates hungry. Since she couldn't forget the days of famine, she insisted on having plenty of food in the house, so there was always plenty to eat. Her body simply rejected the prosperous sign of fat just as she rejected finery.

I had always taken her for granted. She was simply Mother, the woman who still went down to tend her fields like any poor farmer and who was still spry enough to trip her husband two falls out of three when they wrestled. Now, though, I saw the fine little wrinkles that spread from the corners of her eyes like miniature fans. I realized with a shock that she was getting old. There would be a time soon when she really would need my help. After all, she was already in her thirties.

"Sorry," I said, straightening up.

She adjusted my posture with a firm hand. "What

possessed you to fight a Manchu?"

"It was self-defense," I said resentfully. "He mistook me for a rebel."

Mother came from a long line of rebels, so she had to smile. "You are a rebel." But her next words made me feel cold and alone. "Maybe I shouldn't have raised you a Young. Maybe I should have sent you to some Stranger family. Then you wouldn't be in this mess."

"If you'd sent me to some Stranger family, either I'd be a refugee or I'd be dead. They're still massacring Strangers." In the back of my mind I began to wonder what I really was.

There were times when Mother acted as if she were standing upon a high tower from which she was sadly observing people. At those moments, her judgments could be devastatingly accurate. "Instead, you're neither horse nor water buffalo, neither Stranger nor Young."

I hated to hear her talk like that. "I'm your son," I reminded her, desperately wanting her to stop.

She tapped her fingers against my arm. "Yes. Sometimes you're so much a part of me that I forget I didn't bear you. But," she added, "even if I had borne you, you'd still be a halfling. They say there's some serpent's blood on my mother's side."

Over the years, I'd heard rumors, but I'd marked that

off to malicious envy because Mother and Uncle Foxfire were so rich. "I'm still your son," I insisted.

"I nicknamed you, you know." Her hand fussed over my hair. Despite all the Lion Rock woman's lotions, it was still hard as leather from years of field work. "You were so small and wriggly. I said that you were like an otter, and your mother liked the name so much that she used it for you. As she lay dying, I promised to protect you."

She had never talked much about my birth parents before. Now as I looked down at my birth mother's grave, I wondered out loud, "What did she look like?"

There was a strange expression on Mother's face. "Didn't I ever tell you?" she asked huskily.

It was strange, but I felt as if a door were being unlocked inside. "Before this, you were always the one who was my mother."

It took her a moment to recover her voice. "I guess that's why I never brought it up. Aster was small and very lively—like a peppercorn. You've got her tongue."

Suddenly I felt rather shy. "Where do I get my height from?"

"Your father. We called him Tiny, but he was a big, muscular man—a blacksmith." She craned her head back to measure me better. "I'd say that you're just about the same height, in fact. But he had more flesh to him—though I suppose you'll fill out when you get older." She smiled when she saw the flowers in my hand. "I remember a time when your mother and I had to pick those for stew because there was nothing else to eat."

I placed them by her grave. "Then Uncle Foxfire showed the way."

As she stood over the graves of her friends, her mind seemed far away for a moment. "But the cost was high. Your father, I mean Tiny, gave his life for his friends—for my husband and your uncle Foxfire. I've had to remind that Lion Rock woman that her husband is alive because of your father's sacrifice." She added without looking up, "She's all for turning you in to protect the family."

"Go ahead and scold me. I deserve it," I said.

Mother took a box from under her arm and set it in the dirt as she squatted and picked a few weeds from near the bottom of the stone. "Scolding's a luxury. If we had enough time, I'd try to track down Tiny's brothers. I think they fled to Hong Kong. But we have to get you out of the country as soon as we can."

For her sake, I tried to hide my sense of elation. "Do you really mean it?"

"You killed a Manchu." She tossed a handful of

weeds to the side. "We'll have to let time and bribery do the work. Eventually you'll be able to come home again."

I hardly dared hope. "From the Land of the Golden Mountain?"

She straightened, brushing the bits of weed from her hands. "Our name has some clout with the agents. They'll see that you get on a safe ship that'll land you alive on the other side of the ocean. Then you can join your father and Uncle Foxfire. They'll look after you." Mother nodded her head as she mapped out her plan with her usual efficiency. "You'll have to stay up here until I can make the necessary arrangements. Cricket will bring food to you until you leave to join your father."

Now that I had my wish, my throat felt very tight. "I'll miss you."

While she was cleaning the grave, a strand of Mother's hair had uncoiled itself from the bun at the back of her head, hanging down like a limp snake exactly across the middle of her forehead. She grasped it, her eyes crossing as she did so, and tucked it away again. "No, you won't." She hadn't forgotten that afternoon either. "You're leaving, just as you asked."

"Only for a little while," I said quietly. "That's all I want."

Standing up, she wet her sleeve with a catlike lick of

her tongue and began to clean a smudge off my cheek. "Tiny never lived long enough to see ice. He was looking forward to it."

I let her tilt my head to the other side. "What does ice look like?"

Briskly she went about the business of tidying me up. "I've never seen it either. We guessed it would look like diamonds."

Suddenly, now that I had my wish, I could feel a host of fears clamoring inside me. Somehow, though, I managed to keep my voice under control. "I've never seen diamonds either."

Finished, she lowered her arm and slid her hand out of her sleeve once again. "They're like ice." She handed me her box. "Here. Better open this and begin reading."

I looked into the box. There were two neat bundles tied up in ribbons. "These are Father's letters."

Pulling my head down, she brushed her cheek against mine as quickly and lightly as a breeze. I was surprised, though, to feel the moisture on my cheek. "Read them. Study them as if your life depended on them—because it does."

That night, as I lay down among the pine trees, I thought I saw a woman weeping in the cemetery. "Who is it? What's wrong?" I demanded. It took a moment to light the candle in the lantern that Cricket had brought. When I looked among the stones, she was gone; but the wind blew through the trees so that they seemed to whisper constantly, "Don't go. Don't go."

CHAPTER | VII

January to February 1867.
San Francisco.

Through her many business contacts, Mother had found a couple of my uncle's friends, former guests of the Golden Mountain who were returning there after visiting their families at home. My escorts had told me what to expect.

They saw me through the month-long voyage. We were packed into a dark ship's hold on wooden bunks, with the wooden shelves set so close together that they reminded me of the space in a coffin, row after row disappearing into the dark hold.

The food was rice and vegetables; and the sanitation was simply a few buckets without any privacy. Even so, my escorts said it was paradise compared to their first

67

trips to *America*. On one boat, one out of three T'ang men had died. (We called ourselves people of the T'ang after the famous dynasty of some thousand years ago. The T'ang dynasty had been building fabulous cities when the westerners' own kings had been lying in the straw with their hunting dogs.)

When we disembarked in San Francisco, my companions took me to another friend of Uncle Foxfire's, a store clerk named Smiley, who decked me out like a real guest. When they had finished dressing me in boots, denim shirt and pants, and heavy quilted coat and felt hat, I felt ridiculous.

"I had a cousin named Braid. He was working in a cigar factory here with his father, Spider." Smiley gave a start. "Do you know them?"

"No," he said.

"Well, maybe I'll go looking for him," I suggested.

"You've got time to eat and go to bed," Smiley said. "You leave before sunrise."

I figured that maybe he didn't want to be bothered setting up reunions of farm boys; but since I really was feeling pretty tired, I didn't argue. I thought I could look up Braid some other time.

I still hadn't gotten my land legs back, but I was whisked away the next morning onto a riverboat along with a herd of other T'ang men and boys. We sailed in a drizzle across a broad, gray-green bay. My escort's duties ended once they had brought me here.

There were about a hundred T'ang men—I recognized some of them from the ship. All the greenhorns were still dressed for the warm weather back home—cloth shoes and cotton coats and pants. In fact, they were shivering so miserably that they weren't looking at the alien landscape rolling past. As I sat armored in my guestly rig, I was grateful to Smiley.

Though the sky remained overcast, it got a little warmer once we sailed up a river past rich flatlands. As I watched the strange, exotic plants and trees pass by on the banks, I began to feel like one of those travelers in the folktales who find themselves whisked away to some fantasy land.

At a city on the river, we debarked. Westerners shouted in the T'ang people's language as well as in English for us to follow them, and I joined the river of men. Soon, we came to a pair of shiny metal railings that rested parallel to each other on thick wooden slabs. From my father's letters, I assumed that this was the road for the fire wagon.

There was a kind of ruthless geometry about its straight lines. Everything else had to get out of its way.

Soon we came to long, narrow, rectangular buildings mounted on wheels so they could travel along the rails. Through the open doors on the sides, I could see kegs and barrels and crates and sacks of all sizes. Several flat platforms, also on wheels, had been loaded with piles of shining iron rails, and stacks of wooden slabs or longer wooden beams. I counted twelve such houses and platforms.

Walking beside me was a boy a couple of years older than me. He pointed excitedly at a massive black machine at the very front of the wheeled buildings and said to no one in particular, "That's the fire wagon. It can do the work of a hundred water buffalo." He spoke in the dialect of the Three Districts.

Striding along next to him was a tall, pale boy with almost no shoulders. "Thousands," he grunted. Though he spoke Four Districts like me, it was with a slight accent that I couldn't place.

Smoke billowed from the pipe on top of the fire wagon at the very front. It really did remind me of a water buffalo snorting to itself.

"*Locomotive,*" I said in English, and then slower. "*Lo-co-mo-tive.*"

"You look awfully young to have guested on the Golden Mountain," another boy said.

"I have kin here." I felt self-conscious as he continued to stare at me. "Are they the ones who told you to wear that outlandish costume?" He plucked at the sleeve of my heavy coat. "Aren't you hot?"

In Three Willows, the poorer boys and I could be familiar with one another; but a look or a certain tone were enough to remind them of their place. "It's what they said to wear," I said firmly as I stared the boy in the eye.

The boy dipped his head apologetically. "Fancy that."

To show him there were no hard feelings, I smiled. "My name's Otter. From Three Willows."

"Call me Brush." The boy waved a hand at the fuzzy sides of his head. "From Horsehead Village."

"Shifty," the tall boy said. "From nowhere in particular."

It was my turn to stare. Everyone had a home—just like everyone had a family and a clan. The only people who didn't were the Strangers who had fled the massacres. If he was a Stranger, that explained his accent. If so, he was the first of my parents' kind—I mean my birth parents—whom I had ever met; but I was reluctant to say so.

Brush stepped in front of Shifty. "You're awfully tall. Tall enough to be a Stranger. We cut most of your kind down to size."

Shifty turned so he could watch not only Brush but the rest of us. "Why are you picking on me? He's tall." He pointed at me.

I can't say that I liked my first Stranger. Fortunately Mother had anticipated just such an encounter as this so she had rehearsed me in what to say. "I'm no more a Stranger than you," I said to Brush—which was true in a way, because I had been raised as a Four Districts boy.

Brush studied me with renewed interest—like a cat eyeing a parakeet. As a Stranger, I would be fair game. "Maybe we ought to see what you've got in your basket." Several of the other travelers also began hovering nearby.

Suddenly I felt alone and vulnerable. During the trip I'd had Uncle Foxfire's friends to smooth the way and protect me. Now I was on my own.

With a chill, I realized that it was just this kind of feuding that had gotten my birth father killed. "They just grow them this way up in Three Willows."

"Sure," Brush said, and swaggered a little closer. "Your folks stretched you so they wouldn't have to buy a ladder."

Mother had also made me practice what to do if I couldn't talk my way out of trouble. All those White Crane exercises now paid off. Dropping my basket, I slid forward and flung myself to the ground, hooking a leg behind one of Brush's. With a cry he toppled over.

Before he could react, I'd gotten hold of his toes through the cloth material of his shoes and began to twist them. "Didn't your mother tell you it's not polite to steal?"

"It was just a joke," Brush yelped. To ease the stress on his toes, he turned over onto his belly.

"The weather's a safer topic." As soon as I let Brush go, I got to my feet, ready to block a retaliatory blow.

"Just monotonous." Picking bits of dead leaf from his clothes, Brush rose slowly. I waited for him to try something else, but his fall seemed to have taken all the fight out of him. He started on, trailed by the others; and I made a note to myself to keep my back to the wall after this. Shifty glanced uncomfortably at me and headed after them. Getting back my breath, I followed.

The closer I got to the machine, the bigger it seemed, with all sorts of pipes and bits of metal attached to it. It was over seven meters long. The massive machine looked like it could churn its way up to heaven. Joined together with the wheeled buildings, the machine looked like a centipede but it was a train. So this machine was going to make the Middle Kingdom strong.

A westerner with thick sideburns directed some of us into one of the houses, letting us make room where we could among the provisions. As they slid the doors shut, I could smell the salted fish and ducks and vegetables. "At least we won't starve," I joked. We had no sooner settled down than we heard a loud howl from the fire wagon; and the whole train lurched forward. I was already sitting down with Brush, but Shifty had been looking for a spot and took a spill right into a pile of salted fish.

As Shifty emerged, Brush waved a hand in front of his nose. "There won't be any trouble finding you."

Shifty didn't bother to answer. Instead he slid over to look out through the cracks between the wallboards. "We're moving."

The train puffed along slowly with a steady clacking sound; and I could feel the power as it picked up speed. I could understand some of Uncle Foxfire's excitement. This could move great loads over vast distances. Shuffling over, I peered through the boards. As the train wound through the fields, Shifty joined me. "I think it's wheat, like up in northern China."

"You could grow anything here," a Four Districts man said enviously. "And they use hardly any of the land."

Even when the land turved, the tracks tried to run as straight as they could along big holes gouged indiscriminately from the side of the hill. I was shocked; any people clever enough to come up with this machine should know that it was only a question of time before the land itself became angry at such treatment.

As the tracks sloped up through the foothills, it began to get chillier again. Soon great knobs of gray rock began to thrust out of the soil—though the trees still clung stubbornly to patches of dirt here and there on a ledge. Higher up still, we passed by heaps of slag. It puzzled me at first until I remembered one of my father's letters; I realized we were in the old goldfields. After a while, it had become harder to get out the gold on the surface, so the westerners had begun diverting streams and using them to wash down whole hillsides to find what gold there was. When all the gold was gone, all that was left was this debris.

The westerners had made it into a wasteland. Surely Uncle Foxfire didn't mean to bring such destruction home.

"What happened here?" Brush asked out loud. "It looks like a battlefield."

I didn't see what harm it would do to share a little information, so I told Brush about the goldfields. Shifty got annoyed. "Back home, they always talked about a gold mountain."

Brush might be new, but he understood immediately.

"They were playing a joke on a greenhorn."

Higher, still higher the train climbed. Down in the lowlands, my heavy coat and gloves had made me feel odd; but now I was glad I had them. The other passengers huddled together for warmth. Only Shifty and I sat a little apart—no one wanted to be near a Stranger who stank of salted fish. He sat there, long frame bent over, arms wrapped around himself as if he could hold in his body heat. I was the only one who had the energy to watch the scenery roll past.

We rounded a bend. There were hundreds of T'ang men working on some kind of side road for a fire wagon. A crew of T'ang men was setting down the wooden slabs. A crew of westerners rested a pair of iron rails on top of them. To finish up, another T'ang crew was tamping gravel down around the wood. Watching the crews lay track was like watching the different parts of one big machine.

In the distance, I could see hundreds more T'ang men with handcarts, shovels and picks, busily leveling the ground up ahead. They seemed to be heading toward a group of huge sheds that were being built even farther away.

"Hey, it's T'ang people," I told the others. As they struggled to get to their feet and join me, I eagerly tried to see Father and Uncle Foxfire.

However, the train never even slowed down, passing instead through a forest. There were more T'ang men here clearing tree stumps. Beyond the forest, the train crossed over a stone bridge. From Father's letters, I knew that the T'ang men had built it. The blocks had been cut to fit one another without mortar. The fit was so exact that you couldn't have inserted a knife blade between the stones.

Beneath us, in the chasm, lay huge boulders, many of them as big as houses. They just sat in piles as if some giant had dropped them.

On the other side of the bridge, the mountains were too smooth and sheer for even brush to find a grip. The stone rose in diagonal slabs; but here and there were little ledges where some funny white stuff gathered.

At first, I thought it was sand, but as I stared at one small mound we passed, I realized it was too fluffy. Suddenly I realized what it was.

"Snow," I said to the others.

Despite the cold, they all sat up and craned their necks to see the strange stuff. There was snow at home, up in the north, but not down south where we came from.

At home, I'd tried to imagine snow from my father's

letters. All Mother and I could think of was when the petals fell from the fruit trees and covered the ground. Just this smooth, pale sheet hiding the dirt. Except that it was cold.

Only I'd never imagined how cold it really would be.

Streaks of dirty white began appearing on the road where the snow had mixed with the dirt. And ahead of us I saw the real mountains, looming like hard, flat-faced giants. They stood shoulder to shoulder in a long, winding gray wall topped with capes of white.

"There must be some mistake," Brush said miserably from behind me. "We don't have the clothes for this weather."

"I don't think the westerners care," Shifty grunted, his companion in misery.

CHAPTER | VIII

The Snow Tiger, the Sierras

Suddenly it grew dark within the train. "What is it? What's wrong?" voices babbled.

It was only when it was light and I could look behind me that I saw we had gone through a tunnel. It wasn't until after we had gone through a second tunnel that the train finally halted at a small village. There were big buildings with peaked roofs, all of new wood. I took them to be warehouses and the village a storage depot. The place was thick with westerners in heavy, dark clothes, like so many fat ravens. They floundered and high-stepped their way through the waist-high snow to our train, slid back the doors and urgently pantomimed for us to unload the supplies onto a long row of sledges pulled by oxen.

All the while, they kept shouting at us to hurry. I couldn't understand what the rush was, but when the train was empty, we had to find space on the sledges among all the provisions. There were several dozen sledges, all in a line.

We had no sooner found places than our sledge began sliding after the one ahead of it. Just as our sledge's runners started to hiss out of the village, a young westerner leaped off a porch and came running toward us, shouting, *"Hey, wait for me!"* He kept one hand over the bulging belly of his coat.

The others looked at him blankly, but I understood. Our driver heard and slowed a bit—though he couldn't halt because of the sledges coming after us. The westerner thrust out a hand. *"Give me a boost, will you?"*

It took me a moment to realize that he was talking to me. Because of my western clothes and my hat pulled down over my face, he had mistaken me for one of his own kind. Puffing, he started to fall behind the sledge. *"Are you deaf?"* he said. With a sudden burst of speed, he high-stepped through the snow and caught up with me again, his hand bobbing in the air as he ran.

Hesitantly, I stretched out my hand. He caught me by the wrist. Bracing my feet against the sledge side, I hauled him up. He collapsed over my knees. The other T'ang people squirmed and wriggled to get away from him.

"*My thanks to you,*" he panted as he sat up. He seemed surprised to see a T'ang face looking at him from under the hat brim; and we stared at one another for a moment.

It was my first chance to be almost nose to nose with a westerner. His scarf had fallen away from his face, so I could see that it was covered with small brown spots. His eyes were green instead of a normal brown, and his hair was as red as fire instead of black. It was hard for me to judge westerners' ages; but I would have said he was about my age.

What he made of me I couldn't say, but he must have figured it was chance that had made me help him—and not the fact that I understood his language.

The driver glanced over his shoulder. "*Oh, it's you, Sean. How's your pa?*"

Sean laughed and patted the bulge in his coat. "*Da'll be the better now that the booze can get through. What a storm!*"

The driver shook his head. "*There's another one coming in. Let's hope it holds off long enough, or I'll be bunking with you folks.*"

"*He'll not care so long as you leave his liquor alone.*" From inside his coat, he pulled out a bundle of letters, all of them written on blue paper. Pulling off his gloves, he began to read, his lips moving slowly, oblivious of the others' stares.

About a kilometer on, the sledges passed by a huge fire wagon that was joined to a second and both of them to a third. In front of them was another strange device that looked like a giant plow. It had a huge curving front and glittered all silvery. Joined together, they looked like a monstrous arrow aimed at the heart of the mountains. In front of them scurried dozens of T'ang men with shovels.

I figured the westerner owed me a favor so I tapped him.

"What's that?" I asked the western boy.

Sean turned in surprise. *"You speak our lingo."*

"Only a little," I confessed.

"Will miracles never cease." He grinned. *"'Tis a snowplow you're seeing. And the mighty marvel pushes the snow away from the tracks."* He moved one hand slowly in pantomime, with accompanying noises. *"But whoever sold the contraption to the railroad walked away laughing. The blessed thing won't work for prayer or money. You Chinamen are always having to dig it out. In fact, you lads are lucky the sky's cleared. There hasn't been anything going up or down the mountain in a week."*

By now, the T'ang crew had already dug the snow out from behind it so that we could see the rails. The icy metal shone like the slime trails of twin snails moving relentlessly in a straight path.

Brush leaned forward toward me. "What did the demon say?"

I looked in awe at the surrounding white mounds. "Three fire wagons can't push the plow through the snow in front. And three wagons couldn't drag it through the snow in back."

Brush was like a lot of greenhorns—eager to find something to crow about. "The demons thought their machines could conquer the mountains; but it's the mountains that have licked them. But not us—not the children of the T'ang. These mountains couldn't crush our hearts."

"What good is a railroad then?" Shifty frowned.

"As long as they pay me," Brush crowed, "I'll build them a ladder to the moon."

"Tit for tat now." The western boy turned and pointed at a stringed salted duck. *"These things have been bedeviling me ever since I saw them. What in God's creation are they?"*

"Duck. Salted." I flattened one gloved hand on top of another.

He fingered it, examining the bit of frozen grease on his fingertip. *"To be sure. But what's it for?"*

I tried to remember Mother in the kitchen. *"You chop them into pieces and cook them on top of some rice. As the rice cooks, so does the duck and it gets soft so you can eat."*

He pointed at some salted fish. *"The fish too?"*

I nodded.

He seemed to have been waiting a long time for this opportunity to ask about our food. *"And this?"*

It took me a moment to find the right word. *"Squid."*

He grimaced. *"You eat that?"*

"It's good," I said firmly, and tried to give him a quelling look; but it didn't work.

Instead, he simply shook his head at the preposterousness of it all. *"Fancy the stomach you must have. I'd never keep it down."*

I wasn't used to having a stranger discuss my digestion. In the Middle Kingdom, no one would have dared. It made me realize that I was not only exploring a strange new land, but meeting a new people as well. What status did I have with the westerners now?

He grinned at me while I studied him uncertainly. *"My name's Sean,"* he said.

"Otter," I said.

"Ot-ter," he said, and practiced my T'ang nickname several times.

He looked around at the others, who were shivering miserably. *"You tell your mates that they'll be the happier if they find some old newspaper when they get to camp and wrap it around themselves. It'll help keep out the cold until they can afford a coat."*

"*Thank you,*" I said, surprised to find such sympathy.

He touched his fingertips to the visor of his cap. "*And weren't we all newcomers to the mountains once?*"

As he went back to reading, I tried to pass on the information. Shifty, though, was as suspicious as ever. "And when we arrive," he said, glaring at Sean, "he'll happen to have newspaper to sell."

"Some folks are determined to wallow in misery," I said.

Despite my curiosity, I found my eyes closing. I hadn't slept well, what with the crowding on the ship and all the excitement of traveling. In no time I dozed off.

The sledge must have lurched over some snowy mound. The next thing I knew, I had started to go over the side and found myself opening my eyes on four hundred meters of cliffside. Far below, like a silk ribbon, was a river winding its way out of the mountains.

Naturally I grabbed for the first thing I could, which happened to be a hundred-kilo sack of rice; but the sack started to leave the sledge too.

"Help!" I yelped in the T'ang language.

The American driver must have turned around and seen me and the sack half draped over the sledge side. "*Tarnation!*" he shouted in American and for a moment I thought I was safe. "*Get that rice!*" he ordered in American;

"*Rice! Rice! Rice!*" he shouted frantically; but of course the other T'ang men didn't understand, and just sat there.

As I stared down at the river, I thought, Well, now you know what your life is worth over here. Luckily I had a death grip on the sack.

Something fell past me and broke with a crystalline crack against the rocks below. From above me on the sledge, I heard Sean swear. "I'm in for it now." When the red-headed westerner hauled the sack back into the sledge, I came with it.

I collapsed among the bony knees and feet of the other T'ang passengers. "Oof. Get off," someone complained and tried to kick me.

I squirmed back to my old place as the westerner made sure the sack wouldn't fall out again. "*Thank you,*" I said, remembering my manners.

Sean was staring morosely over the side of the sledge. His coat was now flat, so I supposed he had lost his father's bottle. "*There's the devil to pay now—and my da.*"

"*Here, boy. On credit.*" The driver took a brown bottle from underneath his seat and held it behind him.

In his eagerness, Sean clambered heedlessly over everyone to get the bottle. When he sat back down, he kissed the glass and stowed it carefully inside his coat before he went on reading.

Determined to be more alert, I tried to concentrate on our surroundings again. By now, the sledge was creaking along a narrow track that curved away from the river. Ahead of us and behind us, I could hear the other sledges groaning in sympathy.

The first work camp was another eight kilometers into the mountains. Here the workers lived in wooden shacks about four meters by four. The snow rose almost to the peaked roofs. Paths had been dug in the snow so that the camp seemed like a maze of paths between white walls.

We trundled on, but the sledges ahead of us turned off. We watched them bump down the narrow trail until they were hidden behind the snowy walls.

My eyes traced the trails through the snow until they finally led to the mountain. There was a black hole gaping in the side where T'ang men worked.

Sean pointed, *"There's the tunnel we're digging. The big bosses want it ready come the spring thaw. That way they can just keep laying track straight on without having to pause."*

By the late afternoon the sledge followed the trail as it twisted down into a valley full of snow. Walls of cold, gleaming white rose on either side of us like the waves of a sea. Here and there were hints of blue where the snow was thicker. All of us were silent as the snow closed in on either side, leaving only a narrow slot of gray sky above us.

Suddenly I missed the sound of the other sledges and looked behind us. They must have turned off too. Still our solitary sledge kept on. On the other side of the valley, a mountain shoulder provided some shelter, so the snow was less deep and we could all feel less claustrophobic.

However, as the trail circled upward, it got steeper. More and more, the driver had to swear and crack his whip at his team of oxen. Finally, try as they could, the oxen's hooves began to slip on patches of ice. So the driver had all of us—Sean included—tumble out of the sledge and help shove it up the trail. When we reached a path with a more gradual incline, we could climb back into the sledge.

The path ran parallel to a ridgetop, and as we rumbled along beside the ridge's snow-covered sides, the ridge reminded me of a tiger crouching, ready to spring. From one end rose a peak. As we rounded its base, I thought I could almost make out two large eyes glaring down at us in the snow-covered face and a mouth drawn back in a snarl.

"It looks like an animal." Brush raised a hand and traced the general shape along the ridge. It really did resemble a large tiger crouching.

The others had grown so quiet, they hardly dared to breathe, as if they were afraid that the slightest noise would bring the paw smashing down on us. Snow lay piled up on one of the shoulders like a mass of bristling fur.

The driver swore as he stared up at it. *"When are you going to do something about that pile of snow?"*

"They did a couple of months ago." Sean was stowing his letters away. *"But the blizzards piled it up worse than before."*

"Well, I wish you'd do something now. I keep expecting to find the camp gone," the driver said uneasily, looking away from the snow.

"They've needed every keg of powder for the headings," Sean said, but he glanced up just as uncomfortably at the massed snow. *"They don't have the powder to spare."*

I was so busy staring up at the monster in the snow that I was surprised when the sledge gave a bump and half skidded onto a ledge near a huge mound of snow that would be one of the monster's paws. It looked about four meters high and hundreds of meters wide and long.

"This is it, boys," the driver announced.

I looked around. There was nothing but a large hole in the snowy mound about three meters square.

"Is what?" I asked dumbly.

"*The camp.*" Gathering up his things, Sean leaped over the side. "*Come on.*"

I climbed out after him and got my basket. As the others followed me, Sean turned his face so that the wind blew directly against his cheeks. "*The wind's shifting back to the southwest. That means more storms will roll in from the sea. I'm glad I'll be out of it. You're lucky there was a lull.*" And he gave an exaggerated shiver.

"*Hee-yah!*" The driver cracked the reins across the rump of one ox and the sledge lurched toward the hole.

"*See you,*" Sean said over his shoulder to me.

He began to trudge toward a westerner in an apron throwing out a pot of potato peelings, who called, "*Hey, Oofty-Goofty, 'dyou get the mail?*"

"*They're all love letters from your sweethearts, so I threw them away,*" Sean said, and barely jumped back as the westerner threw the pot at him.

In the meantime, my sledgemates had gathered around me. In their uncertainty, they didn't even object to having Shifty join us. "What's happening?" Brush asked.

I pivoted and nodded toward the sledge disappearing into the dark hole. "I think we're supposed to go in there."

"Why?" Shifty demanded.

"I don't know." Despite the coat, I was beginning to feel the cold.

"I thought you knew everything." He snorted.

"Only your people make that kind of claim." He'd stung my pride, so I felt obligated to go inside. So I started along the slushy track after the sledge.

Brush swung in beside me. "Didn't your relatives' letters say? Or is this something new?"

I tried to stride along with more confidence than I felt. "It takes a while for their letters to reach us. For all I know, my boat might have passed the boat with their letters telling about this."

The slush hid a patch of ice and suddenly I went flying and landed on my back. Brush helped me to my feet. "This can't be real," he muttered as he looked around the snow.

We found if we moved in a kind of shuffling slide, we could move faster than we could walking. The walls of snow closed all around us. They were white above and on either side, but the floor itself was a dirty, slushy gray.

As we entered the tunnel, the air was filled with a strange whistling sound. Brush jumped. "What's that?"

A shaft of gray daylight fell like a column through an airhole that had been dug straight up through the snow to the surface above. I looked up through it. "It's the wind blowing over the airholes."

The sledge's tracks were all mixed up with other tracks now in the slush. "Which is which?" Brush scratched his head as he looked at the crisscrossing trails. The light was so dim here that it was hard even to see my feet.

Then, through some trick of the tunnel shape, we suddenly heard a sound like the clopping of hooves. On impulse, I began to make my way down a side tunnel. "I think this is the most recent."

On either side we saw wooden doors that seemed to appear mysteriously from within the snow. A chain of small icicles hung like a shining glass fringe around each doorway.

I pulled my coat collar tighter around my neck. "Diamonds," I murmured.

Snow suddenly puffed down one of the airholes, and the others ducked. "What?" Shifty asked.

Curious, I reached a hand out and touched one of the icicles, and then snatched my hand back from the chilling cold.

Over our heads, the wind had picked up strength and was howling now. I had to talk louder to make myself heard. "Just something my mother said once."

And I found myself sliding my hand back inside my

sleeve so I could break off one of the icicles without feeling pain. And then, as if there were someone else using my hand, I held it up against the light falling from an airhole and watched the yellow dot slide outward to either end of the icicle as if the light were alive inside the ice.

Snowflakes floated all around the air like tiny ghosts, and Brush swatted at one. "Where are we?"

Suddenly I understood and looked around. "The shacks are buried right in the snow." My voice echoed eerily in the narrow tunnel. The walls of snow seemed to stretch on forever.

The others didn't say anything, as the knowledge of their situation slowly sank in. Even the tough Shifty looked a little scared. "Why build a camp here?"

"Maybe this was the only area big enough for the camp. Or maybe they built the camp where the sledges could reach it." I shook my head. "But it's left the camp exposed to the storms." I couldn't even begin to calculate the amount of snow that had been dumped on the camp.

"I didn't know it was going to be like this," Brush complained.

The chill of the icicle began to make my fingers ache. Suddenly frightened, I tossed the icicle away. "We'd better catch up with the sledge and find out where we're supposed to go."

We kept moving on. The tunnel was filled with the whispering sound of our feet. Still, there wasn't any sign of the sledge. Just more wooden doors opening eerily from within the snow.

Over our heads, the wind had risen to a high keening sound; and when it blew across the airholes, I felt as if I were walking inside a giant flute. The deeper we went into the snowy maze, the more I felt like the wind's tune was a funeral dirge.

CHAPTER | IX

B y the time we had gone a hundred meters, I had lost track of the number of intersections. When I told the others that, Brush gave a wail. "How could you get us lost? I thought you hicks had a sixth sense."

My own temper wasn't the best right then. "I thought you city slickers knew everything."

We were discussing the matter rather forcefully when a door slammed open. A T'ang man stood there in a padded coat. One hand was holding up his unbound pants. "Shut your traps or I'll shut them for you. We're trying to sleep." He was a Four Districts man.

"It's still daylight outside," I objected.

The man squinted at me through sleep-encrusted eyes. "My pet pig, you must all be Tiger meat."

Brush smiled warily. "What sort of insult is that?"

"Look, meatball, if you don't want to get your head knocked in by a shovel, get lost." He tried to wave us away so vigorously that he almost lost his grip on his pants.

I reluctantly decided that I wasn't going to get any help unless I used the magic name. "Just give us directions to my uncle Foxfire and we'll leave."

The man straightened as if I had just dumped snow down his back. "Uncle Foxfire, did you say?"

"I'm his nephew and I'm joining him." I tried to look modest, but in my mind I was thinking: And then I'll help him in the Great Work.

The man shook his head as if he couldn't quite believe his ears. "Leave it to him to make his own kin into Tiger meat."

There was that term again. "Tiger meat?"

He was more cooperative now. "When you arrived, did you see the bluff above the camp?" With his free hand, he tried to shape it.

Brush chimed in. "The one that looks like a crouching animal."

"Well, you're riding the Snow Tiger now. And you can't stay on, and you can't get off." He closed the door; and when he opened it again, he had jammed his feet into a pair of boots and was tying a rope around his waist.

"Come on, Tiger snacks. We'll find Shrimp. He's the big boss of all the work crews."

"My name's Otter," I said.

"Till you prove you can survive the Tiger, you're nothing but a meatball," he said.

He didn't seem to have trouble finding his way through the maze of dim tunnels. In the distance, we started to hear the clinking of pickaxes on stone. "Generally we work from sunrise to sunset in the open. Inside the tunnels, though, we work in three shifts of four T'ang hours each," he explained, and added, "supposedly."

I didn't like the sound of that. "What do you mean by 'supposedly'?"

He moved easily through the icy slush. "Westerners will waste most anything—food, money, land—but not time. One T'ang hour makes two of theirs. And they slice up the hours into finer and finer portions—like a stingy cook with an expensive piece of meat. Hours are diced into *minutes* and *minutes* into *seconds*."

I did some quick math in my head. One of our hours equaled two of theirs, and I had to allow for the shorter day during the winter. "So," I said slowly, "it's four of our hours or eight of theirs."

"And every one of them has a little pocket clock so

they can keep track of the time." He held up his cupped palm to give us some sense of the size of the device. "The funny thing is that they can't count."

"Anyone can count to eight," Shifty protested.

The man eyed Shifty in a superior manner. "You'll learn soon enough, meatball."

In their wet, cold, cloth shoes, Brush and the others began to fall behind. "How can anyone sleep in this cold anyway? And what about the noise?"

"That ain't the half of it." He grinned like the cat that ate the duckling. "Say good-bye to Mr. Sun."

For some reason, the snowy ceiling hung lower here, and we each, in turn, had to duck under the puckered pale flesh. "Will you quit dropping hints and tell us what you mean?"

He eyed me sideways. "Hey, meatball, I ain't the smart one."

At that moment, a tiny, middle-aged man turned the corner. He had large, bulbous eyes that seemed as large as a duck's eggs. In his hand, he held a kerosene lantern. "There you are—sightseeing when you ought to be working." He spoke in the Three Districts dialect like Brush.

"Try not to lose the meatballs this time, Shrimp," the man grumbled.

"Very funny, Lamper." Shrimp sniffed. I noticed that he had his queue pinned up under his hat.

Spinning around without reply, our guide disappeared into the dimness before I could even thank him. I guessed he was eager to get back to sleep.

Shrimp spoke to each of us officiously, checking off each name on some mental list. "The fat rat sat on that hat. The quick tick jumped over the stick. Singing and dancing, the dying man is changing the bedding." It took me a moment to realize he was using the sentences as a quick way to distinguish our dialects.

As soon as he interviewed the last, he jerked his head impatiently. "Come on." He strutted along hurriedly like a man who thought he was busier than he was.

I held up my basket. "I'd like to leave my things at my uncle Foxfire's."

He stuck the stinking lantern close to my face to examine me. "You don't look like him; but you're smart-mouthed enough to be his kin." And he set off at such a brisk pace that we all had to trot to keep up with him.

I could keep up with him in my boots; but the others were falling behind. "Wait up," I said.

Shrimp hurried along like a worried little rooster, though. "Step lively now. We don't want any lazy bums here. The railroad has a dozen tunnels they're trying to dig. But the Snow Tiger is the key. It's the tallest and the toughest and the meanest. Either we beat it or the railroad never gets finished."

As we walked, he explained that we had come up on the wagon road. The actual path for the railroad followed a straighter line. A bridge would have to be built spanning the chasm between this ridge and the next. In the meantime, though, we were digging the tunnels from both ends. To speed the process, a shaft had been driven from the ridgetop downward into the middle of the railroad's route, and crews were digging out from the middle. If all went well, the four headings would meet. A third of a meter a day was good progress for each heading.

I was full of questions after Lamper's hints. "How long are we supposed to work?"

"Four of our hours, eight of theirs." Shrimp flipped his hand over and back several times. "But there has to be some give and take."

"Just who does the giving and who does the taking?" I wondered out loud.

Shrimp gave me an odd smirk. "Don't tell me you're going to make trouble like your uncle."

"Because he's not afraid to ask questions?" I challenged him.

"Because he tried to lead a couple of strikes," Shrimp said.

I was proud to follow in my uncle's footsteps. "We're obviously replacements. What happened to the men we're replacing?"

Shrimp, though, ignored me as he pointed down a tunnel. "Report to Keg Mouth. You and you." He pointed at Brush and another Three Districts boy. "It's the third door on the right."

Shrimp sent two Fragrant Mountain boys to another shack. From the way the men inside the shack were talking, I knew they were from the same area. In the meantime, I couldn't help noticing a shed off to one side with a big padlock on the door. On the surface was painted a skull and crossbones and the western words *Do Not Enter*. "So that's where you keep the powder," I said to Shrimp.

"So you can read, too." Shrimp nodded grudgingly. "It's a problem trying to keep it dry during the winter with the snow all around."

By the time we reached the mountain itself, I was the only one left with Shrimp. Even Shifty had been dispatched to a crew of Strangers—each to his own kind.

The snow tunnel now extended another seven meters through the snow to the side of the mountain itself, where a hole had been painstakingly chiseled out of the rock. It was some five meters wide, and its sides curved upward into an arch. The shape reminded me uncomfortably of a mouth—the Snow Tiger's mouth.

From within, over the scraping of shovels, I heard a strange metallic song. Western-style kerosene lanterns hung from poles at regular intervals down its length. Even at this short distance in the dim light, their wicks seemed to dance like yellow ghosts; and it was hard to tell what was frost and what was smoke.

Just before the mouth of the tunnel stood a huge barrel, with little ribbons of steam twining upward from under the lid. Just as I was going to ask what was in it, I heard a familiar voice. "There you are, Shrimp. I've been looking all over for you."

I whirled around to see Father coming up from behind us toward the mountain. In his early thirties, Father had liked to smile a lot. When he came back to Three Willows to visit Mother, he always brought along plenty of jokes as well as presents. He was the kind who was always looking for an excuse to laugh and make others laugh. Resting on his shoulder was the most outlandish object: A meter long and of black iron, it looked like a short spear.

"How've you been eating, Father?" Almost shyly, I gave the customary greeting.

Father started, and he stared at me now as if he were seeing a ghost. "What are you doing here?"

I felt my ears burning. "Mother sent me. I . . . I got into a little trouble."

His hat brim touched mine. "Like what, boy?"

I wanted to postpone that moment as long as I could; and with all the company around us, I had an excuse. "We should talk about it when we're alone."

For once, he forgot about propriety and used his free arm to reach around me and give me a quick hug. "Well, you hopped out of the soup pot into the fire." Stepping back, he adjusted his grip on the spear. "My letter warning about this winter is probably reaching your mother just now."

I looked around at the cold, white cavern that surrounded us. "I don't think this is what she had in mind for me."

"You can catch up on family secrets later," Shrimp snapped. "Here's your replacement."

When Father turned, his spear scraped the roof of the tunnel, and snow plopped onto Shrimp's hat. "We asked for three men. Not just one. When are you going to stop shortchanging us? If it isn't supplies, then it's our gear; and if it isn't our gear, it's bodies."

Shrimp took off his hat and shook off the snow. "You

know how many crews are shorthanded? Be thankful you even got one man. You wouldn't need so much help if you just worked instead of gossiping in the tunnels."

"I can't help it if this rock is harder than your heart." Father patted the spear. "It blunts the drill tip in no time flat. And since I had to get the toothpick sharpened, I got that taken care of and came looking for you." Father dug the drill into the roof again so that the snow plopped directly onto Shrimp's bare head. "We've got some trouble."

Shrimp brushed the snow off. His voice rose a notch. "I knew I shouldn't have put your crew at the point."

I'd had just about my fill of Shrimp. While his back was turned to me, I scooped some slush from the floor of the tunnel and deposited it in his hat.

Somehow Father managed to keep a straight face and nod humbly. "You're the big boss."

"I'm glad you're finally learning who's in charge up here." Drawing himself up to glare at Father's chin, he clapped his hat on his head.

He just stood there for a moment with one leg raised. His eyes rolled upward as the snow began to melt and send little trickles down his forehead. He got so mad then that I was surprised the snow didn't turn to steam.

"Tsk, tsk, tsk." Father clicked his tongue. "Such

language before an impressionable boy. Come, Otter. Let's leave the wretched cur." As he turned, he swung his drill off his shoulder, bringing a bushel of snow down from the wall upon the head foreman.

"I'm going to report you to Mr. Kilroy," he shrieked. "To Mr. Strobridge himself!"

"Actually," Father said, with his familiar mischievous smile, "they're the ones causing all the trouble."

"What? Why didn't you say so?" He bulled past us as if his coat were on fire.

Father made a point of strolling along jauntily, but under his breath, he asked, "All right. What did you do, boy? Kiss the emperor?"

"It was an accident," I whispered back.

He eyed me sardonically. "Don't kid the kidder. I know my Cassia. Nothing short of calamity would have pried you from her side."

I glanced around and then leaned my head in close. "I killed a man."

"You what?" His eyes went wide.

"This Manchu was chasing me and fell on a stiletto," I explained hurriedly.

His eyes got even bigger. "You killed a Manchu?"

"I told you it was an accident," I insisted.

"Well, now I understand Cassia's haste." He put his

free hand on my shoulder, and his face grew worried. "I'm sorry, boy; but she sent you to a place worse than any prison. Somewhere that Manchu's ghost must be laughing his head off."

As I followed him into the tunnel, the metallic song became the cold, hard laughter of a ghost in hell. Like the laughter of someone who knew I was going to join him soon.

CHAPTER | X

I thought it was cold outside in the snow; but it was even colder within the mountain—like wandering into the hollow heart of the world. Snow, tracked into the tunnel, had melted and frozen again, forming scummy patches of ice. I didn't see one patch until the last moment, when the lantern light suddenly gleamed beneath my boots. It was like a hole opening up to another world. I started to slip, but I managed to shuffle my feet and get my balance on the slippery surface.

"Like this." Helpfully, Father shuffled his feet back and forth in small, sliding steps.

Outside, even at night, there is some kind of faint light from the stars. Light had never before entered this deep in the mountain, though. The walls seemed to suck up not only the heat but the light as well. If I paused, I felt almost as if the very darkness would swallow me up forever. The hardest thing to shake was the feeling that we shouldn't be there at all.

Shadowy men worked in the dim light, breath steaming from their mouths as they used hammers and chisels to smooth the walls. At the point where the tunnel began to narrow, men swung pickaxes to widen it chip by chip.

The crew lifted the big pickaxes over their heads in a slow, ragged rhythm and smashed at the rock, each at his own pace. Their lean bodies contorted with the effort as they threw all their weight into their blows. Despite the padding in their coats, I could see muscles rippling beneath the cloth. Even the muscles of their throats strained as they tried to crack the walls.

The dim light glittered off the sharp tips of the pickaxes; and as they dove toward the stone, they seemed more like weapons than tools.

"This is like a battlefield," I said to Father.

"It's war," he grunted. "Because the mountain can kill you in a dozen different ways before you can blink an eye. And victory is twenty centimeters a shift."

As we passed, men turned to stare at me curiously and stopped what they were doing. Father signed to a middle-aged man with a sour face like a pickled cucumber. "Bright Star."

Bright Star gave him a sour look. "Why do I have to

work at the point all the time?"

"Do you have to argue every time? It's your turn."
Then Father nodded to a fellow as thin as the shaft of
his pickax. "Noodles."

Setting down their tools, the two men reluctantly
stepped in behind us.

The tunnel grew narrower the farther in we went.
Pretty soon we were picking our way over mounds of
rubble. The walls were rougher here and marked by black
blast marks. When I looked closer at the rubble scattered
around, I noticed that it too was sooty.

Curious, I worked my way slowly down the tunnel,
mound of rubble by mound, meter by meter, toward the
source of that strange song. As we passed a lantern, its
light shimmered in broken waves along the dark, cold
walls of the tunnel until it was just a distant glow.

With each meter the walls grew rougher and the air
more and more stifling. And with each step, the metallic
music grew louder and louder until I was at the end of
the tunnel before a blackened, jagged wall. Pitting its face
were lines of holes, as if giant bullets had been shot at
the rock.

Before that wall was a man with a drill to match
Father's. He was standing with his legs braced, holding
the tip of the drill against the wall. As he worked, he

sucked at something that hung on a gold chain around his neck and his head wagged from side to side as if he were some mechanical toy.

In front of him was a man swathed from head to toe in scarves. Only his eyes showed through the mask made of the scarves. He wore so many coats it was a wonder he could swing his big sledgehammer; but swing he did, and with such violence that if he missed the butt end of the drill, he was sure to smash the skull of the man holding it.

The only light came from a kerosene lantern on the floor, so their shadows reared behind them, almost appearing to belong to two giants rather than to ordinary men. The air was so bad at the end of the tunnel that I didn't see how they could breathe, let alone work.

Standing right before the wall was Uncle Foxfire: a little leaner, a little grayer, a little dirtier. He seemed as wide as he was short, with a round face and broad cheeks that hid his small eyes. Leaning wearily on the shaft of a huge sledgehammer whose heavy head rested on the bumpy floor, he didn't look like the king he had seemed back in the Middle Kingdom.

He was arguing vehemently with Shrimp, and with a thin westerner with a long, dark, curly beard that hung down to his chest and a second westerner in a fur cap like a cylinder and a long red suede coat that hung down to his knees with black fur trimming the collar, cuffs and hem. His pants were bright blue and striped with yellow designs while his boots, which matched his coat, were also trimmed with fur. Standing behind them were two more westerners covered with hair. I mean, not just hair on their heads and jaws, but even hair down the backs of their necks and down the backs of their hands. Both of them gripped pickaxes, which they held menacingly. As we entered, one of them studied me suspiciously.

Father whispered to me, "The thin man is Strobridge, the head of all the operations. And the man in the cap is Kilroy, our overseer. He supervises the crews at the heading. That's what they call this side of the tunnel. There's a group drilling from the other side as well. In theory, we should meet in the middle—if there isn't some mess-up."

"Who are the hairy men with the pickaxes?" I asked.

"Sometimes they drive wagons," Father told me, "but most of the time they're Strobridge's bodyguards."

Kilroy was nodding to the thin man. *"Mr. Strobridge wants the holes drilled closer together, John."* As I was to learn, westerners called every T'ang man John.

Mr. Strobridge himself added, *"I want to double the number of holes in the same space."*

Uncle Foxfire had whole arguments in his head; and

I could see it frustrated him to have to use only a few words. *"More hole then. Take longer."*

Shrimp raised his index finger. *"He say, you do."*

Uncle Foxfire lapsed into the T'ang people's tongue. "Dog, why do you always take their side?"

Shrimp, aware that the westerner was watching the exchange, swelled with self-importance. "It's give and take."

"Yes," Uncle Foxfire glowered. "With us giving and them taking. You're supposed to see that they keep our contracts. We've been in the mountain for six hours and we're only supposed to be in it for four." I did some quick figuring for practice: It was twelve western hours instead of eight, which sounded even worse than our six longer hours. Since I couldn't see spending even one hour in this awful hole, I had to marvel at their powers of endurance.

Shrimp rocked up and down on the balls of his feet. "The longer you jaw at me, the longer your shift will take."

Uncle Foxfire swore. "You're scared of losing your cushy arrangement with these westerners. That's the real problem."

Kilroy was tired of being ignored. *"Look, John. We're falling behind schedule. You got no choice. Sabe me?"*

I waited for Uncle Foxfire to rear back and let them

have it. Back home, if someone tried to make fun of *America*, he would browbeat that critic until the man had to apologize. I was shocked when Uncle Foxfire just grimaced. "All right."

Shrimp turned to Kilroy and Strobridge. *"He do."*

Strobridge nodded in satisfaction. *"I knew you'd come to your senses, John."* With a nod to his bodyguards, he moved around Uncle Foxfire.

Kilroy followed them. *"Call me when you're ready to set off the charges,"* he instructed Uncle Foxfire. *"I'll be wanting to check them."*

When he saw them coming toward us, Father made me stand to the side. Shrimp scurried in their wake. *"I watch 'em, boss. I make sure they work hard."*

"I'm surprised Shrimp doesn't leave a trail of slime," I said in a low voice to Father.

"He would if he thought that would please the westerners." Father chuckled and then presented the drill to Bright Star. "Time to spell the others." Then, with his arm around me, he shoved me forward. "Foxfire, look who dropped in for a visit."

Uncle Foxfire blinked; it looked as if the grimy sweat stung his eyes and he was having trouble seeing. With his slender build, Noodles easily slipped around us and took the hammer from him. "Give us some room."

The air was even worse at the end of the heading. I could see why Bright Star had objected to going. Around his neck, Uncle Foxfire had a kerchief, which he untied as he stepped back. While Bright Star braced the drill against the partially dug hole, Noodles lifted the hammer from the ground and brought it down hard against the drill. He swung with such force that I thought he would miss the drill and hit the man holding the drill instead; but the hammer clinked against its target.

When Uncle Foxfire had wiped his face, he stared in astonishment. "Otter, what're you doing here?"

Despite all my good intentions, I knew already that I couldn't match his powers of endurance. The cold and noise and bad air were just too much. "I thought I'd come up and help you; but maybe a job in the city would be better. I mean, until I get used to this country."

Uncle Foxfire and Father exchanged somber looks; and it was Uncle Foxfire who first overcame his reluctance to speak. "Once you're up here, you're stuck."

"It's a rule the westerners have," Father added quickly. "Otherwise they'd lose half their crews. It's not the hard work. It's the cold."

"And the accidents," Bright Star said grimly as he pounded at the drill.

I thought of the men we had replaced; and the cold and the dark seemed to seep into my bones. I started to feel a chill that no fire would ever warm. "I don't understand. Why wouldn't the westerners listen to you?"

Uncle Foxfire seemed in genuine distress. "Because I'm not the boss here."

Puzzled, I refused to believe my own ears. "But you're . . . well . . . you." He was such an important man back home that it was hard to believe he wasn't the same here. "I mean, you're helping them build their railroad."

Uncle Foxfire draped his kerchief around his neck. "In the Middle Kingdom, I'm somebody; but here I'm just one more worker."

"But I thought——"

"——that I was a somebody." He gripped my shoulders. "Get it through your head, boy, or you won't live out a day. In the Middle Kingdom, you and I were on the top of the heap, but here we're on the bottom. Question the bosses or talk back, and they'll kill you in a dozen different ways."

I thought back to the scene I had just witnessed. "You argued with them."

"I gave in before I went too far." His fingers knotted the kerchief around his sweaty neck again with quick, abrupt movements. "It's not like I lie about things back home and claim to be a boss. People there just automatically assume that I'm the top dog. And since it doesn't seem to do any harm, I let them think what they want."

"At first, Foxfire used to tell people the truth, but they thought he was only being modest," Father explained. "People believe what they want to believe."

I tried to control my growing sense of dismay. I was just as gullible as the rest of the folks back home. "But the fire wagon and all the other marvels—"

"You've seen them," Uncle said, "haven't you?"

"We're learning about them from the bottom up," Father said, trying in vain to add humor to the moment.

Uncle tried to pat me on the shoulder. "When we're finished here, we'll know what we need to know. Then we can take those lessons home. Don't worry. We'll still further the Great Work, just like I said."

I wasn't any better than some country hick, I realized. "But you lied," I said.

Father was going to defend his brother-in-law, but Uncle Foxfire held up a hand, and Father stopped. "No, I only told half the truth," he admitted. "And I'm afraid that you're going to have to pay the penalty."

I shook my head, things still didn't add up. "You said everyone was free and equal in *America*."

He spread his arms in exasperation. "They're better in theory than in practice."

Desperately, I used his own arguments about *America*. "But they fought a whole war."

"But not for us."

This was the man for whom I had crossed an ocean? "So you told half-truths about the *Americans*, too."

"Just because there's tarnish on the copper, doesn't mean there's not a shine beneath." He adjusted his kerchief slightly. "Don't judge the truths I told by the ones I didn't tell."

I stared at him, feeling betrayed. "You're worse than a liar, because a liar actually tricks people. You're only a humbug who doesn't have the energy to trick people. Instead, you let them trick themselves."

"You'll see I'm right," he insisted.

I laughed at him. "And the worst part of it all, is that you've tricked yourself."

"Show him what to do," Uncle said to Father.

"I just traveled the whole day," I objected.

"There's still a couple of hours of our shift left. You have to try," Uncle said.

"I see," I said stiffly.

Father couldn't wait to drag me away. "I just wish we had a drill as hard as your head," he scolded me. "We'd knock a hole into this mountain in no time. Foxfire's trying his best."

Twisting my head, I stared back over my shoulder at Uncle Foxfire. He just stood there, a shadow against the lantern light . . . a very small shadow. Then he looked away.

CHAPTER | XI

Still in a state of shock, I stumbled after Father. All my life, Uncle Foxfire had been a real legend. Now it was almost as if some stranger had taken his place. "How can you make excuses for what he's done to us?" I asked Father.

Father halted so abruptly that I stumbled into him. "Because he sees more than any of us."

I laughed harshly. "Did he see this?"

"The contract we signed was a fair one. Only now that we're up here, the *Americans* won't honor it because they're behind on their schedule." Since we were alone in that section of the tunnel, Father took the opportunity to give me another encouraging hug. "We just have to make the best of it, boy. You know I'd cut off my leg before I let anything happen to you."

I was so frightened that I sought comfort in his arms as I had when I was small. "Yes, sir. I know."

Subdued, I followed Father to where the rest of the crew toiled. It was only then that I noticed that we had been followed by the mechanical-looking man who had been holding the drill for Uncle Foxfire. His head continued to wag back and forth as Father led us both to the outer tunnel, where the others were scraping at the walls.

"Shaky," Father said to him, "this is my son." He indicated me.

At the mention of his name, Shaky paused and grinned at me as he picked up a pickax.

"How've you been eating?" I asked politely.

"Don't mind him if he doesn't talk to you," Father explained. "He hasn't been right since Cape Horn." Cape Horn, as I learned later, was part of the mountain here.

"What happened there?" I wondered as I stared at him.

"There wasn't enough room for a goat to walk. So they hung men like him in baskets from on top of the cliff. They had to chisel holes and pack powder and blast until there was finally enough of a ledge to work with." Father mimed so well that I could see Shaky dangling high in the air in a basket while he tried to hammer a hole into the stubborn stone.

As he walked, Shaky began hauling at a rope as if he were lifting something, and then his hands flew up to shape an explosion.

Father interpreted for me. "Once they set the charges, they had to be hauled up. Shaky was one of the lucky ones. He didn't get blown up."

Shaky spat out of his mouth the object that hung on his necklace, and I could see it was a gold coin. "That's the charm that kept him alive when all the rest of his crew were getting blasted to bits." Father said it as calmly as if he were talking about a list of groceries.

Next to Shaky was a man who dressed in an elegant velvet coat cut to some western design. "We'll all be like that soon." He spoke in the dialect of the Three Districts, which I thought was odd. I would have assumed that he would have been assigned to a bunch from that area so I was surprised to see him in my father's crew.

Father introduced me, "Dandy, this is my Otter."

I bowed nervously. "How've you been eating?"

Dandy's eyes insolently raked me from head to toe. "More Tiger snacks." Pivoting, he called over to another man with thick ringlets of hair who was shoveling debris into a basket. "What'll you bet, Curly?"

"Let me check the goods." Curly spoke with a Fragrant Mountain accent, so it seemed even odder to have him teamed up with men from the Three and Four Districts.

Taking a lantern from the floor, the short man held it up so close to me that I had to squint and try to shield my face with my hand. He grabbed my wrist.

I tried to pull free. "What do you think you're doing? I'm not a buffalo."

"Hmm, he may look scrawny, but he's actually pretty strong." Curly grunted and twisted my wrist so that my palm was showing. "It's as soft as a baby's bottom." He finally let go. "He's never done a day's work in his life. Five dollars says the meatball doesn't last the winter."

"They're just having a little fun with a greenhorn," Father whispered to me. He picked up one of the pick-axes. "Now you swing like so." Spreading out his legs, Father swung the pickax easily over his shoulder and down against the rock. Though he put his whole weight behind the motion, the point barely dented the rock.

Looking at the little scratch, I began to realize that

this mountain taming wasn't going to be easy.

Setting down my basket, I took the pickax from Father. "This stone's like steel. Is it because it's frozen?"

"I can chop frozen rock just like it was mud. It's the mountain. It's got a hide harder than a landlord's heart. In fact, the stone's so hard that we don't need much lumber to shore up the tunnels." He took a big step backward and to the side. "Now show me what you've got, boy."

I brought the pickax up and then down against the wall—and almost had the pickax bounce out of my grip. As it was, my forearms felt numb from the blow; and when I leaned forward, I could see that the hole was not any bigger. "It's like trying to knock a wall down with a piece of straw."

When Curly laughed, he sounded like a donkey braying. I would have hated to lose any kind of bet to him. "Would you like it if someone was nibbling at your innards?"

"Hmm" was all Father said. I could see that he was trying hard to be tactful. "Let's try you at shoveling." Father headed over to him. "Curly?"

He held out his tool with an insolent grin. "Does this mean I get to go back to the cabin now?"

"Hardly." Father took the shovel and demonstrated in his usual quiet, patient way. "Stick your foot in." With his boot, Father jammed the shovel into a pile of rock chips, and then lifted it and dumped the rubble into a basket, all in one smooth motion. Then he handed it to me.

Resolved to do better, I gripped the shaft of the shovel.

"Not from the waist," Father corrected me gently, "or your back will be aching in an hour." He demonstrated. "Bend from the knees, not the waist."

Face reddening, I squatted slightly and jabbed the shovel into the debris pile. When I lifted the shovel into the air, Dandy laughed. "He looks like a stork trying to juggle. Awk, awk." He made bird noises as I dumped the load into the basket.

"Ten dollars. Who'll make it ten?" Curly pleaded. If I hadn't thought I would miss, I would have used the shovel on him.

"Shut up. We all had to start sometime." Father patted me encouragingly on the shoulder.

Dandy surveyed me with a puzzled grin. "You'd think he'd never shoveled manure before."

"Two dollars will get you one that he never did,"

Curly said. He was taking a vengeful pleasure in my clumsiness. "He's another one of those spoiled little princes back in China living off his daddy's money."

"Never mind them," Father instructed me, trying to ease the sting of their words. "You've lived the way those clowns would have liked to. But you're here now. So lift that shovel from the lower half of your body, not from your shoulders."

I wanted to do well this time just to show those two smart mouths. Dutifully I dug up another shovelful. "Got it."

"Easy," Father coached reassuringly. "Let the load carry itself to the basket."

I tried to twist from the hips; but my momentum carried the shovel too far, and I fell.

Overhead, Curly and Dandy were laughing so hard that the others in the tunnel turned to watch. Curly's laugh echoed and reechoed cruelly.

"Twenty bucks," Curly begged. "I'll bet twenty bucks the meatball doesn't last the winter."

Dandy wiped the tears from his eyes. "That's a sucker's bet."

Embarrassed, I tried to scramble to my feet; but I had managed to fall on a patch of ice. When I wanted to be at my most dignified, my feet kept sliding right out from underneath me until I finally gave up and just lay there panting.

Father came over to me with an extended hand and helped me to my feet. He didn't want to discourage me. "I think we'll put you on basket duty." Getting a long pole, he slipped either end under a rope attached to a basket of debris. "When the baskets are full, you take them outside and empty them on a disposal cart."

I held the pole awkwardly. "How do you use this?"

By now, the incredulous Curly was beyond betting. "Haven't you ever carried something heavy?"

Dandy shook his head in amazement. "Not him. His servants did everything." He began mincing about on tip-toe. "His feet never touched the dirt. Servants carried him everywhere in a chair."

"Back home, I used my mind, not my back. Can you write your own letters?" I challenged him. "Can you even sign your own name, donkey?"

Curly hitched up his pants. "What counts over here is shoveling, not poetry. So what if I'm a donkey? So are you!"

Grabbing my shoulders, Father turned me away forcibly before I could answer my tormentors. "Razzing greenhorns is the major sport up here." In a louder voice, he said, "Pay them no mind. When Dandy first came to our crew, he put his boots on the wrong feet."

Curly let out one of his loud, braying laughs and nudged a chagrined Dandy.

Father calmly swung his gaze toward Curly. "And Curly got his tongue stuck on a frozen shovel."

"You talked me into it," Curly mumbled, but he went back to work.

Crouching, Father got his shoulder underneath the pole and then rose slowly. The pole sagged at either end with its heavy load; but the baskets rose, swaying. "You do it like this."

He went a few shuffling steps and then crouched again so that the baskets rested on the stone floor. "Now you try it." He looked worried now—as if he were afraid I was too delicate for the work.

Determined to allay his fears, I took the pole from him as if it were made of glass and squatted down so abruptly that my knees popped.

"Easy." Father slid over so I could take his place underneath the pole.

I eased into the weight. "It hurts my shoulder."

Anxious as a mother hen, he repositioned the pole on my shoulder and then readjusted my grip. "Now get up slowly."

I took my time getting to my feet. The ropes grew taut, and then the front basket began to rise.

"That's it," Father encouraged me.

When I tried to straighten up, though, the rear basket rose and the front basket fell. Immediately I tried to compensate by shifting my hands farther along the pole.

"Squat down," Father ordered.

"I've got it," I insisted. I tried to overcompensate by lifting the front basket more. The result was that the rear basket thumped hard against the floor, spilling the contents all over. Startled, I tried to look behind me. The pole rolled from my shoulder and the front basket thumped to the floor, sending rocks and pebbles rolling amid a cloud of fine dust.

Curly rested his elbow on Dandy's shoulder. "I think we ought to call him 'Prince Useless.'"

Father took the pole from me. "Don't say anything," he counseled. "Until you pull your own weight up here, you have to expect to get hazed." For the first time, I thought I saw fear in his eyes—as if he were now certain the mountain was going to kill me.

Wanting to escape that look, I dropped to my knees and began scooping handfuls of pebbles and dust back into one basket. "I'll get the trash out to the cart my way, even if I have to take one rock out at a time."

Father hesitated, and then he squatted down beside me. "I'm sorry, boy. If I had my way, I'd assign you to something light; but if I played favorites, the whole crew would rebel."

I refused to lift my head. "Don't do me any favors."

He gave me an anxious pat on the back. "Let me show you where to haul the baskets."

Picking up the basket with my things, he led me outside the mountain to a two-wheeled handcart. "I'll see that your things get to the shack. Put the debris in there. When the cart's full, take it outside and dump it." He gave me directions for the labyrinth of tunnels to the trash heap. "Want me to repeat it?"

I tried to answer, but my throat and insides felt as if they were coated with layers of dust, so I only managed a croak. To ease my thirst, I scooped a handful of snow from the wall and started to lift it to my mouth.

Father slapped my wrist so that the snow spilled onto my boots. I looked at him, stunned, because it was the first time he had ever hit me.

"Sorry," he said contritely, "but up here we drink only boiled water. People who eat snow get sick." He led me over to a barrel near the mouth of the tunnel. Steam rose from around the edges of the lid.

I managed to find my voice. "What's wrong with the

snow?" I demanded. "It looks clean."

"It may look clean, but it isn't. The westerners get sick all the time because they don't drink boiled water." He flung off the lid.

The aroma filled the tunnel. "That's tea."

"You bet," Father said. He dipped up a ladle full of tea for me to drink. "If you're careless you can be your own worst enemy up here."

As much tea spilled on my coat as down my throat. I was just taking a second dipper when Shrimp materialized at Father's elbow. "Has your brother-in-law lost his senses? You can't argue with the westerners that way."

Apparently, Shrimp and Uncle Foxfire differed on the lengths one could go to—and I had criticized Uncle for not going far enough! "What do you want him to do?" I asked sarcastically. "Lie on his back and stick his legs up in the air like he's dead?"

Shrimp rounded on me as a convenient target. "You're not in the Middle Kingdom anymore, Your Highness. You're nothing here, so don't play the Little Emperor."

"If I have to die, I might as well die like a man," I said haughtily.

Shrimp gave me a sour grin. "You're Foxfire's kin all

right—a regular idiot. So you belong with his crew of misfits."

"Misfits?" I demanded.

He ticked them off on his fingers. "Shaky's lost his mind. Honker's a hypochondriac. Doggy's the biggest thief in the country. Noodles would eat the bark from trees. Bright Star lives in a perpetual bog. Curly would bet that the sun will rise in the west if you gave him the right odds. No one else will work with them." He waved his hand at Father. "And we have these two trouble-makers who can't keep their mouths shut."

I looked at Father, remembering what I had just said to Uncle. "And you thought we didn't complain enough," Father said drily.

Shrimp squared off at him. "You may have been important men in Chinatown, but you're up here now. You can't go around criticizing everything and making the westerners mad."

Things suddenly clicked into place after Shrimp had spoken. That's why there was such a wide variety of dialects and types in this crew. The truth finally dawned on me. Uncle Foxfire and Father had been put in charge of a crew of outcasts—the ones that had been expelled from the other crews.

It didn't seem as if Uncle and Father could sink

much lower on the ladder; but I wasn't about to let scum like Shrimp mock them. "They know what they're doing. They're the only ones capable of molding them into a crew."

Shrimp laughed harshly. "Meatball, have you got a lot to learn."

CHAPTER | XII

Father looked at me gratefully. "You have to understand, Otter. This is the first time we've worked for westerners. Until now we've always worked for other T'ang people or for ourselves. When the westerners fell behind on their schedule, they forgot all about their promises."

I was still hurt and angry, so I wasn't about to forgive quite yet. With a grunt, I went back to work.

However, after what I had learned at the tea barrel, I now started to notice little things—like how grudgingly the members of the crew cooperated with one another. It was clear that none of the crew liked one another. Friendship wasn't necessary for an efficient crew; but they were a team only in the loosest sense of the word. I could expect no help from them.

So I began to drag the baskets out, one at a time,

along the rock floor. After a while, my body ached too much for me to feel afraid or even angry. As I worked, the ringing of the hammers on the stone walls became some strange metallic song—like swords beating on shields or spearheads clashing on spearheads.

The longer I cleared away rubble, the more stifling the air felt inside the mountain. In fact, whenever I was outside in the snow tunnels, I noticed that the ventilation was better, so that I didn't have any trouble breathing. The bad air inside the mountain must have made it even harder to swing a tool. And yet Uncle Foxfire and his crew put up with it.

It seemed to take forever until my preoccupied Uncle Foxfire passed by. "Uncle—" I began.

He didn't even glance at me as he disappeared outside into the snow tunnels. He returned a moment later with Shrimp and Kilroy. The three of them looked a little worried as they returned to the end of the tunnel. When the westerner shoved Shaky out of his way, I saw that one hand was missing a finger.

A moment later, Noodles and Bright Star came out, carrying the drills and hammers. "What's up?" Curly demanded.

"Kilroy's checked," Noodles announced. "The holes are packed okay."

"For our funeral," Bright Star grumbled.

I hadn't heard a more misplaced name—he was the gloomiest fellow; but then he was already an old man, almost in his forties. "What holes?" I tried to ask them. "You mean the drill holes?" They simply ignored me as they headed for the mouth of the tunnel.

"Fire in the heading!" Kilroy shouted from the tunnel's end.

Almost like an echo, Uncle Foxfire yelled in the T'ang people's tongue, "Fire in the heading!"

Curly and Dandy, tools in hand, trotted past me. "Better hurry, boy. Fire in the heading."

"What fire?" I called out to them in bewilderment; but they were already out of the tunnel. The rest of the crew began to pelt past me, looking over their shoulders in surprise as I just stayed where I was.

"What's going on?" I yelled after them.

"There you are," Father said with relief. Jogging over to me, he forced my hands away from the basket. "Foxfire's setting off the charges in the holes we drilled."

Together we went outside to the snow tunnel, where the crew had gathered around the tea barrel.

"Fire in the heading." Kilroy puffed as he went out.

Uncle Foxfire followed him with a lantern in his hand—it was probably the one I had seen on the floor of the tunnel. He wasn't the most graceful runner—or even very fast actually. In fact, he looked like a water buffalo trying to speed up into a charge. Panting, he skidded to a halt, kicking up the snow, and knelt.

"I'm getting too old for this," he wheezed to Father.

He was just bending his head and trying to get back some of his wind when the first charge went off. There was a bright flash of light from within the tunnel and then a rumbling that came through the mountain and the snow tunnels. We all heard the roar as fist-sized chunks of snow fell on top of us. The next moment there was another flash of light and another explosion.

Uncle went back up in my estimation. At least he was braver with the mountain than he was with the westerners.

As one explosion after another went off, I thought of a battery of cannon firing. And as each charge went off, it was as if the Tiger itself were roaring in agony.

As a cloud of dust rolled out of the tunnel, I was glad to wait until it settled before moving to the barrel. My ears were ringing from all the explosions and my arms and my whole body were aching. In fact, I don't think I could ever remember feeling more sore.

Opening my coat, I began to rub my aching sides. Almost immediately Father came over and began to fasten up the front of my coat as if I were a child. "You won't get down from this mountain if you catch pneumonia. The only thing keeping you warm up here is your body. It's like a small stove. You want to keep that heat wrapped up and close to you. And all the time, the Tiger is trying to steal that magic fire."

I tried to raise an arm to shove him away, but it ached too much. "I can do it myself."

"Sure, you can," Father soothed. "How're your hands?"

I was sensitive after the crew's hazing. "They're okay."

"Don't be a martyr." Pulling off one of my gloves, he examined my hand. The fingers and palm were covered with blisters, and where the blisters had broken the flesh was raw and sore.

Turning to a man who had a scarf wrapped around the lower part of his face, Father asked, "What do you think, Honker?"

With his hat pulled down, all I could see were Honker's eyes. He batted his eyelashes in greeting and mumbled something that got lost within his scarves. As he bent over my hand, I could smell him. It was as if Mother had dumped her whole medicine chest on top of him.

Straightening, he muttered something indistinguishable through his scarf. Father interpreted for me.

"Honker says they'll toughen up soon enough."

With a nod, Honker slipped away to mingle with the rest of the crowd. Father handed me back my glove. "In the meantime, I have an ointment."

In spite of everything, I had to grin. "Another one of Mother's herbal cures?"

Father let go of me. "She would have sent over a whole shipload of medicines if I'd let her. If Cassia doesn't kill you," he said chuckling, "she'll certainly cure you."

As he moved away to supervise something, I used my free hand to wipe the sweat stinging my eyes—and found that my fingers ached so much that it hurt to bend them.

"Sore?" a voice asked me.

I turned to see a boy about my age, but there was something old about his eyes—a kind of sadness.

"A little," I said, and introduced myself. The boy said his name was Doggy and that he came from the city of Canton.

With difficulty, I flexed my fingers. "How many parts is Kilroy missing, anyway?"

Doggy did an exact imitation of Kilroy down to his squint. "He lost an eye to an explosion. He lost a finger in another accident. And a third took off part of his foot." He dropped his pose and nodded toward the tea barrel, where Curly was taking bets on something. "When you get some money, you might consider getting into Curly's betting pool. We're trying to figure out how much of him will be left when the railroad is done."

Bright Star nudged him. "Give it back."

Doggy drew his eyebrows together, the perfect image of puzzled innocence. "Give back what?"

Bright Star grabbed him by the coat collar and hoisted him into the air. "Give it back, you little rat."

Doggy was now the picture of indignation. "It was just a joke." From a coat pocket, he produced my glove.

"You'd steal the hair from a man's nose if you could sell it." With a growl, Bright Star dropped Doggy onto his feet. "Keep a tight hold on everything when this one is around."

"It was just a prank," Doggy insisted lamely, but he sidled off.

As I pulled the glove back on, Kilroy ordered us back inside. There was still enough dust to make me cough and to sting the eyes; but while he went back with Uncle Foxfire and Shrimp, we took up our places in the tunnel. No time was going to go to waste if Kilroy could help it.

From the end of the tunnel, we heard Kilroy's voice echo. *"So, John, did you do more than scratch the mountain today?"*

I couldn't hear Uncle Foxfire's reply; but when they

came out a moment later he was smiling. "How much?" Curly asked eagerly.

"Twenty-two and a half centimeters." Uncle Foxfire held out his hands in the approximate measurement. *"Almost nine inches."*

"We've been averaging eighteen centimeters for a whole day," explained Father.

"Darn," Curly swore.

Noodles punched him in the arm. "You bet against your own crew?"

Kilroy surveyed the cheering work crew and then turned to Uncle Foxfire. *"You did good, John. But you got to do better if we're going to catch up with the schedule. Tomorrow drill the same number of holes, but double-charge them."*

It took Uncle Foxfire and Shrimp a moment to work their way through the western words. As they did so, Shrimp's face grew uneasy, while Uncle Foxfire seemed downright panicky. *"No, pack too tight, powder not burn,"* Uncle Foxfire protested.

"It's orders from Strobridge, John." Kilroy slapped his leg in exasperation. *"Hang it all. I don't like it any better than you do. I wish the rock was softer, but it ain't."* Kilroy began to walk outside. *"Get the next shift in here,"* he said to Shrimp.

Some men at the mouth of the mountain began moving past us into the interior as if under some sad, terrible spell. I suppose their shift had already reported but had been keeping out of our way by working at the mouth of the tunnel.

Resentfully, Uncle Foxfire looked at Shrimp. "Aren't you going to say anything?"

"Better use longer fuses," Shrimp suggested, and brusquely shoved the workers out of his way.

CHAPTER | XIII

Uncle Foxfire fell into step beside Father and me. "So, boy, you survived your first day on the Tiger."

It's strange, but back in Three Willows anybody would be glad to have him pay attention to us—even if it was only to make small talk. However, that seemed like a century ago, back in the Middle Kingdom; and we were here now. I could see how uneasy he looked—as if he wanted to reestablish that old rapport.

And I realized that I was as much at fault as he. He hadn't made up anything that I hadn't wanted to hear. I thought over what Father had said back by the tea barrel and realized that Uncle couldn't help it if he was fooled. It was just unfortunate that his letter had crossed the ocean at the same time I had.

"Yes, sir," I said with a slight smile. "It's certainly different up here."

"You'll get the hang of it," Uncle Foxfire said, reas-suringly. We squeezed in among all the other T'ang men, moving along through the snow tunnel as if floating on a black, sluggish river. "You're young yet, so things are either black or white, and there's no such color as gray. When you get to be my age, you'll realize that you can't set the world on fire right away."

I thought he was beginning to sound like Shrimp, but I refrained from saying so. "Maybe," I said carefully. "Do we at least get the same pay as the western workers?"

"I'd love to know," Uncle admitted, "but we'd have to look at the records; and they'd never let us do that."

"Will you quit talking shop when we're on our own time?" Father snapped impatiently. "How's the family?"

The thought of home made me ache inside; but I tried to forget my homesickness, because that would do no good. "Fine."

I filled them in on the latest happenings in Three Willows. Both of them were hungry for even the most trivial tidbits; and I found that it reminded me of what we had in common.

As we walked, I found I had to speak progressively louder, because the farther from the Tiger, the more relaxed our neighbors became and the more they talked. I heard the dialects mingling—Four Districts, Three,

Fragrant Mountain, even Stranger. It was like having the province shrunk down to one little town.

As we continued down the tunnel, T'ang men began streaming away into side passageways. Finally we turned to our right. Uncle Foxfire paused before a wooden door in a wall of snow. "Here we are. Home sweet home."

He opened the door; I could see that the shack was a log cabin some four meters on each side. There was barely enough room for three tiers of bunks on three of the walls. Each tier had four beds and each bed was little more than a wooden shelf, with only two thirds of a meter separating each shelf. It reminded me a lot of the bunks on the ship coming over.

Slightly off the center of the cabin was a western-style stove, all of iron and shaped like a barrel. As we entered, its warmth wrapped itself around us like a blanket.

On top of the stove was a big pot of hot water—melted snow, I supposed. Another pot sat on the floor keeping warm near the stove. Steam rose in cheerful silver ribbons.

Despite the stove's roaring fire, I could feel all the little drafts in the shack as if heat leaked out between the logs. Sheets of western newspaper, pieces of scrap lumber and even tin had been put up in a vain attempt to add another layer; and here and there were patches where I could see mud packed into the gaps.

Tending the stove was a wispy little man with a goatee consisting of six whiskers; but what his beard lacked in quantity, it made up for in quality, for the whiskers were thick as hog bristles and long as chopsticks. As he talked and moved, they wriggled and curled with a life all their own.

"There you are," he scolded Uncle Foxfire. "Well, your dinner's probably turned to charcoal, and it serves you right." He spoke with a Fragrant Mountain accent.

Uncle Foxfire dragged me inside after him. "Packy, this is my nephew, Otter. He's Squeaky's son."

Packy assumed a mock-mournful look. "I pity you, boy—having to put up with these tardy ingrates. They'll be late to their own funeral."

"I hope so." Father showed me over to a vacant bunk where I could put my things. "Packy's official title is Chief Cook, but he's also a dozen other things. If we could survive without the grumpy old goat, we'd chuck him right out into the snow."

"I've got a good mind to go anyway," Packy declared; but there was a twinkle in his eye, as if he enjoyed this solid exchange of insults.

Uncle Foxfire caught the washrag that Father threw to him. "Otter, if you've got any hobbies, let Packy know. He might be able to trade what you make for something we need."

Father began taking off his coat and shirt. "Doggy tickles the strings. Noodles does a little painting. Bright Star's learning how to carve from Shaky. Every little bit helps when Packy has to work one of his deals."

Personally, I wasn't sure if I would have trusted Shaky with a knife; but I didn't say anything. "I don't have any." I climbed onto my bunk.

Uncle Foxfire stripped to the buff without any sign of self-consciousness. "Then get one." He nodded toward a bunk that I assumed was his. Its wall was decorated with all sorts of intricate pictures cut from colored paper. "I nearly went crazy until I found out I had a knack for snipping."

One by one they washed, Uncle first and then Father. By the time Doggy finished his turn, the water in the pot was scummy—especially after Honker had washed off his medical ointments (he applied a new coat right away). Puddles lay all around the floor. With an elaborate flourish and a bow, Doggy indicated the pot. "Your turn, my dear fellow."

I wasn't about to undress before all these strangers. "Let's eat."

Doggy grabbed my ankle. "Not before you wash." He tugged at my leg.

"Easy. He's Squeaky's son," Packy warned. He started to move toward the pot of hot water; but Uncle Foxfire held up his hand.

He looked at me warningly. "Up here there are three rules of survival."

Curly slid out of his bunk, his feet splashing in a little pool of water that lay on the floor. "Keep warm," he recited as he stood up.

"Keep dry," Noodles added as he got to his feet.

"And above all, keep clean." With one fierce yank, Doggy tumbled me off the bed and into the others' arms.

"Help me," I appealed to my father and uncle.

Father began to swing his legs from his bunk, but Uncle Foxfire stopped him. "He broke the rules, Squeaky." Then he turned to me as I dangled helplessly in my captors' grip. "Aside from sprains and colds, this cabin is the healthiest one in camp. You're part of a team now. Your health affects your crewmates."

Feeling betrayed, I struggled wildly, kicking with my

legs and thrashing with my arms. "I'll get you all. I swear. If it takes ten lifetimes."

"Anytime," Curly grunted as the three stripped me efficiently. "Knife, club, boot."

I was so outraged over the humiliation that I was almost ready to cry. "Is that how you take care of a son? A nephew?"

Uncle Foxfire didn't say anything as the others started laughing in their bunks. When I was naked, the three of them dropped me into a puddle, where I sat trying to hide my nakedness with my hands.

Curly towered over me with a bar of western soap in his hand. "Do we have to soap you down too?"

If I could have obliterated him from existence at that moment, I would have done so cheerfully. As it was, I could only shake my head and take the soap from him, wincing as the wet soap touched the sores on my hands.

Embarrassed now, Noodles handed me a rag to use for washing myself. Still trying to hide as much of myself as I could under the circumstances, I soaped myself. The whole cabin had fallen into an uneasy silence, as if they had expected me to enjoy their prank.

When I had lathered myself all over, I remained

sitting while I tried to figure out how to stand up modestly and rinse myself. Curly had wrapped his hands in rags, though, and he grabbed the pot of hot water. "One, two . . ." On "three," he threw the water in a scummy arc that drenched me.

I rose, coughing, my shame replaced by outrage, but not at being seen in this state. What truly hurt was that Uncle Foxfire had not raised a finger to defend me—in fact had stopped Father and encouraged the others to abuse me. Even if the westerners held all the power in the tunnels, he could have protected me here and now. And that I could never forgive.

Father finally intervened. "All right, you three. You've had your fun and he's had his bath."

Packy had climbed up into an upper bunk to get a better view and keep out of the way of the splashing. He jumped down now. "Doggy, Curly, Noodles, help me clean up before the water turns to ice."

"By rights, he should," Doggy complained.

"Shut up, or you won't get supper," Packy snapped.

As they cleaned up, I got dressed and lay down on my bunk, turning my face to the wall.

"Here's the ointment I promised," Father said. I heard a clunk as he planted it near me. "Make sure you

put your gloves on. You could lose a finger to frostbite."
He hesitated when I still said nothing. "Don't be harsh
on Foxfire. This crew barely holds together as it is. It'll
fall apart if he's partial to his kin."

"Adopted kin," I muttered.

From above me, Bright Star declared, "You're a fool."

"Maybe," I snapped, "I don't want to be his nephew."

"I don't think you're even human," Bright Star shot
back.

Wrapping myself in my clothes, I lunged outside
into the tunnels, walking and walking endlessly. In the
snow tunnels, I felt free.

The lanterns gleamed like small frosted stars. They
seemed to pull me from one tunnel to the next. I had just
rounded a corner when I bumped into another bundled
up figure. *"Watch it,"* he said.

He wore a muffler wrapped around the lower part of
his face while a hat covered his head, leaving only a thin
strip around his eyes exposed to the cold. In the dim
light, it took me a moment to realize how pale that strip
of flesh was.

"Sorry," I answered, and tried to shuffle on.

However, he put his hand on my shoulder. When I
stopped, he pulled the rag down from my mouth. *"'Tis the
new boy,"* he said.

I finally recognized him. *"Sean?"*

He lowered his own muffler to reveal his face. *"How do you like our homes? Aren't they the grandest thing? And isn't the weather lovely? Puts the regular nip into you."*

I covered my mouth back up with the rag. *"Yes,"* I said, expecting him to move on.

He seemed disappointed, though, by the shortness of my answer. *"And how have you been keeping yourself? Lazing in the manor like a regular lord?"*

I couldn't understand why he wanted to stand and chat rather than head for his cabin, which I was sure was kept warmer and drier than ours. *"I have a lot to learn."*

"And who would think I'd find company in the tunnels at this time of night?" He covered his own mouth with his muffler.

Could he be as much of an outcast among his own kind as I was? But why? Suddenly I wished I had more of the western tongue. But even if I had, I don't know if I could have asked. Instead, I tried to make conversation since he seemed to want to. *"I thought you'd be outside enjoying the full moon."*

"No, 'tis the quarter moon." He started to sidle down the hallway until he found an airhole.

Together we craned our heads back and studied the matter. *"It's dark,"* I said.

Suddenly Sean seized a lantern from its nail on a

pole. *"The only way we'll settle this, new one, is to go outside and find out what phase the moon's in."*

Almost jauntily, he set off to find the moon; and I shuffled after him.

He led me through the main tunnel, holding the lantern before us, and we turned into a side tunnel where I could see the double furrows of the handcarts in the slush.

At the end of the tunnel was a curtain, of swirling snowflakes; but I thought I could make out a bright dot of light. I felt my pulse quicken, and I began to jog forward. *"I see it."*

The same need seized the western boy, and he began to run too. Together, we slid and slipped in the snow until we reached the end. The light seemed larger now and bobbed and weaved in the air like a firefly.

"It isn't the moon." Disappointed, I started to sit down on an overturned handcart, but then I noticed that a rope had been tied to one wheel while the other end disappeared somewhere outside in the snowy landscape.

Sean caught my hand before I could touch it. *"Leave it be. Someone's outside."*

Suddenly the rope went slack and a silhouette appeared in the curtain of snow. It was a T'ang man in a straw hat with a lantern in one hand and snow covering his clothes. The rope was tied to his waist. He gave a start when he saw me. "Are you a relative?"

"Of whom?" I asked.

"The man who got lost." The man went to the wheel and began to untie the rope. A moment later another man entered, carrying the legs of a frozen corpse. A third man followed, carrying the corpse's shoulders. Both of them were also tied around the waist with the same rope.

As they lowered the corpse to the tunnel floor and freed themselves from the rope, I stared in horrified fascination at him. His arms were extended in front of him and his legs parted in mid stride. "What happened to him?"

The first rescuer was coiling up the rope, using the hand and elbow of one arm. "It's some boy. He went out with a handcart to dump some debris on the trash heap and got lost."

Snowflakes had limned the wrinkles in his face so that his features were outlined in white. There was something familiar about it, and I bent over to look closer. It was Shifty, but looking more peaceful now than he had in life.

Sean's voice caught. *"'Tis he that's the lucky one."*

I looked at him sharply. *"Don't you want to be here?"*

He laughed, and the sound echoed oddly in the

tunnel. The rescue party turned in surprise. Then I started to laugh too.

The first man glared at me. "I don't expect any manners from a demon, but don't you have any shame?" "Demons" was the word that ignorant and superstitious people used for westerners. My English instructor had made a point that it was the wrong term, because in English it was equated with evil creatures called demons, while in the T'ang language it referred more generally to creatures who were ghosts or spirits.

I went right on laughing. "We're all going to wind up like him." I glanced at Sean to see if he needed a translation, but from his eyes I saw that he comprehended.

Still chuckling, Sean and I trudged back into the maze of tunnels. *"I have to go. My da should have drunk himself to sleep by now,"* Sean said.

Suddenly I understood a little about why he had been out wandering in the tunnels when everyone else was either working or resting. He was as much of an outcast as me.

I stared at him, and he returned my gaze steadily, almost defiantly. I found it disconcerting. Eyes should be brown, not green like his.

"See you tomorrow?" I asked.

"It could be the next day already for all we know. It's Central

Pacific that keeps the clock and the calendar." He stuck out a mit-
tened hand. On the ship and the city, I had seen westerners say good-bye. I took his hand and shook it.

When I was alone, I suddenly became aware of just
how tired I was. I tried to head for where the cabin was.
It didn't take me long to realize I was hopelessly lost.

Then as the wind keened over the airholes above,
I heard someone begin to play on a moon guitar. The
musician took that sad, mournful tune of the wind and
made it strong and hopeful. He could play the sun up and
the moon down. For a moment, I stood, just listening,
with the snowflakes floating all around like tiny ghosts.

Suddenly, I forgot the wind and the cold. And
instead I was back home . . . on a hot sunny day, and I
was riding on top of a buffalo, kicking with my heels as
I guided it to the pond.

I followed the music until I was standing right before
our shack. Squaring my shoulders, I plunged inside. It
was Doggy, playing as he lay on his back. Even though he
was a thief and a nuisance, he certainly could play.

"Where did you go?" Father asked, worried.

Sean was my secret. "I just walked around."

Faces smirked at me as I threw myself onto my bunk.
Staring up at the planks above me, I felt as if I were in a
real coffin.

As I lay there, I thought of that crazy tour guide by the Dragon's Gate. His curse had seemed so strange at the time. Now I knew that having your wish come true could be the cruelest thing of all.

CHAPTER | XIV

The next workday was much like the first—except longer. When I woke up, I was already exhausted. My back ached and every limb felt rubbery. I couldn't clear up the rubble fast enough, and Uncle Foxfire had had to assign some of the crew to help me—which got me some hard looks.

By midday, though, I got the hang of the carrying pole, which speeded up carrying out the trash. I was shuffling along with a triumphant smile when Bright Star saw me and gave a sarcastic cheer. "It's about time you started pulling your own weight."

When Packy brought us our supper, I sat off a little bit to eat. *"Don't you just love the weather now?"* Sean said.

I looked up to see him in an apron. He was pushing a handcart in front of him with a small bucket on it. *"It's very refreshing."* I pointed my chopsticks at the bucket. *"But wouldn't it be easier just to carry the bucket instead of carting it around on that big thing?"*

"I had to deliver supper to the lads." He lifted out the bucket. *"I work in the mess. Just how do you eat with those things, anyway?"*

"I was born with them." I clicked my teeth in illustration.

"Aren't you the clever one?" He dug a miniature metal rake out of his coat pocket. *"I meant those things."* He used the tiny tool to indicate my chopsticks.

"You get the hang of it." I was surprised when he sat down next to me.

At home, I was friendly with the poorer boys and had been their leader in the school games; but there were certain things they would never have done—like eat with me. However, I was glad. His friendliness was as unstoppable as a sunrise.

I now began to see a glimmer of what Uncle Foxfire had tried to describe when he said all westerners were equal. Sean had no sense of status, which gave him an open-mindedness that I found refreshing.

"I'd starve long before that." Prying off the lid of his bucket, he dipped the rake into the stew and, lifting up a hunk of beef on the points, jammed it into his mouth.

The old guest at home had told me about forks, but that had been theory rather than actual fact. I watched

Sean spear a carrot next and cram that into his mouth. *"How do you keep from hurting yourself with that thing?"* I wondered.

"You get the hang of it." He grinned. *"I never had grub so good."*

I used the tips of my chopsticks to shove some rice into my mouth. *"You don't miss home cooking?"*

"And what's to miss?" He snorted. *"Ma loved her whiskey even more than Da, and she took it out on me when there was none in the house."*

I shook my head in disbelief. *"So you prefer it up here?"*

He hesitated; and his hesitation told me more than his words. *"Most of the time. What about you?"*

Until this trip, I would have said that my home was in Three Willows; but traveling had been "educational"—to say the least. And I wondered what would have happened to me there if I hadn't had Mother's formidable protection. The clan probably would have planted me in a grave beside my birth parents.

It hurt me to admit it. *"I think I was always pretending my home village was home."* There was so much more I wanted to tell him; but where do you begin when you have to describe an entire world?

I could see a whole world behind his eyes too as he struggled to find a place to start. *"And then it's like you become unstuck. And there's nowhere else to stick,"* he said.

I became excited as I thought I'd finally found someone who understood. *"Yes, like you're on a patch of ice and sliding and sliding and you can't stop."*

He held his fork over my bowl and raised his eyebrows. When I nodded, he speared a vegetable. *"Exactly. I think that's why geography was always my favorite subject in school. We were always moving because of me da. Always looking for the end of the rainbow, he is. And when he realizes that he won't find it in this spot, it's off to the next. Even so, no matter where we wound up, I'd get meself to the school. And I'd always be good at geography."*

He sounded almost wistful—as if he missed being in the classroom. *"I didn't like anything about school. The teacher in our village wore out three bamboo sticks switching me,"* I bragged. Mainly because I kept playing tricks on Uncle Blacky.

Sean nibbled the vegetable, and when he found it was all right, he ate the whole stalk with open curiosity. *"Sometimes it's easier to be as bad as they expect you to be."*

"And to see how much they will stand before they squawk like ducks." I thought I would test him and picked up a flake of salted fish, which is salty and pungent and not to everyone's taste, and held it out to him.

Sean slid his fork under my chopsticks and then transferred the salted fish to his mouth. I was impressed when he ate it with gusto. *"If I had listened to me da and his yahoo friends, I would have left school ages ago and let him put me to work.*"

In a way, he hadn't stopped being curious about the world. I had become his textbook. "*Instead of now.*"

"*Me ma got sick; and I knew we couldn't count on Da to send his wages home.*" He held out his supper bucket to me and motioned for me to sample his meal. I fished up an over-cooked piece of meat that I ate with far less relish than he had shown for my supper.

Even if his mother had been mean to Sean, he had still forgiven her. "*Is she getting better?*"

He shrugged. "*She died a month ago.*"

"*I'm sorry.*" I concentrated on my own supper.

"*Don't be. If you could ask her, she'd say she's happier.*" To change the subject, he asked me about China.

Talking to him, I realized how little I really knew, so I wound up asking him about *America.* Apparently he'd seen a lot, and I told him so.

"*We moved just about every six months.*" Twisting, he scooped a handful of snow from a tunnel wall and started to bring it toward his mouth.

"*No, drink the tea. Snow can make you sick.*" Setting down my bowl, I rested my chopsticks across it and got up and went over to the barrel nearby. I took off the lid and handed him the dipper. But Sean had no sooner begun to drink than Dandy boomed, "You've ruined the tea. Are you crazy? Now we'll have to refill the barrel all over again."

No Four Districts person takes guff from a Three Districts one. Sweeping my arm through the tea, I splashed it over him. "There. Is that better?"

Father slipped in between us before the man could charge at me. I thought he was going to stand up for me, but I was wrong. "Forgive the boy, Dandy. He's so stupid, he could use his skull for a hammer."

"It's probably thick enough," Dandy conceded as he wiped at the tea on the front of his coat.

As he walked away, Father turned and nodded to Sean. *"You go."*

I slammed the lid on the barrel. "He wasn't doing anything."

"His kind doesn't mix with our kind," Father explained in an overly patient voice—as if to a three-year-old.

"You like western ideas and machines," I argued.

"But not them." Father jerked his head at Sean. *"Go."*

"Shouldn't you be back at work?" Kilroy threw an empty meal bucket into the handcart with a clank.

I glanced down the tunnel, but the others were still eating. *"We just started our meal."*

Kilroy turned toward me. His eyes were even more unnerving than Sean's green ones, because Kilroy's eyes were gray—the color of stone, the color of the mountain. I felt almost as if the mountain itself were staring back at me—as if I were not a human but simply some bug waiting to be squashed. *"Well, I say it's over."*

I got my bowl and chopsticks. *"Thank you."*

However, that still must not have been fast enough for Kilroy, because he grabbed me by the collar and hauled me to my feet. *"I said go, you filthy little heathen. You eat with your own kind."*

I realized with a start that he considered it a comedown for Sean to eat with me—when I had thought it was the opposite. Uncle Foxfire had been wrong. All westerners might be equal among themselves, but we were not westerners. I would have laughed if it had not been so dangerous.

Sean rose. *"He was going, Da."*

I stared at him and then at Kilroy because I had thought Sean was his last name. Kilroy let go of my collar. *"You wait here, you young guttersnipe. I have something to say to you."*

"You always do," Sean countered. Sullenly he handed me the bowl and chopsticks. *"Thanks."* As he leaned in close, he whispered, *"Meet you by the trash heap."*

It didn't matter where we were from, or who we had once been. On the mountain, he and I were in a secret conspiracy against the world. It didn't matter what our fathers thought, and I nodded my head before Kilroy motioned for me to follow and started bellowing, *"Get back to work!"*

Noodles was still stuffing his mouth. He looked over at Uncle Foxfire. "It's too soon."

"I know." Uncle Foxfire stood up and walked over a few paces. He and Kilroy had an animated conversation while I plodded away. In the meantime, Noodles was eating as much as he could. "What did you do to make him so angry?"

"I was just trying out some *American* food with his son. I met the boy on the way up here." I put the bowl down with the other dirties. "I thought his name was Sean."

Honker piled his on top of mine. "They reverse things here. Family name comes last instead of first. So he'd be Sean Kilroy, not Kilroy Sean."

"They get everything mixed up," Bright Star said. "That's why like should stay with like."

I stared right back at him. "Back in the cabin, you said I was a fool. In fact, I wasn't even your own kind. So why should I eat with you?"

"The boy," Bright Star declared to no one in particular, "will never learn."

Doggy held up his hands. "Soft hands, soft brain."

Father came over. "Stay away from him, do you hear?" he asked sternly.

Usually he left the discipline to Mother when he came home, so it was hard to take him as seriously as I was supposed to. Besides, if they could lie to me, I rationalized, I could lie to them.

"Yes, sir," I said.

I moved away from them, an outcast among the outcasts. If anything, they had made me all the more determined to keep Sean as a friend. And for the first time in my life I would even disobey Father.

CHAPTER | XV

It was snowing after the shift, so I waited at the mouth of the tunnel leading out to the trash heap; and Sean found me there. I found I could talk to him about things; and he could do the same with me. He told me that his time in this camp had been the longest his father had stayed in any one place.

After that, when work was done, we would meet somewhere in the tunnel at a spot we had arranged the day before. Tempers were getting thin in camp. The storms had come back in; there was no longer enough firewood, and our meals were rationed. So we were grateful for one another's company.

On the mountain, we had founded our own country with just two citizens; and it didn't matter what the westerners or T'ang people thought. Sean and I did what the others preached. Uncle Foxfire had been right about learning things from the *Americans*. He had just been wrong about the source and the scale.

Sean had even asked to learn some of the T'ang language, so I began to instruct him. *"Now let's try this one. How are you?"* I said.

"How are you?" he repeated.

He had an amazing ear for tone and sound. *"Very good."*

"You sound like a jackass braying, Oofty Goofty," growled a voice. I whirled around to see the man from the mess crew.

I was all for advising caution, because the man was several heads taller and had a much longer reach than Sean's; but he spoke up before I could stop him.

"'Tis better to sound like one than look like one," Sean snapped.

The man raised a fist as big as a ham and shook it at Sean. *"If you weren't that devil's own son, I'd teach you a lesson."*

"And why should that be stopping you?" Kilroy asked from another tunnel. He strolled up through the slush and glanced down at his son. *"Let's see if you got any sand."*

The man warmed up by punching the air, his muscles flexing under his coat. One of the trash haulers stopped at the junction. *"Fight!"* he shouted up one tunnel. *"Fight!"* he shouted down another.

As excited as small boys, westerners and T'ang men

came tumbling out of their shacks or away from work, each shouting in all kinds of languages. Among them, I saw my own crew.

"Fight!"

"Fight!"

"Come on. Let's go," I said in a low voice to Sean.

The man still managed to hear me. *"You're yellow—just like the Chinamen you love,"* he said.

When Sean didn't say anything at first, Kilroy jerked his head at him. *"Will you not do something?"*

Sean folded his arms. *"And isn't nothing something?"*

Kilroy turned from his son and nodded to the man; and the man struck Sean with his fist. My friend staggered back and shook his head as if to clear it. With a grin, the man launched another blow, but Sean ducked. When he straightened up again, he had both fists raised.

I had never seen westerners fight before, and it seemed a bit strange when the man just shuffled his feet occasionally. When I saw that Doggy had squeezed in next to me, I asked him, "Why don't they kick? Don't they know they have feet?"

Doggy was so excited that he forgot he was angry at me. "Most of the time, they use their fists. They don't think it's honorable to use their feet."

Sean may have been shorter, but he was quicker. He

easily ducked under the man's swings; and his own punch smacked solidly against his opponent's stomach. It was so hard, it sounded like a sledgehammer hitting a side of beef.

All the man did was grin broadly and wave a hand for Sean to hit his stomach again.

"It's going to be a long fight," I said to Doggy.

Sean tried to dodge back when the man swung at him, but the snow slowed him down and the man clipped him.

"Or a short one," Doggy observed.

Instinctively, Sean kept backing up even though he looked groggy now. All the spectators had begun shouting hoarse encouragements as the man plowed after him. His head was bent and there was an ugly glint in his eye.

Sean tried to keep him off with quick jabs; but now that the man could smell a kill, he kept trying to close. He blocked some of the jabs with his fists, but others landed. *Whap. Whap. Whap.* Each time, the man's head jerked back; but they might have been gnat blows.

"He's got a head as hard as rock," I said to Doggy. Doggy, watching the fight intently, didn't say anything.

Finally the man dropped his left fist and pretended to swing his right. Sean ducked instinctively; but it was only a feint. The man whipped his left fist up, catching

Sean right on the chin.

His head snapped back and he tumbled backward into the snow. There were groans from the few who had bet on Sean, while the man's supporters began to cheer. I was amazed that anyone would have bet on Sean; but as Shrimp said about Curly, you could find people who would bet the sun would rise in the west—provided you gave them high enough odds.

The whip crack silenced everyone. Kilroy stood with it dangling like a long black snake from his hand. "All right. You've had your fun, now back to work."

The man was going to help Sean up, but Kilroy barked, *"Leave him."*

With a shrug, the man turned to his friends, who swaggered around him, slapping him on the back.

"Come on," Father said to me as the crowd began to drift back to work.

"He could be hurt," I said.

Father grabbed my arm. "He doesn't keep that whip around just to make noise."

I pulled free and started moving toward them. Kilroy was shaking his head at his son. *"It's proud of you I am. In five minutes you've destroyed our name and undermined my authority."*

Sean sat up, blinking his eyes. *"Not to mention puffing up my lip."*

When Kilroy saw me, he growled, *"Haven't you done enough damage?"*

The closer I got, the bigger and meaner that whip looked. It took all of my nerve to take another step. For a moment, I wasn't sure if Kilroy would use it on me.

"We take care cuts." It was Uncle Foxfire. He and Father had followed me over to Sean.

Kilroy relented, so I guessed he wasn't a complete monster. *"Get the fool out of my sight,"* he ordered me.

Uncle Foxfire positioned himself between Kilroy and me. "And then get to our cabin on the double."

At the same time, Father crouched beside me to help Sean to his feet. "And don't push your luck anymore today," he whispered to me. "It was a near thing."

"Come on," I said to Sean.

As Father let go of Sean, he looked at me. "You disobeyed me, didn't you?"

"I'm sorry," I said, "but I had no choice." And I hunched my shoulders, preparing for the tirade.

Father was a gentle soul who rarely got angry. Instead, he looked thoughtful. "Wasn't there anyone else you could talk to?"

I stared at him defiantly. "What do you think?"

He stepped away sadly. "Now it's my turn to be sorry."

As I helped Sean to his cabin, he murmured, *"Poor Da, I'm such a disappointment to him."* He started to laugh and then winced.

Their cabins were in better shape than ours. Though they were the same size, they were less crowded and had tables and chairs as well as beds. *"Which one is yours?"*

"That one." He pointed to a bed. At the foot stood a trunk, on which I saw a picture in an ornate silver frame.

I eased him into the bed. *"Where do you have your medicines?"*

"There's a small medicine chest over there." He pointed to a small black bag.

I tended his cuts under his direction; as I returned the bag, my eye happened to fall upon the picture. The woman in it didn't look painted or drawn. *"What's this?"* I asked.

He mistook my question. *"Me ma."*

I leaned closer to it. *"No, I mean how did the picture get made?"*

He winced again as he sat up and took the picture. *"'Tis a daguerreotype."* He went through several English words that I did not know; but eventually I gathered that people sat in front of a device and it captured their images onto a plate.

When I looked at it more closely, I could see the

resemblance between them. *"You look a lot like her."*

"And nothing like me da," Sean said ruefully.

I restored the bag to its corner. *"It must be marvelous to capture someone's image that way."* I was thinking how I would like to have Mother's picture.

At that moment, the door creaked open and a gust of cold air blew in. When I saw it was Kilroy, I checked his hand for the whip, but it had disappeared. I guessed he kept it coiled up on his belt somewhere underneath his coat.

"Are you all right?" he asked.

Sean set the picture down quickly, as if it were shameful to look at his mother. *"Yes, sir."*

He closed the door. *"Can you work tomorrow?"*

Sean began to slide off the bed. No matter how it hurt, he seemed determined not to show it to his father. *"I'll manage. I'll not embarrass you anymore."*

Kilroy cleared his throat. *"Try to understand. It wasn't for me, lad. It was for you. Without respect, you're nothing."*

"'Tis money that buys respect—like the brigands who own this railroad," Sean said bitterly.

Kilroy crossed the room. *"I'll not have you speaking about them that way."* His voice took on an urgent, pleading tone, as if he were begging Sean to understand. *"They're grand dreamers. Giants. If we can join California and its resources to the* rest of the country, there's no stopping America."

"How convenient to have a destiny." Sean spoke in a bored voice—as if he had heard or read the sentiments often enough.

"And it's for all those families who want another chance." He stood over Sean. "Me da, your grandda, nearly died trying to make it on foot across the mountains. When he sent for us, he thought it would be easier by boat. But me ma got sick crossing the Panama Isthmus." He ran a hand through his hair. "We were so desperate for workers, we were even willing to work with Chinamen."

"And what has America ever done for you?" Sean asked stubbornly. "Except squeeze you into a bottle?"

Strange to realize that a westerner could dream. In his own way Kilroy's dreams were as grand as Uncle Foxfire's. Maybe the deeper he slipped into the bottle, the more he clung to the dream. Or maybe it was the dream that kept him afloat and kept him from drowning. In any event, it was sad that Sean had to pay the price too—especially since Sean didn't seem to share the dream.

Embarrassed for Sean and his father, I sidled behind Kilroy toward the door. He hadn't noticed me yet, so he was surprised when he heard the door open and saw me. I didn't like the way his eyes narrowed—or the look he gave me, which would have withered grass. I don't think he enjoyed the notion of having anyone, T'ang or west-erner, know so much about him. *"You."*

"Excuse me," I said quickly. I slipped through the door-way, half expecting to feel the whip fall between my shoulder blades. I felt grateful when I was able to slam the door shut behind me.

CHAPTER | XVI

When I got back to the cabin, most everything was torn apart; and Bright Star was swearing. "I can't find my carving knife."

"Some thief must have come in while we were gone." Packy began to hit his head as if he blamed himself.

Uncle Foxfire stopped him. "It can't be helped. Everyone check your things."

"I've got all my stuff," Father said after a moment.

"Same here," Curly said. "I don't think the thieves had enough time to do a thorough job of it."

Doggy set his feet on the floor. "My moon guitar is missing." He lowered his head into his hands.

I went over to my bunk between Doggy's and Bright Star's. My own basket hadn't even been touched; but the outrage was burning inside. Even if I didn't like Doggy, I liked his music. "We'll look in each cabin till we find it."

Doggy swung his leg out like a gate to block me. "It's probably kindling by now."

I think everyone felt bad, not just for Doggy, but for themselves, because his music had eased our stay up here. Everyone was on edge that night.

Uncle Foxfire held up his brush with the blunted tip. "The bath water's icing over."

"It's been snowing for the past ten days." Packy shrugged. "We're running low on firewood."

"And on chow," a disgusted Noodles said. "The last three days we've had nothing but some rice and pickled vegetables. Rice and vegetables were all I used to get at home. I could have stayed back there."

Packy frowned. "We're starting to run low on supplies too."

"I'd give my souls for a piece of meat," Curly swore.

We all wound up turning in early; but I couldn't sleep. Doggy may have been a thief and a troublemaker, but his music had become part of my life. I thought of evenings without it—like tonight—and I ached inside, as if there were something missing.

Just when I didn't think I could stand it anymore, I had an idea. When I heard the bunk creaking and groaning above me, I whispered, "Bright Star, are you awake?"

In the dim red light of the coals in the stove, I saw

his head appear over the side. "Obviously."

"I was thinking—" I started.

"What a novelty," he grunted.

My first inclination was to shut up, but that would not help Doggy. "Is there any chance we could pool our resources and buy another moon guitar?"

"These misfits? Everyone hates the others. What would we get out of it?" he demanded in a low voice.

"His music," I whispered back.

I figured if I could win over Bright Star, who was the most uncooperative of the crew, that I might have a chance of getting the entire bunch to accept my idea.

I considered it a good sign that Bright Star didn't lie back on his bunk. Instead, he drummed his fingers thoughtfully on the side of the bed. "On the other hand, who wants to listen to your idle chatter all night? At least when Doggy played, you had to shut up."

It was Bright Star's backhanded way of saying that it was a good idea. The important thing, I reminded myself, is to get a moon guitar for Doggy, so I didn't let myself stay insulted. "Well, Packy's a clever fellow. Maybe if we got together, he would have enough to use in trade."

When his head disappeared, I thought he had broken off the discussion. I was surprised and pleased when his legs appeared and he hopped down to the floor. Doggy lay on his side, with his face to the wall. Careful not to wake Doggy, he went over to the next bunk.

I crept out of my bed just as quietly and went over to Father and Uncle's bunk. With only the coals left in the stove, it was icy cold in the cabin; but their bunk was closest, so they got a little warmth. Gently I touched Father's shoulder. "What?" he asked.

I held a finger to my lips, and he looked at me questioningly. Once I had whispered my plan, he nodded and pointed below, so I woke Uncle Foxfire next while Father woke Packy.

I had expected some of that misfit crew to refuse; but everyone gathered around Father's bunk. When Bright Star had outlined my idea, he asked Packy in a low voice, "So do you think you can get another moon guitar?"

Packy tugged at his thin goatee. "I might, but it'll be expensive."

"Doggy cheats at cards and every other gambling game," Curly complained.

"Think what his music meant to each of you," Father said. He was the first to hand over some money to Packy.

"I saw your faces when he played," I urged them. "He could take you home. He could make you forget you were here."

"We need that." Uncle Foxfire gave as well, and then

waited; but there weren't any more volunteers.

Packy jingled the coins in disappointment. "This wouldn't even buy the strings back."

Still the crew hesitated, each thinking of himself. Uncle Foxfire looked around until his eyes settled on Bright Star.

Bright Star squirmed. "My family's been demanding more money lately."

"And mine," Curly said.

As the echo went around the group, I began to think that another good idea had been smashed by life on the mountain.

But then Shaky seized Packy's hand and turned it palm upward. As we watched in puzzlement, Shaky slipped his lucky charm from around his neck and tried to lower it onto Packy's outstretched hand.

"That's your good luck," Packy protested in a low voice.

Closing his fingers around the charm for one last squeeze, Shaky gave it to Packy. Turning, he nudged Bright Star.

"Not so hard," he complained. As he rubbed the sore spot, he sighed, "Well, if Shaky can make that kind of sacrifice, I guess my family can too. They can use silver buttons instead of gold." He dug some coins from a pocket and added them to the charm.

Uncle Foxfire looked around at the crew. "If you don't chip in, you won't get your music anymore."

Curly got out some coins. "And then you'll have to pass the time by talking to Bright Star. That'll put you into a permanent bog."

"Heaven forbid." Dandy gave some money too.

Dipping into their pockets, one by one, the crew added to the coins in Packy's hand. Father and Uncle Foxfire seemed pleased. I think this was the first time that the crew had cooperated. No matter what personal grudge each might have had against the world, Doggy's music had touched them all.

"I don't have any money yet," I whispered. "But you could take part of my salary."

Packy began counting the coins. "Strictly cash. No I.O.U.s."

I felt helpless at the moment; and this made me feel even more miserable. The cabin would feel like a tomb without Doggy's music.

When Packy finished counting, he put it into a sack. "Do you think that will be enough?" Uncle Foxfire asked.

Packy shook his head slowly. "I don't know. I hope so."

If Shaky could make the supreme sacrifice, so could I. Going to my bunk, I climbed into it carefully—so as not to wake the still-slumbering Doggy. There was a space between the logs, and I eased out my slab of beef jerky. "I've been saving this. Home-grown and home-cured."

To be honest, I'd been nibbling at it for the last three nights when everyone else was asleep. And I saw from their faces that everyone knew it. I think Father and Uncle might also have suspected that this was supposed to be their gift; but they hadn't said anything. The shame of being caught was almost as bad as the hunger.

"Holding out on us." Noodles glared at me contemptuously as if I had just confessed to being an ax murderer.

Packy took it from me. "He's giving it now." He waved it over his head like a prize. "And it's worth its weight in gold." Slipping it inside his sack, he slung it over his shoulder. "Wish me luck," he whispered, and slipped out of the cabin.

It wasn't until several hours later that I felt someone shake my shoulder. When I opened my eyes, I saw Father beside my bunk. He motioned for me to be quiet.

Over his shoulder, I could see the rest of the crew out of their bunks, standing around the stove. Uncle Foxfire was holding a candle in his hand; his breath was wreathing around his head. "Packy's back," Father explained.

Unwrapping myself from my blankets, I slipped out of my bunk and followed him over to Packy's bunk.

Packy was sitting there with a blank expression, .determined not to give any hint about success or failure. Apparently I was the last, because when I joined them, Uncle Foxfire poked him and whispered the question that was on all our minds. "Did you get it?"

Packy had been holding his sack behind his back. Now he brought it around and opened it. "It was the beef jerky that did it." And he lifted out the moon guitar.

Uncle Foxfire clapped him on the shoulder. "I knew we could depend on you." He glanced over his shoulder at the still sleeping Doggy. "We'll surprise him in the morning."

Packy held it out toward me. "Here. Think you can keep from rolling over and smashing it in your sleep?"

"Sure," I said, puzzled, "but why?"

"So you can be the one to present it to him," Packy explained.

I tried to shove it toward Shaky. "You're the one who gave the most."

Shaky pushed it back at me.

Bright Star slapped his arms. "You had a good notion. Take it so we can go back to bed."

Slowly I wrapped my hands around the neck of the

guitar. "Thank you," I said to Shaky, and then I glanced at Packy. "Thanks."

Packy's mouth stretched into an enormous yawn. "Save the speeches." He began shuffling back toward his bunk. "Now for a little sleep."

As we began to move toward our bunks, Father whispered, "You did well, boy."

"But I held out on you," I said, cradling Doggy's precious instrument.

"I meant your idea for trying to buy another guitar." Father squeezed my shoulder approvingly.

From his bunk, Uncle Foxfire gave me the thumbs-up. And though it was frozen in the cabin and my body was shivering, inside I felt warm.

CHAPTER | XVII

For the first time since I'd left the Middle Kingdom, I actually looked forward to waking up. And when I looked out from my bunk the next morning, I saw that most of the crew were already awake and waiting for Doggy to get up.

"This could take forever." Father waved his hand at me. "Get that slug out of his bed."

Climbing out of my bed, I carefully laid the moon guitar where I could reach it. Then I gave Doggy a poke.

Doggy tried to shove me away. "Quit it."

I poked him again. "Look at what we got for you." I held out his instrument.

Doggy rolled over onto his side and his eyes widened. "How . . . ?"

"Never mind," Bright Star urged from his bunk. "Just try to keep that one in tune."

"I don't know how to thank you." He started to reach out with his right hand and then stopped and used his left hand instead.

Honker unwound his scarf so he could be clearly understood. He pointed at Doggy. "What's wrong with your right hand?"

Doggy set the moon guitar down on his bunk. "Nothing. I must've slept on it funny, so it went to sleep." He began to use his left hand to massage his right.

"Maybe I'd better check it," Honker said.

"I just need to get the circulation going. I'm fine." Annoyed, Doggy headed for the stove and tried to lift the kettle in his right hand, but the kettle clunked on the floor, spilling the hot water. "I'm fine," he insisted in a frightened voice.

Honker got out of his bunk. "Let me see."

Steam rose all around Doggy as he laughed nervously. "I'm just clumsy this morning."

Uncle Foxfire joined Honker. "Let me see that hand."

Doggy licked his lips nervously. "Haven't you ever been clumsy?"

"Come on." Uncle Foxfire held out his hand.

Reluctantly, Doggy held out his right hand. "Quit fussing. They're just a little stiff." However, we could all see that the third and fourth fingers of his hand were as rigid as sticks.

Honker studied the fingertips as he rubbed them. "Last night, didn't you wrap rags around your hands?"

Doggy shrugged. "I forgot."

"What do you think?" Uncle Foxfire asked, worried.

Honker looked up somberly. "They're frostbit."

"No!" Doggy snatched back his hand.

"That's what I thought too. They have to come off," Uncle Foxfire said.

As Honker got one of the knives, Doggy protested, "How can I play without fingers?"

Noodles tugged off the glove so we could see that his little finger was missing the top two joints. "It could be worse," Noodles said to Doggy. "You'll be able to work. You'll be able to eat."

Honker opened the stove and put the knife blade into the fire that Packy had started. "So it's your choice. But you could get a lot worse if you don't cut off those fingers now."

It was silent in the cabin while Doggy went over to his bunk and thought. "I guess it could be." He smiled sadly. "There's a fellow three cabins over who lost his nose. Now he can't keep his spectacles on." He reached his left hand out and tapped on the back of his moon guitar. "I can always use this for a drum."

Astounded, I looked at Doggy. "How can you joke at a time like this?"

"Because it's easier to laugh than to cry." Doggy gave one last caress to the moon guitar.

Honker handed him a chopstick. "Put this between your teeth."

White-faced, Doggy set the chopstick in his mouth and planted his hand down on top of his bunk. Father and Uncle Foxfire came over to hold him. No one said anything while Honker shifted the knife around in the stove, heating the blade. When he finally took it out, it glowed red-hot.

I wanted to go outside; but when no one else did, I didn't want them to think I was a coward, so I stayed. But I didn't look. Even so, I don't think I'll ever forget the smell of burning flesh or the funny little crunching sound. Doggy let out a muffled little scream like a toy whistle.

And I heard an ugly snap.

"He's bitten clean through the chopstick," Father swore.

"I'm finished," Honker said in a strained voice.

I turned to see that Uncle Foxfire was bandaging up Doggy's hand. A piece of chopstick angled up on either side of Doggy's face like odd whiskers. As I watched, Father pried the pieces of chopstick from Doggy's clenched teeth.

As they swathed his hand in bandages, Doggy forced himself to laugh.

"At least . . . I won't have to worry . . . about that hand . . . getting frostbit for a while."

Honker began wrapping some rags around his other hand. "There's always rags to keep you warm. You should've asked."

Uncle Foxfire was cleaning the blood from Doggy's bunk. "Lie down in my bed and take it easy today."

As Uncle Foxfire and Father helped him, I gazed around the cabin. The crew looked just like corpses in narrow coffins. And overhead the storm winds howled triumphantly; and the snow . . . the white, white snow piled even higher above us.

Uncle Foxfire straightened and looked at me without saying anything.

"This mountain," I said, "kills singing. It kills laughing. It kills everything. Every day we're here, we die a little."

CHAPTER | XVIII

As we got ready to leave the next day, I said to Uncle Foxfire, "I want to use a pickax today." When he hesitated, I insisted. "I need to hit something."

Curly looked at me sympathetically. "He could use Doggy's today."

With a thoughtful nod, Uncle Foxfire got the pickax from the stack in the corner and handed it to me.

That day, I felt like I was marching with the others through the snow tunnels to a battle. Glancing around, I saw the same grim look on all the others' faces, and I realized they felt as much grief as I did and were determined to do something about it. Bright Star glanced at me and nodded as if he understood my thoughts. The loss of Doggy's music had bound us even more tightly together than the initial loss of his moon guitar.

Once we reached the tunnel, everyone sprang willingly into action. No one hesitated. No one held back or complained that someone else was doing more work. A few quick orders sent drill teams to the end under Father's command. The others began scraping and clawing at the rock while Uncle Foxfire tried again to teach me to use a pickax.

He swung it, twisting from the waist with his whole torso and shoulders, aiming a blow that would have crushed a water buffalo's skull. He did it effortlessly, ready to deliver one crushing blow after another for twelve hours if he had to. The pickax rang as it bit into the rock; and yet despite all the noise and the force, he hardly seemed to have scraped the rock at all.

Then he had me try the motion without the pickax, correcting a few things. When I finally picked up the pickax, it felt heavy as I lifted it over my shoulder and swung, trying to copy Uncle Foxfire. I let the motion itself bring the weight of my body into the blow. The pickax hit the wall with a clink. As before, my forearms felt numb.

"Good," Uncle Foxfire grunted. "Now get into a rhythm."

I swung the pickax again with all my strength; but the point hardly seemed to dent the hard granite.

"Hit it," Uncle Foxfire goaded me. "Don't pat it."

I aimed the pickax at the wall, and the point landed with a clank.

"I thought you were angry." He pretended to look disgusted.

"I am." This time when I hit the wall, I could feel the vibrations shake my whole body.

"Attack it," Uncle Foxfire urged. "Lazy monkey. Monkey! Monkey!"

I could feel the anger and fear swell up inside me and explode, and I began to pound the pickax in rhythm to his chant. I hated the slab of stone in front of me—hated it for being hard, hated it for being in the way of the westerners, hated it for making me come here to this crazy place, hated it for a lot of reasons that didn't make any real sense.

I hated the mountain for being so hard. I hated the pickax for not being sharper. My whole world narrowed to a sharp point. I wanted to drive it right through the heart of the Tiger.

Then, as if from a great distance, I heard Uncle Foxfire saying to me, "Easy. That's it. Get into a steady rhythm now." And I became aware of his hand on my shoulder.

I looked to the side. He smiled as if he knew just

how much I'd needed to hit something. Then he stepped back so I could begin to swing the pickax in an easier, steadier rhythm. Each blow was still solid; but the stone was so hard, it felt like it was hammering back. It seemed strange to measure my life in millimeters.

Rock had always seemed like rock to me; but as I stared at the wall now, I could see that it was not one sheet of bland gray. Instead, there were little bits of white and black mixed in—each about the size and shape of rice grains—as if someone had cooked up a paste of different-colored rocks and then dried it.

As I used the pickax, it seemed as if the mineral specks began to move in the dim lantern light, squirming like tiny bugs. Sometimes they would almost seem to form complicated patterns—like dots in a picture. All I had to do was stand back far enough to understand what I was too close to see. Perhaps I would see whole words written in great sweeping strokes—as if the tunnel were the pages of a giant, secret book.

Next to me, Uncle Foxfire had gotten a pickax and was swinging it just as hard. What had seemed like a wide enough space for one became very narrow as we swung our pickaxes in wide arcs that seemed to just miss one another.

Suddenly he began chanting, "Hit, hit. Work, work.

Get rich. Go home." Our pickaxes began moving in the same rhythm. I was so taken up with concentrating on my own motion that I didn't notice it at first. Finally, though, I became aware of something odd. It took me a moment to put my finger on it, but then I noticed that the noise all around me had synchronized itself to the chant. The crew were hammering and swinging their pickaxes to Uncle Foxfire's chant. They were working as a team. It was just a shame that it had taken Doggy's double tragedy to draw them all together.

As I worked, I gradually felt as if the stone in front of me were only a thin shell. And the next blow would shatter it and pierce right into the mountain's heart. I felt so certain that I lost track of time.

It was as if my arms and body had their own momentum now. Dimly I became aware of how our pickaxes filled the tunnel with that strange, hypnotic song full of bell-like clinks. Even through several layers of clothes, I could feel the sweat staining them all and the granite dust and gunpowder smoke streaking my face.

In the dim lantern light, I thought of those tableaux in the temples back home that showed the various tortures sinners suffer in the afterlife. Surely they should add this tunnel in the Tiger: men hammering at a mountain as if their salvation depended on it.

Then, with a shock, I realized that if some temple did add the scene, I would not be a bystander but a figure right in the middle of the tableau.

Uncle Foxfire must have seen me losing my concentration. "How're you holding up, boy?"

"I'll hold up longer than this mountain," I grunted as I swung again.

Uncle Foxfire nodded approvingly. "We'll make a guest out of you yet."

I stared at the wall. For a moment I thought I saw little specks of rock dance and swarm together into the shape of a giant gate there; but when I blinked my eyes, it was just a lot of dots again. "Maybe," I said.

I had just started to raise my pickax when an explosion rumbled through the tunnel. It knocked me off my feet and on top of Uncle Foxfire.

Dust and smoke rolled outward toward the tunnel mouth.

"Father?" I called toward the end of the tunnel.

From beneath me, Uncle Foxfire wheezed. "Oof, get off, boy."

I rolled onto my side. "What happened?" Uncle Foxfire gripped my shirt so I wouldn't get lost. "I don't know; but let's not get separated."

The dark dust cloud made it impossible even to see

the lanterns. My groping hand found and clung to his wrist. "I wouldn't think of it."

As we got to our knees, I tried to look toward Father's end; but the dust was even thicker now.

"What's wrong?" someone was shouting.

At the same time, someone else was babbling hysterically, "Which way is out? Which way is out?"

In the confusion of voices, Uncle Foxfire got to his feet, pulling me up with him. "Let's see. I think the mouth of the tunnel is this way." But we blundered right into a wall. Somehow in the dust and the confusion, we'd gotten turned around.

I shoved myself away from the wall and bumped into a man stumbling around. Dust had painted his face and clung to his hair, but I managed to recognize Curly. I grabbed him with my free hand. "What happened?"

"I don't know," he said. "Have you seen Dandy?"

A shadowy figure suddenly knocked right into us. "Here." He panted. "Honker, over this way."

"Crew! Foxfire's crew! Over here!" Uncle Foxfire began to shout desperately. "Crew——!" He broke off in a cough.

Somewhere to my left I heard someone hawk and spit. "Where are you?" Bright Star called.

Uncle Foxfire was still coughing, so I shouted to him. "Over here."

"I got Shaky and Noodles," Bright Star yelled back. He sounded closer.

"What about Father?" I demanded.

Bright Star, groping through the dust, found us. He shoved in so close that his face seemed like a dirty, disembodied mask floating in the dust. "I don't know. We were just starting to drill when there was this sudden flash of light. Then the explosion knocked us down."

"We've got to find him," I said, and started to turn.

Uncle Foxfire had kept hold of my shirt all this time and turned me around. "Later."

"He's your own brother-in-law," I protested.

"He'd do the same thing. Now form up," Uncle Foxfire ordered. "Curly, you in front. Bright Star, take hold of him. Then Shaky. Then Noodles. Otter. Dandy." He formed us into a line next to the wall. "I'll take the rear. Keep one hand on the wall and the other hand on the man in front."

We blundered along, sometimes treading on the heels of those in front. Up until then, I had been too confused to become frightened. However, as we made our way blindly out of the tunnel, I began to wonder if it was a cave-in. And what if we were going in the wrong direction?

The other crews and their headmen were still shouting in confusion in the dark dust cloud. I didn't know what had happened to the light—whether the lanterns had all broken or the wicks had blown out—but it was pitch dark. Even at night outside, there's the moon and even if there isn't a moon, there's some faint light from the stars.

However, inside the Tiger, there were tons of stone cutting us off from the light. It was a blackness that I could almost feel wrapping itself around us. Suddenly I wanted more than ever to get out of the tunnel.

Noodles must have felt my hand tightening on his shoulder. "Easy." He tried to encourage me. "This is the last place you want to panic."

I felt as if a whole mountain were about to fall on me. "I don't want to be buried alive." I could hear the shakiness in my own voice.

"Don't be morbid," Dandy said from behind me.

I thought I could feel the rock begin to shake underneath my feet again. Any moment, it seemed, the whole tunnel would collapse, burying us all forever. "Well, I don't," I insisted.

"Bet you five dollars that you get to ship my bones home," Curly called back to me. I thought he intended it as a joke. "How would you collect it?" I laughed nervously.

"He'd find a way," Noodles chuckled.

Then, in the cloud ahead of us, I saw a lantern gleaming like a large, yellow eye. *"Hel-l-l-l-o-o,"* a westerner called.

"Hello," I shouted back, my voice echoing against the stone walls. I felt better, knowing that I was going to make it.

The light seemed to drift toward us. And then I saw Kilroy holding a lantern toward our faces. "How many are inside?"

"Two men from our crew," I said. *"And the other crews."*

He nodded anxiously and squinted back inside the tunnel. If wishes truly worked, he would have asked for the magic to see right through the dust and the dark. "Keep going," he said.

As we stumbled past him, he cupped a hand by the side of his mouth to amplify his voice some more. *"This way,"* he called. His voice boomed and echoed within the narrow space.

A few meters on, we saw a large circle of soft, silvery light. I knew it was only the mouth of the tunnel; but right then it looked more like the gates to Heaven.

CHAPTER | XIX

As we stumbled out of the mountain and into the tunnel of snow, I heard a roar go up. At first, I thought it was another explosion, and I started to throw myself at the ground.

"You okay?" Curly caught me as I tripped.

I realized that it was the other crews cheering. "Yes," I said sheepishly, and stood up again.

I blinked my eyes and then had to shade them. After the inky darkness inside the heart of the Tiger, the dim light of the tunnel seemed as bright as day.

The tunnel was crowded with the rest of the crews, both T'ang and *American*, with shovels in their hands, as if they had all been ready to dig us out. The explosion had shaken some of the snow down from the ceiling, so they were standing ankle deep in the stuff.

As I stood there dazedly listening to the cheering,

Dandy headed for the barrel of tea. Flinging off the lid, he thrust his head into the barrel and drank thirstily.

"Hey, don't drink it all," Noodles croaked, and joined Curly in trying to wash the dust out of his throat.

I lurched after them, squeezing into an empty space so that I could cup the hot tea in my hands and bring it to my mouth. The next moment Bright Star was next to me, slurping down the tea as if his life depended on emptying the barrel. Dandy gave way to Shaky, who didn't drink. Instead he splashed tea onto a gash on his forehead.

I straightened up to give someone else a turn. We were all a sight: between the smoke and dust and tea, we were all striped like tigers. Behind us, another cheer went up; and I turned to see that other men had staggered out, having finally reoriented themselves.

Uncle Foxfire was right there by the entrance, surveying the faces anxiously. He half turned, his lips moving as he counted his crew by the barrel. Taking the unused dipper, I filled it with tea and made my way carefully among the dirty survivors streaming toward the tea barrel. Bright Star obligingly slipped in front of me to act as a shield.

In his wake, I made it easily to Uncle Foxfire. He drank thirstily, not caring if tea washed down the front of his padded jacket.

By the entrance, a lantern had crashed on the snow and the spilled oil had burst into flame. Snow melted and bubbled and hissed around the edges of the fire and ribbons of steam drifted out like the ghosts of worms.

"There's two missing," he said.

"Honker was with Squeaky," Bright Star said.

Uncle Foxfire sniffed the air. "Wait. I can smell Honker's medical balm."

The turbaned Honker shuffled out of the darkness, his long muffler trailing behind him like a tail. I grabbed his arm as he tried to pass. "Did you see Father?"

Honker shook his head as he tried to gather up the excess length of muffler on his arm. "I don't know. He was holding the drill, and I had the hammer. All I know is I hit it good and the next moment the whole world went up. There were rocks flying all around, ricocheting off the walls." He held up his hand to reveal a gash. "That must be how I got this." He tore a strip from the bottom of his shirt to use as a bandage.

Kilroy came over with Shrimp. *"What happened?"*

Handing the dipper to me, Uncle Foxfire stared at him accusingly. *"You make triple pack. Powder not all burn same time. Some go off later."*

Kilroy squinted. *"We don't know that for sure."*

Shrimp was still trying to make excuses for his bosses.

"Maybe one of the holes didn't go off. Or it was just smoldering. Maybe some snow got tracked in and wet the fuses somehow."

Uncle Foxfire rounded on Shrimp. "Whatever it was, the charge just blew out of the hole like a cannon. And it sent rocks out like bullets."

Even if Kilroy couldn't understand T'ang, Uncle Foxfire's tone was plain. He stepped in between Uncle Foxfire and Shrimp to keep them from coming to blows. *"We ought to check to see if more charges are still smoldering."* He waved a hand at all the men standing idle.

"All you think about is tunnel, tunnel, tunnel," Uncle Foxfire said accusingly.

Shrimp sucked in his breath sharply. "Mind your manners."

Kilroy, however, was unrepentant. *"That's right, John. We've got God's country sitting west of the mountains and a whole continent wanting to get to it; but it can't because of these mountains. So are you going to ask for volunteers, or do I have to pick some?"*

"I go myself," Uncle Foxfire snapped.

Honker shook his head. "He was right in front of the hole. I don't think you can help him. He never answered when I called."

Right then I thought I knew how Doggy had felt when he had lost part of himself. Losing Father would be like losing my smile or my laugh.

"He could be out cold," I said worried. I kept hoping that Father would bull out of the tunnel. He had survived over here almost as long as Uncle Foxfire; he seemed almost as indestructible.

By then, the rock dust and smoke had settled on the snow, but it was still dark inside. Even the kerosene was burning itself out. All I could think of was Mother and what would I say to her.

Going over to a pole outside the tunnel, I lifted down a kerosene lantern. "*I go.*"

Kilroy, Shrimp and Uncle Foxfire twisted around and looked at me in surprise. "Stay out of this," Uncle Foxfire snapped.

I simply skipped over the puddle surrounding the broken lantern, which was already icing over. "I don't have any children."

"That's just the point." Uncle Foxfire caught up with me within the tunnel. "You're a fool."

I tried to grin as I listened for some sound from within the tunnel. "Then you ought to be happy that I'm adopted."

When he hugged me clumsily, the lantern swung in my hand, sending shadows whipping back and forth with its motion. "No, it's the way Cassia brought you up."

As we made our way slowly down the tunnel, I checked around anxiously. The tools lay where they had been dropped and the baskets were overturned. There was no sign of Father.

"Squeaky?" Uncle Foxfire called.

"Please answer us," I yelled.

When our voices echoed mockingly off the cold, stone walls, I began preparing myself for the worst. Then, at the end of the tunnel, we saw a figure lying among the rocks.

"Father!" I hopped over a large rock and nearly fell on the icy floor. So, as much as I wanted to run, I shuffled painstakingly through the rubble.

He didn't move or say anything when I shone the lantern on his face; and his face was bloody. Around his head there was a dark red pool that was beginning to freeze.

Kneeling, I took his wrist. The flesh was still warm; I felt for a pulse. It was so faint at first that I couldn't tell if I was imagining it or not. Then, to my immense relief, I felt his pulse grow stronger—as if he were taking energy from the touch of my hand. "He's alive—barely."

"Thank Heaven." Uncle Foxfire opened his coat and began to tear a strip from the bottom of his shirt.

Laying down Father's hand, I set the lantern on the

floor and examined a wound on his shoulder. "He looks like he's been shot several times." I lifted my head to gaze around and saw fresh nicks in the wall. "It must have been just like Honker said: rocks bouncing all around."

"It's my fault for giving in," Uncle Foxfire said.

I looked up at him in surprise. "I never thought I'd hear the almighty Foxfire admit to being wrong."

He motioned for me to lift Father up. "I'm wrong lots of times. Squeaky wanted to stay home on our last visit; but I wanted to find out about the fire wagon."

"You talked him into it?" Carefully I raised Father's torso.

"Like Tiny, your birth father." Uncle Foxfire began to wind the bandage around Father's wounded shoulder. "There isn't a day that I don't send him a prayer of apology."

It was all very well for dreamers to have dreams; but the rest of us got hurt too.

"A lot of good it does him." I helped knot the bandage while Uncle Foxfire made more bandages from his shirt. "And a lot of good it does my father."

He seemed genuinely distressed as he tore strips from his shirt. When he was done, he had only half a shirt left. "He came here to build a future for you."

I thought, This is as bad as any war. If I don't get

blown up or crushed, I'll freeze. However, I forced myself to act calmly and used a rag torn from my own shirt to try to clean Father's face as carefully as Mother would have. "A fat lot of good that future is if I'm going to die too."

As I held Father's head, Uncle Foxfire began to bind it. "I swear to you, boy. You'll get down from this mountain and home if it's the last thing I do."

When we had finished bandaging Father's wounds, I felt his wrist again. "His pulse is stronger than before."

"What—?" Father's eyelids fluttered open.

Relieved, Uncle Foxfire straightened up. "There was an accident. Fortunately, most of the rocks hit your noggin rather than your body."

Father's eyes rolled in the direction of his brother-in-law's voice. "Who's there?"

I began to feel a sense of panic; but I fought to keep it from my voice. "It's Uncle Foxfire and me, Otter."

Father turned toward me and stared at a spot above my head. "Didn't you bring a lantern? It's so dark. How did you ever find me?"

Uncle Foxfire snatched up the lantern and held it near Father. "We've got a lantern right here."

Father's eyes flicked around the tunnel as if he were looking for it. "I . . . I can feel its warmth." He raised his hand to find the lantern and yelped when his groping fingers touched the lantern's hot chimney.

"Sorry." Uncle Foxfire snatched the lantern back.

"This is some kind of joke, right?" Lifting his hand again, he spread his fingers and flapped his hand back and forth before his eyes. "I can't see my hand." The panic made his voice rise higher. "I can't see."

I knelt there, watching in horror as his hand skittered over his face like some giant spider. "I'm blind."

Uncle Foxfire took Father's hand and drew it down. "It's probably just something temporary."

Father clutched at Uncle Foxfire's wrist as tightly as a drowning man. "Don't try to trick the trickster. My days of riding the Tiger are over."

For a moment, I felt an irrational surge of anger: Legends weren't supposed to give in so easily; but then I managed to tamp it back down. "What would Mother say?"

"Cassia," he groaned. "I completely forgot about her. Cassia's going to be so mad."

"Let's get you out of here first before we buy your boat ticket." Uncle Foxfire got a hand under his shoulders. "Can you walk?"

Father bent one leg and then the other, rotating his ankles experimentally. "I think so."

I got hold of Father's other hand. Together, Uncle Foxfire and I supported him so he could sit up. "I feel dizzy," he muttered.

"You lost a lot of blood," Uncle Foxfire said. He nodded for me to pick up the lantern. "You're lucky your skull's so thick."

Father's mouth twisted itself into a tight, crooked smile. "Yeah, lucky."

Uncle Foxfire and I helped him to his feet. "We'll take it slow," Uncle Foxfire reassured him. "The footing's treacherous."

Father was so boyish that he had always seemed of a young if indefinite age. Now, however, he suddenly seemed to have aged sixty years. He clung to both of us desperately.

Uncle Foxfire took most of the burden as we helped him shuffle along. "Walk in short steps. Mind the rock to your right."

Father nodded dumbly. I could feel how every muscle in his body was stiff as he stepped around the unseen rock. "Let's just take our time," he said.

Moving slowly, we picked our way through the rubble and back along the tunnel. The light from the swinging lantern seemed to ripple along the rough-hewn rock, making the rock itself seem to pulse like living tissue.

More than ever, I felt the Tiger begin to close around me; and the fear was like a mole living inside me, its claws scrabbling deeper and deeper into my mind.

As we neared the mouth of the tunnel, I heard Bright Star shout from outside, "I see a light!" He must have yelled into the tunnel, because his words bounced from the walls like so many rocks. "How's Squeaky?"

Uncle Foxfire and Father hesitated, so I called back, "He's blind." I added, "Temporarily."

When we emerged from the mountain into the snow tunnel, the silence was like some living thing. It was strange, but I don't think I had ever heard it on the mountain. Even when the shifts changed places, there was always the sound of voices and the clink of a pickax somewhere.

Now, the silence was so great you could have heard a snowflake drop.

CHAPTER | XX

Kilroy was the first one to speak. *"All right,"* he said in a deep growl, *"get back to work, John."*

He was addressing me, using the name he used for all the T'ang men. I stared up at him in disbelief. He couldn't be ordering us back into that deadly tunnel—not after what had just happened. *"No."*

"I said to get back to work. Sabe?" He aimed a kick at me; and I had to leave Father to Uncle Foxfire so I could dodge him.

Then, as I stood there panting, all the fears, the cold, the very strangeness of the land suddenly became a tidal wave that threatened to drown me. *"My father and I quit,"* I said.

Kilroy stared at me as if I were a dog that had just done something on him. *"Eh?"*

"We quit," I enunciated the words carefully and slowly, but Kilroy's face was still as blank as if I had spoken T'ang words—or rather as if I were some animal that had just barked at him. So I repeated rapidly, *"We quit, we quit, we quit."*

Alarmed, Father thrust his hand out, his fingers trying to grab me. "You're upset. Be quiet."

"No." I stayed away from the spiderlike hand—as if that hand could shove me back all by itself into the tunnel. "No. I'm going home. It's too cold here. And it's too dangerous. And I'm scared. No one said anything about getting blown up. This is like living in the middle of a battlefield."

Uncle Foxfire let go of Father and clutched at my arm. "They won't let you leave."

By then, other western engineers and bosses shoved their way to the front and had formed a line between us and the rest of the T'ang people, including our crew. I saw Sean trying to break through.

Kilroy unbuttoned his coat to expose the whip coiled on his belt. "You work," he said in mangled T'ang words.

The sight so shocked me that I just froze there while Father, now unsupported, stumbled in the direction of Kilroy's voice. *"No trouble. I talk to him,"* Father tried to reassure Kilroy. He tripped and fell to his knees.

Uncle Foxfire stood uncertainly, torn between help-ing Father and stopping me. *"I explain everything to him."*

Father held out his hands urgently. "Otter, come here."

Still stunned, I just stared at them both. Back in the Middle Kingdom, Father and Uncle had seemed so power-ful; but now I realized just how helpless they really were here. "I'm not going to wind up like you. I'm leaving."

Kilroy lifted the coiled whip from his belt. *"John, you're scared of the mountain when you really ought to be scared of me."*

Uncle Foxfire seemed to be speaking to both Kilroy and Father. *"Is okay. I fix."*

Kilroy hesitated; but then, with a little shrug, he shook out the whip so that it lay like a long, black snake in the snow. *"I'll tell you one last time. Get back into that tunnel."*

"No." Uncle Foxfire started to reach for the whip.

Kilroy swung the whip up so that the butt caught Uncle Foxfire right under his jaw and sent his uncon-scious form right into Father. *"I can't have you starting a riot,"* Kilroy warned me.

Father lowered Uncle Foxfire to the ground and moved forward on his knees, hands still fumbling in the air. *"Please, boss. Let me talk this boy. This my son."*

"Get back into that tunnel!" Kilroy roared.

Instead, though I was so afraid that I could only walk

stiff-legged, I took a step away from the Tiger. *"I was born free. I am free. This is a country where you fight wars to be free."*

I heard the crack as Kilroy raised and lowered the whip. *"Not on my mountain!"*

I froze for a moment and then took another step. *"I'm going home if I have to walk across the ocean."*

Kilroy swung his arm around, and with the lash he flicked snow centimeters from my right foot, to demonstrate that he could direct the whip wherever he wanted. However, I kept right on walking.

"Halt!" Outraged, Kilroy drew his arm back.

"No," I said.

I didn't believe my ears when I heard the crack of the whip; but the next moment, I felt a fiery pain across my back. The heavy whip had ripped through even the thick padding of my coat and my shirt as if they were paper.

With a scream of pain, I fell to my knees. I put a hand to my back and winced as I felt the wet stripe across my back. When I brought my hand in front of me again, I saw the blood. As I held out my hand to him, drops fell from my fingers to stain the snow. *"You hurt me."*

This time when the lash struck, I had no strength in my legs, and its force sent me sprawling on my face.

"There's only one way down from this mountain and that's my way. You sabe me, John?" Kilroy demanded.

I remembered a curse I'd heard a westerner use. *"The devil take you,"* I said as I tried to stand.

He whipped me again. *"I gave him my soul a long time ago,"* he said.

My back felt on fire as I tried to push myself up. Behind the line of westerners, there were maybe a hundred or so T'ang men with pickaxes, shovels and chisels and hammers. "Help me!" I begged.

Father was crawling on his hands and knees. "Quiet, boy, or you'll just make things worse."

Instead I called to the other T'ang men. "We outnumber them."

At first, they only stared at me silently; but then I heard Brush's high, taunting laugh. "Where's all your bragging, Mr. Know-it-all, Mr. Show-off?"

Kilroy gave me eight more strokes. When he cracked his whip for the ninth time, I simply cringed, and fell screaming in terror— and was surprised when the only thing that touched me was snow falling from the ceiling. He must have swung the lash over my head.

"Let that be a lesson to you all," Kilroy announced.

When Father finally found me, his hands patted my arm clumsily. Instinctively I drew away, afraid he might touch my back, but he clutched at my arm again. "Don't make him madder."

"I want to go home," I whispered, and then screamed as the whip cracked overhead again. Kilroy hadn't touched me, but the sound was enough to shatter my raw nerves.

Father bent, putting his arms around me so that his own body acted as a shield. "You will," Father said gently, "but just not as soon as you'd like."

As I sat up with his help, I gasped in pain. "How can you stand it?" I broke into sobs. "I'm not tough like you."

Despite his own terrible accident, his only thought was of me. "I'm a fool, boy. I've always been a fool. But I've always taken things one day at a time. I'll do that with blindness now. So," Father whispered in my ear, "we're going to stand up. Can you do it?"

I nodded my head tentatively.

"Try." Father got up and I rose with him. *"You not need whip now,"* he said to Kilroy.

Kilroy coiled up the whip, looking almost guilty. *"You know I hate to use this. But I'll not have him spread a panic."*

"It wouldn't look good in the reports," Sean said drily.

"It won't look good anyway." Kilroy shook snow from the whip. *"The whole day's shot."* He began coiling it up as if in a hurry to hide it.

"And isn't it inconvenient that a Chinese had to get himself blown up like that?" Sean asked sarcastically.

"*This whip can stripe a white back too,*" Kilroy warned; but he attached it to his belt and pulled his coat back down.

Father was smiling reassuringly at Kilroy as if trying to calm a vicious dog. "*No trouble. No trouble,*" he said to Kilroy. "*He good boy now.*"

"*You make sure of that, John,*" Kilroy warned and nodded to Uncle Foxfire. "*Some of you get this other man back to his cabin. And the rest of you get back to work. You sabe?*"

"*Sure, sure, everybody sabe.*" Father began to maneuver me back into the tunnel; but I got us turned in the right direction. By then, the rest of our crew had been let through to pick up Uncle Foxfire and to take Father and me back to our log shack.

CHAPTER | XXI

Honker threw off his scarf. "It's going to hurt," he warned me as I lay on my stomach on top of my bunk. I just bit my lip as Honker began to put on one of Mother's ointments. It stung at first; and despite my best intentions, I took my breath in with a hiss.

Uncle Foxfire sat on his bunk, rubbing his jaw. "Oh, no," he said when he saw me.

However, the ointment had begun to cool the lacerated flesh, and I kept a sullen silence as Honker bound me up in bandages. Uncle Foxfire stood up and swayed slightly, and he had to grab hold of his bunk for support.

Honker flapped a hand toward Uncle Foxfire's bunk. "Sit back down. I'll tend to you in a moment."

I rested my chin on my forearms as a new thought finally sank in. "We either finish this railroad or die, don't we?"

218

"What do you expect when you strike a bargain with demons?" Honker asked as he tied a knot in the bandages. I stared at Honker.

Uncle Foxfire, though, did not try to correct him. "I swear to you again: You'll get off the mountain alive and whole." Uncle Foxfire tried to pull the blanket up over my legs.

But I shoved his hands away, as he became the target for all my rage. "How? When I'm crippled like Father?" I regretted my words the moment I spoke; and I looked guiltily toward him. "I'm sorry."

"Anger is a luxury up here," Uncle Foxfire warned. "Listen to me."

If my uncle had kept quiet, I might have simply mourned for my father; but his words made my wrath blaze up again so white-hot that I felt as if I would burn to ash the next moment. "Like he listened to you? Like my first father did too? What kind of future is that?"

Uncle Foxfire jerked back as if I had just lashed him. "You respect me, boy."

"Respect what?" I demanded bitterly. "The Almighty Foxfire. Your crazy notions got my adopted father injured and my birth father killed. You're an idiot and worse than an idiot. You're a jellyfish, too."

A muscle twitched on Uncle Foxfire's cheek, but he

said quietly, "Have your say, boy. I owe you that much."

"What are the white demons going to teach us?" I deliberately used the insulting name for *Americans.* "How to make a wasteland? How to turn people into slaves? You put your faith in them, and they betrayed that trust." I tried to work up the phlegm to spit, but my throat was too dry. "Your Great Work is nothing but lies."

"Finished?" he asked.

I glared at him scornfully. "And I'm as good as dead—thanks to you."

"No," he said. "Because this is one promise that I'll keep."

Father rose on one elbow on his bunk. "Maybe you should go," Father suggested, "before you excite my son anymore."

"But I swear—" Uncle Foxfire began.

Father cut him off. "Don't make promises you can't keep."

Uncle Foxfire's shoulders sagged guiltily. "You don't believe me?"

"All my life, I've lived in your shadow; but no more," Father said with quiet conviction. "From now on, I do what's best for me and mine."

Shaken, Uncle Foxfire retreated to the door. "If there's anything you need, send Packy."

Doggy was still slumbering in Uncle Foxfire's bunk. Honker went over to check on his bandages. "I will."

A draft of cold wind blew in when he opened the door. When he shut it again, Father leaned out. "Packy?"

Packy bustled over from the stove. "Here. What do you need?"

"I'd like my son's coat. And then thread a needle for me." He managed a smile despite everything. "I'll mend it."

I felt mortified. "Don't fuss over me, Father. I can fix my own tears."

As Honker draped the coat over his lap, Father said, "I have to learn. I'm not going to be carted around like a load of old wood."

It grieved me to hear Father say things like that. It made me feel terribly helpless. "This is just temporary." I tried to comfort him. Silently I raised my eyebrows at Honker. When Honker shook his head, I felt my own heart sag.

Taking out a needle and thread, Packy smoothly slipped the thread through the needle's eye. "That's right. Just think of it as a rest from my ugly face. You'll be seeing it all too soon."

Father waited patiently with a palm thrust out. "Don't try to trick the trickster. I know this is permanent."

Packy tied off the thread. "At least you'll get to go home."

Father accepted the needle from him. "I just wish I could take Otter with me."

For Father's sake, I tried to keep up a bold front. "Don't worry about me. I'll get home soon. Then I'll be your eyes."

Father began painstakingly to sew up the rips in my coat. "You couldn't be any closer to me than if you had been born my own son."

I felt a lump in my throat. "I know."

He went on sewing. "Do what you have to do, but come home alive."

Though it sent a pain ripping through my back, I pulled the blankets up over me and lay on my stomach. "I will," I promised. Then I closed my eyes and tried to forget that I was caught in a death trap.

When the crew got off their shift, they came into the cabin as if they were going to a funeral. There wasn't the usual joking and roughhousing when the shift was done.

Curly took off his hat. "How . . . unh . . . are you feeling?"

Father tried to joke. "Fine—now that I don't have to look at your ugly mug."

The others began to smile in relief, and Dandy turned to me. "You're not a real guest till some American marks you." He started to draw up his pants leg. "I still got a dent in my leg from a sailor's club."

"I don't want to see," I growled. "I don't want to talk. I just want to get off this mountain."

Bright Star headed for the stove. "If he wants to be a ghost, let him be a ghost."

"Leave him alone," Father counseled. "His temper will heal when his back does."

Only it didn't. Every morning I woke up hating the Tiger and hating Uncle Foxfire for getting me stuck here.

Sean came by after a few days. *"It's sorry I am that I couldn't visit you before, but Father watches me like a hawk. He says our friendship undermines his authority. How are you?"* he asked.

"How do you think?" I snapped.

He touched a bruise on his cheek. *"Whoa, now. I got this trying to help you. So don't be getting mad at me."*

My eyes raked him contemptuously from head to foot. *"But you could leave anytime."*

When he flushed, his bruise got even more purple. *"I can't help that."*

"Then get out," I said.

Though Father's eyes still hadn't healed, he remained as optimistic as ever. *"He's still a little upset. Come back in a few days."*

"I will." Sean left the cabin resentfully.

They left me alone after that. I lay there for a long time, unable to sleep because of the pain and yet unable to collect my thoughts into a coherent pattern. Bitter, alone, lost.

Somehow I eventually slipped into a kind of half sleep, and in my dreams, I saw my birth father, a big, dark shadow, smelling of smoke from his blacksmith's forge— with iron arms that could have tossed me up to heaven but that remained by his sides as if he were bound.

CHAPTER | XXII

When I went back to work, I could see the other crews snickering as I passed; the story of my humiliation must have spread through the whole camp. The only ones who didn't mock me were my own crew. I challenged Bright Star about that, and he just shook his head.

"There isn't one of us who hasn't wanted to run away," he explained. "It could have been any of us. And it could have been any of us who were blinded. All we have is one another. We have to cooperate if we're going to get off this mountain alive."

It was true that the crew worked even more smoothly and efficiently than before. My punishment and Father's blinding had shown them that they would have to depend on one another.

It became a real pleasure to take a pickax to the

mountain. Sometimes I would pretend it was Kilroy, sometimes it was Uncle Foxfire, sometimes it was just simply the Tiger.

Outside, the sky was just as angry as I felt. The storms just kept piling in, one after another without any apparent break, so it was impossible to send Father home. Eventually there was so much snow that the camp was shut off from rest of the world by a cold, white wall of snow.

When we started to run out of fuel, we began wearing spare shirts and coats or whatever we could scrounge. Even old newspaper became hard to find as people used it for an extra layer of insulation.

By then, one bowl of rice gruel seemed like a luxury. Finally we were down to eating what the westerners ate— watery cornmeal. Most of the others went to bed as soon as they could, to try to keep warm and forget how hungry they were.

"You know," Father said to Doggy one night, "we could use a good song."

Doggy had kept the moon guitar out of sentiment, but of course he never played it. "I can't sing unless the moon guitar can accompany me."

"Your voice isn't that bad," Bright Star said.

"If you could strengthen it, you might go into the

theater when you're done here," Uncle Foxfire suggested.

Encouraged by the rest of the crew, Doggy tried a song. As he had implied, his voice was a little on the thin side; and he sang so softly and tentatively that it was difficult to hear him. Despite that, we all told him how fine it was—even Bright Star.

As Doggy's confidence grew, so did his voice, so his singing was soon the one bright spot. Even so, it couldn't keep us from forgetting the cold and our hunger for long.

One morning we got up amidst much coughing. Breakfast was weak tea and cornmeal. All around me I heard my usual breakfast music of coughs—from small, throat-clearing ones to chest-wracking growls.

Dandy shuffled over and felt his wash. He spat out a half-frozen lump of cornmeal. "It's frozen already. And look at this. None of my wash dries. It just freezes." He took a shirt off the line strung between the bunks and held up the shirt by the stiff sleeve. "We need more heat in here."

Packy took it personally. "We have only enough to cook our meals. Your clothes don't stink any worse than we do."

Noodles slowly swung off his bunk. Curly tried to pull him back. "Noodles, don't."

"I came to America so I wouldn't starve." Picking up the chunk of cornmeal, Noodles crammed it into his mouth. It made a lump in his cheek.

Uncle Foxfire filled a cup from the kettle and frowned when he had sipped it. "This is awfully weak tea." He fished his finger around in his teacup. "And it's only lukewarm."

Packy stirred the pot of cornmeal with difficulty. "Be glad of what you have. By tomorrow, there'll be no more wood, no more tea and no more cornmeal."

Noodles began to stuff his foot into his boot. "Then what are we supposed to eat?"

Packy pointed a ladle toward Bright Star's boot. "You're looking at it."

"If I had stayed home, I'd still be hungry, but at least I'd be warm." Doggy looked down at his mutilated hand. "And I'd still be able to play."

Suddenly we could all feel a rumbling under our feet. Father turned his head toward the mountain tunnel even though he couldn't see it. "Funny. That sounded like it was away from the tunnel. Why would they be blasting there?"

Suddenly the cabin began shaking, and there was the loud roar like an explosion. Plates and cups rattled, and Packy clutched at the stovepipe. He jerked his hands down as quickly as he could because the metal was so hot.

Uncle Foxfire flung him a shirt, and Packy wrapped it around his hands so he could steady the pipe. "Avalanche!" someone shouted outside.

The word echoed and reechoed down the tunnel as others took up the cry. "Avalanche! Avalanche!"

It was like some strange, terrible bird had swooped into the cabin.

A boy came pounding at our door. "Avalanche!"

Doggy threw open the door. "Where?"

The boy looked about my age. He pointed to the end of the tunnel. "It took out a bunch of cabins at the end." He was so agitated that he slipped into the Fragrant Mountain dialect, and spoke so rapidly that we couldn't understand him.

"What did he say?" Uncle Foxfire demanded from Packy.

Packy was taking off his apron. "He says that the snow just swept them all away."

Nodding his head like a puppet, the boy pivoted and started to slog down the tunnel again. "Avalanche! Avalanche!"

As others repeated the cry, Father struggled to rise from his bed. "So much for a quiet breakfast."

Uncle Foxfire made him sit back down. "You stay put."

As the others began to pick up their shovels and pickaxes, Packy threw the tea on the stove, extinguishing the fire.

Bright Star pulled up the collar of his coat. "I knew it. There was just too much snow piling up on top of the mountain."

By the time we emerged from our shack, the other crews were marching into our tunnel. One man was wiping the lather from the crown of his head; he must have been shaving when the call went out. As they tramped on by, the light of their lanterns and candles winked off the sharp points of their pickaxes and the edges of their shovel blades. They looked like a company of soldiers moving to meet a surprise attack.

I pointed at some drillers as they paraded by with their long iron poles bobbing. "We're not going to blast."

Bright Star stood within the doorway like a diver about to take the plunge. "We need them as poles," Bright Star explained. "You want to find where there might be air pockets. A man could live for hours in there. There could be survivors."

We surged as a group after Bright Star into the crowd. "There." Dandy pointed to a solid wall of white where a cabin had been. "That's where the snow fell. It's Mouse Ear's crew."

While Uncle Foxfire surveyed the area with a professional eye, several headmen were already shouting directions. "Here," a barrel-shaped man was saying to his Three Districts men. I saw Brush among them.

"There, there," a headman called Nosey was saying to the Four Districts men. With all the other headmen also shouting orders, we were like ants scurrying around helter-skelter after water had been poured down their colony.

"Hey, Keg Mouth," Uncle Foxfire shouted to the barrel-shaped man. "We need one headman."

"And I suppose you're the one?" Keg Mouth asked suspiciously.

"I'll take orders from you," Uncle Foxfire offered.

Keg Mouth was still suspicious of a Four Districts man. "Why?"

"Because we call ourselves children of the T'ang," Uncle Foxfire explained desperately, "but we don't act like it. Everyone thinks of his family first, and then his clan, and maybe his home district. But that's it. That's how the Manchus stay in power, because they play us off against one another. And that's how the westerners control us."

Keg Mouth nodded his head slowly. "Let's talk to Nosey."

I jumped when I heard Kilroy's whip crack. *"Get back to work!"*

I turned to see him limping into the tunnel. Sean and some of the American bosses followed him.

Uncle Foxfire stood his ground. But it was always difficult to argue in a foreign tongue. Instead of using complicated, well-reasoned arguments, you could only put your conviction into a few forceful words. *"We look for men in snow."*

"For Heaven's sake—" Sean began to argue, but his father cut him short.

"They could be halfway down the mountain. You could look all day and not find them," Kilroy said; but he didn't look too happy.

"We not send bodies home, their ghosts not happy," Uncle Foxfire argued.

"Then we'll find them in the spring when the thaw comes." Kilroy raised his voice. *"Third shift, get back to work. The rest of you back to sleep, or you'll be too tired to work when your shift comes."*

"You heard Kilroy," Shrimp called. As usual, he was late.

Uncle Foxfire looked at the crews. "Stay. We outnumber them. If we stick together, there's nothing we can't do." He was brave enough—I had to give him that much.

For once, Keg Mouth nodded his head in agreement. So did Nosey.

Kilroy gestured impatiently toward the mouth of the tunnel, and the other American bosses began taking out their pickax handles and whips.

Men began looking around uncertainly. "Keep on digging," Uncle Foxfire ordered. "If you were under that snow, you'd want us to keep looking."

"But you're not," Shrimp argued. "You're still alive. Keep it that way."

The Americans began laying on forcefully with their clubs and the butts of their whips. The bosses never hit hard enough to break any bones. At first, I thought it was from a sense of shame. Then I realized that they couldn't afford to put that many men out of action. Though the workers had their pickaxes and tools, they did not use them as weapons. Instead, they just stood there stubbornly, submitting to the blows.

Shrimp pointed at me. "They could whip you just as bad as they did him."

"He's bluffing," Uncle Foxfire called. "They need us more than we need them."

The crowd stirred and then, by ones and twos, the men began to drift past the headmen and back up the tunnel. One boy darted back and forth among the workers.

I recognized him as the boy who had first knocked at our door. "No, no, my brother's under there. Help me."

He jumped when Kilroy grabbed his shoulder and spun him around. *"You heard me, John. Get going."*

The boy dropped to his knees and bowed; his face disappeared into the slush. "Please, please, save my brother," he wailed.

Kilroy didn't understand a word. Impatiently, he grabbed the screaming boy by the queue and jerked him to his feet.

"Let him go," Uncle Foxfire pleaded. *"His family under snow."*

"For the love of God, Father," Sean begged from behind Kilroy.

Kilroy dropped the boy back into the snow and spoke with exaggerated slowness—as if to a toddler. *"We'll assign you to a new crew, John. But you got to leave now. Sabe?"*

"Please." The boy got slowly to his feet. Pressing his face against the snow had turned his eyebrows white and given him a frosty beard. His head bobbed up and down as he continued to beg. *"Please."*

Shrimp's voice grew harsh. "They could whip you just like that dog." He nodded to me again.

The boy shook his head back and forth. "I don't care."

"They could whip you so bad that you'd be laid up for months and no money going home." Shrimp had finally found the right threat. Failing the family was far worse than personal pain.

Like most of the others, the boy had probably come over on credit. He probably owed money to the labor contractor and others who had paid for his ticket.

The boy began walking away from the wall of snow, his legs moving stiffly as if they were made of stone. Outraged, I tried to pull him back. "Where are you going? You can't leave your brother."

The boy whirled, sending up a flurry of snow. "I have a mother at home. I'm all she's got left." In his own mind, he had already accepted his brother as dead.

I watched in disgust as the others began to follow him, even Nosey and Keg Mouth. "You don't have any more spine than a jellyfish."

Keg Mouth shrugged. "After all, Mouse Ear's crew were Fragrant Mountain men."

Shrimp taunted me. "You're a fine one to talk about courage. You're the one who wanted to run away. How's your back?" He put his arm around the boy's shoulders. "Come on. We'll find you a good crew."

"No," Uncle Foxfire called to the others; but the men flowed away like dry sand poured between open fingers.

In the end, it was only Uncle Foxfire and his crew facing the bosses.

"Da, this is barbaric," Sean protested.

Kilroy looked hurt. "I've lost friends to this devil mountain myself. But I can't bring them back by throwing a tantrum. This railroad is going to get built, whether you believe in it or not." He stared past his son at Uncle Foxfire. "John—"

"Young Foxfire," Uncle Foxfire corrected him.

However, Kilroy ignored him. "You've given me nothing but trouble."

"Big talker, big notions," Shrimp chimed in.

"You're out as headman!" Kilroy said to Uncle Foxfire, and then turned to Shrimp. "Appoint someone reliable to head up the crew."

"Him." Shrimp pointed at Bright Star.

"Me?" Bright Star asked in surprise.

"You want the job?" he asked Shaky.

"Well, I . . ." Bright Star licked his lips and then glanced nervously at Uncle Foxfire.

"We're a team," Uncle Foxfire insisted.

"I'm sorry," Bright Star said. He began to walk away. One by one the others followed until it was only Uncle Foxfire and I and the two westerners.

Kilroy saluted Uncle Foxfire. "See you later, John." Sean would have stayed, but his father wouldn't let him.

Finally it was only Foxfire and I. He looked at me, pleading silently. "Otter?"

"Let's go inside, Uncle," I called gently. "It's almost time for work."

"You go if you want to," he said grimly.

"Come with me," I urged. "There's no point anymore."

"Someone has to care." Uncle Foxfire pivoted and walked over to the collapsed end of the tunnel and began to dig.

For all of my life, he had been some mighty legend; and yet in the end no one would listen to him. In the end, he was just as much an outcast as I was.

He was still digging when I left.

CHAPTER | XXIII

When Uncle Foxfire joined us after an hour, Bright Star broke off his chant and the crew stopped whatever they were doing as he walked by. He looked tired and damp, but still proud as he marched past. I tried to catch his eye, but he ignored me too as he headed for Bright Star. "Where do you want me to work?"

Bright Star shook his head. "I just pretended to take over so Kilroy wouldn't go crazy with his whip. As far as I'm concerned, you're still the headman."

"The crew voted with their feet," Uncle Foxfire said gracefully, and he wrapped his fingers around the handle of Bright Star's pickax. "So where do you want me to go?"

Bright Star shifted his feet uncomfortably. "Don't be like that."

With a sharp tug, Uncle Foxfire took the pickax and

walked over to a spot on the wall. "Is this okay?"

Bright Star spread his arms with a sigh. "Anyplace you like."

Uncle Foxfire attacked the rock with a grim little smile. Wherever I went, I couldn't help but be aware of him. The rest of the crew tried to speak to him because they all thought of him still as the headman. However, for all the notice he took, they might have been a breeze huffing and puffing at his back.

I felt especially bad because of the harsh things I had said to him. He had fallen from being a legend to merely being a man who made mistakes like the rest of us—but even so, I was beginning to realize he was some kind of man. If I had been him, I would have been sulking in the cabin, unwilling even to go near those who had betrayed me. Whatever I thought of him as a prophet, I had to admire him as a man.

And I thought of all those wonderful homecomings back in Three Willows and how kind and generous he had been. So finally I stepped up beside him and began to work. "I'm sorry, Uncle."

He glanced at me but went back to swinging his pickax. "Don't be."

"But I am," I protested.

The pickax fell to the floor with a clang. "I said not

to be sorry. Maybe you were right. Maybe I was so busy walking in the clouds that I ignored what was happening down here on the earth."

I felt as if I were meeting my real uncle for the first time. "They were good dreams, and still are."

He rested his hands on the hilt of the pickax handle. "They weren't worth blinding your father—or getting you whipped. I kept overlooking things and giving in because I told myself what was important was the Great Work."

The point of my pickax bit into the rock. "It's this country. The sooner we get away, the better."

He began gnawing at the rock again with his toothpick. "You don't understand, boy. You can never go home now. When you go to Three Willows, you'll see things with western eyes."

I thought back to those long discussions with the elders, when he had tried to convince them how necessary it was to modernize the Kingdom. "Like a halfling," I said.

"Just so." He gazed at me with new interest, as if surprised at my intuition; and the man who could be so eloquent about American machines struggled to find the right words. "Once you guest on the Golden Mountain, you change inside. Only some of the guests don't realize it's happened."

"And when you're here?"

"I see things with T'ang eyes." He gazed at me sadly.

It was strange to realize all the loneliness that lay behind the legend. I realized how disappointed he must have been that day so long ago back in Three Willows when I had let the clan's opinion make me stay.

"Still, we'll be safer," I said.

"Yes," he admitted with a slight smile. "Cassia will see to that."

As I worked beside him, I found I liked the real Uncle Foxfire far more than the clan's false image. Briefly he told me about his childhood, about which my mother had rarely spoken. Though no one else in the clan liked the Manchus either, they were also afraid of the rulers; so Mother's family had been very unpopular. Worse, on their mother's side, they were believed to be not quite human. In their own way, Mother and Uncle Foxfire had been outcasts as much as I was.

"Though you'd never know that from the way the clan talks about us now."

I was so fascinated by what Uncle Foxfire was telling me that I lost track of the time. So I couldn't have said when Shrimp and Kilroy came over to our crew.

The first thing I knew, Shrimp was shouting for our attention. When we stopped, he spread his legs and planted a fist on either hip. "The superintendent is calling for volunteers."

There was an awkward silence while we waited for Uncle Foxfire to speak; but he hesitated as if he were no longer sure he was the head of the crew.

With an uncomfortable glance at Uncle Foxfire, Bright Star finally asked, "What is it?"

Shrimp turned to Kilroy with such smoothness that I suspected they had repeated the announcement many times that day.

Kilroy shaped the mountain in the air with his glove. *"I went out when there was a temporary calm. The snow that wiped out that cabin was only a fraction of the overhang. There's still enough up there to wipe out the whole camp. It could happen any moment."*

As Shrimp translated his words, I thought of my first sight of the Tiger, when I had seen all that snow piled up on the head of the mountain. It had seemed like an incredible amount then. Since then, the storms must have deposited even more.

When Shrimp finished, Kilroy plowed on. *"We have to put a charge in there and make the snow come down in a different direction,"* Kilroy explained.

We could hear the wind howling overhead. Uncle Foxfire eyed Bright Star; but Bright Star did not dare respond.

Only Uncle Foxfire was willing to ask Kilroy, *"Storm back?"*

"Yes, and if we don't do something now, we could all wind up like those poor devils in that cabin." Kilroy slapped his hands on his cold arms.

Uncle Foxfire swept his hand through the air like a fierce wind. "Out in the open. No shelter. No protection—"

Shrimp interrupted. "Things are desperate."

"It's the same danger for Kilroy as it is for us," Uncle Foxfire argued. "So let him go. Why should we have to take all the risks?"

Kilroy could understand Uncle Foxfire's expression even if he didn't know the T'ang words. *"I could order you to go."*

"You whip me, then no can go," Uncle Foxfire pointed out.

Suddenly I saw my chance to escape the Tiger. *"If I save the camp, what do I get?"*

I don't think Kilroy even recognized me as the boy he had whipped—any more than he might remember a dog he had kicked out of his way. *"You want a bonus, John? I'll pay you out of my own pocket if I have to."*

"I want to leave," I said. *"When the snow stops, I get to go."*

I saw a flicker of recognition at that moment. He drew his eyebrows together in puzzlement, as if a water buffalo had just asked the farmer to unyoke it. *"I don't have the authority,"* he muttered, more to himself than to me.

"When the road reopens, you could look the other way when I depart," I argued. *"The teamsters would do what you say."*

He was annoyed by my continuing to talk back to him. *"But if word got back to Strobridge . . ."* He shook his head.

"What would he say if he lost the whole camp? How many men will go out in this storm?" I jerked my head at him. *"How many will blow up the top of the mountain?"*

He drew his bushy eyebrows together. *"Do you know how to use powder, boy?"*

Now that I had my chance to get off the mountain, I wasn't about to lose it. *"You can show me what to do. I learn things quickly,"* I said.

The discussion disturbed him so much that he looked away from me and studied his boot tops instead. It was a measure of his desperation that, when he raised his head, he nodded. *"I guess I got no choice. All right. You blow up that snow bluff, and you'll be off in the first wagon that comes through."*

The worried look on Uncle Foxfire's face had been growing as he had listened to the exchange. "You'll get lost ten feet from the tunnel."

"You could have a compass," Shrimp offered.

"He doesn't know how to use it," Uncle Foxfire objected.

I wasn't going to lose my chance of gaining my freedom. "Have someone show me. I learn fast."

Shrimp leaned back and whispered a quick summary of the exchange to Kilroy. *"Why, sure. Using a compass is as easy as pie."*

Uncle Foxfire scowled. *"You'd do anything to finish this railroad."*

Kilroy fixed Uncle Foxfire with his intense look—it was like being at the wrong end of a gun barrel. *"That's right, John."*

"And write off another dead Chinese." Uncle Foxfire pointed at me. *"One way or another."*

Kilroy's fist jerked up, and I thought he was going to hit Uncle Foxfire; but the fist stopped and he spread his fingers out and wiped at his face as if he were trying to rub something from his memory. *"And that's why there's going to be a railroad. This railroad will be a better monument to him or me than any slab of marble."*

Bright Star jabbed a finger at me. *"He boy."*

Kilroy put his hands on his hips and looked at Bright Star. *"Well, you're not, John."*

It was really quiet in the tunnel right then. In the distance, I could hear the clinking of pickaxes and hammers.

Bright Star had a look on his face as if he had swallowed a bucket of icy cornmeal and it was just sitting on his stomach.

Uncle Foxfire stepped forward. *"I go too."*

"So you've had your fill too." Kilroy seemed almost amused. *"Well, I say, Good riddance to bad rubbish."*

As Kilroy and Shrimp left, I guiltily tugged at Uncle Foxfire's arm. "You don't have to go."

He shrugged off my hand. Despite his earlier show of humility, he hadn't given up. The pride was burning so fiercely in him that it almost could have warmed my hands. "I said I'd get you home, and I will."

CHAPTER | XXIV

When father heard the plan, he lost his temper. "No, I absolutely forbid it." He scowled.

However, I wasn't about to let Father's anxieties keep me from leaving this cursed mountain. "It won't take long, and then I'll be able to go down with you to the city," I said. I still figured that I would have to wait awhile for Mother to make it safe for me to return to the Middle Kingdom.

Father looked blindly for Uncle Foxfire. "Foxfire, tell him he can't."

"I'm going with him." Uncle Foxfire tried to reassure him.

Father was even more surprised—as if he already knew the odds against the mission. "You are?"

Uncle tried to put the best complexion on the situation. "I'll see that he gets back."

"I won't have it," Father said. "Foxfire, don't let him go." He started to get out of his bunk.

Uncle caught his wrists and forced him back onto his bunk. "He's going whether we want him to or not."

Father struggled clumsily. "You're supposed to help me protect him."

"I'm going with him," Uncle snapped in exasperation. "That's all I can do."

Father lay back on his bunk. "Is this what I get for helping you for twelve years?" he said bitterly.

"I'll do what I can, old friend," Uncle said. Father sighed.

On the other hand, the rest of the crew couldn't do enough for me. Bright Star even offered me his spare shirt.

I caught it when he threw it to me. "You said I was a fool."

He jammed his arms back into his coat sleeves. "But you're *our* fool."

The only one who tried to argue against our going was Father.

"I don't want to sit and wait to be carried away like that other crew," I told him. "At least I'll be doing something."

Father extended his bowl of cornmeal. "Your mother

would say I was getting too fat anyway."

I tried to shove it back. "You need it."

"No, you need it more." Noodles thrust his bowl out impulsively. "Here."

"I don't have much of an appetite," I confessed. I was nervously jiggling my knee up and down.

However, Uncle Foxfire took the bowls and set one down near me. "This is no time to be polite," he said pragmatically. "Eat it. We'll need every ounce of strength for the climb."

Noodles gave a quick jerk of his head as if he were unused to being generous. "This is only a loan, mind you. I expect a five-course banquet someday."

I knew that Uncle Foxfire was right; but as I forced the slushy cornmeal down my throat, I couldn't help wondering if it was a favor to Noodles after all.

After breakfast, I suddenly had an idea and went over to Packy. "Can I have the rest of your rags? I want to use them as markers."

"They'll just blow away, boy," he said, but he lifted the lid of his basket.

I dipped my hands inside the brightly colored patches and strips. "No, they won't. I've got a notion."

Uncle Foxfire was swirling some water around his mouth before he swallowed. "What is it?"

I draped the streamerlike pieces over my hand as I lifted them out of the basket. By the time I had piled them on the floor, everyone else had drunk his water and wolfed down mouthfuls of half-frozen cornmeal. "If everyone's finished with the water, could I have it?"

"Don't try to drink all that." Uncle Foxfire held up a button. "You'd do better to put something in your mouth to keep your throat moist. We don't have any tea today." He placed the button on his own tongue in illustration.

"It's not to drink." I dipped the first rag into the water and lifted it out, laying it out carefully on the floor. "I got the idea the other day from Dandy's laundry."

Uncle Foxfire immediately saw what I was up to. He mumbled from around the button in his mouth. "You're going to freeze them."

I went on dipping the rags. "They'll be as hard as sticks, so we can mark our trail."

"I think it's hanging around me that's making him smarter." Bright Star came over and began helping me lay the rags out. Curly and Noodles pitched in too. And one by one so did the others.

By the end, the whole floor of the shack was covered with frozen rags—like long, painted sticks.

"We'll need a sack to carry them," I told Packy.

"One sack, coming up." And from his bottomless trunk came a sack with a strap I could carry over my shoulder. The rest of the crew helped fill the sack. When it was full, they wouldn't let me carry it, though. Instead Doggy took it.

"I can't talk you out of it?" Father asked.

"No, sir," I said politely but firmly.

"Don't take any unnecessary risks, boy. If it gets too dangerous, turn back," Father said.

"I will," I promised. I took one last look at him. Father's face was made for smiling. His eyes and cheeks were covered with laugh lines, so when he was sad they made his whole face sag—not just his mouth.

The sight of him almost made me stop; but then I reminded myself that if I didn't blow up the rest of the bluff, none of us would get out alive. So with the rest of the crew, I headed for the tunnel that let out on the slope.

"Good-bye," Uncle Foxfire said to Father.

Father simply said nothing as Bright Star helped him out of his bunk. It was clear that he blamed Uncle for everything. Uncle, it seemed, had lost his one last friend on the mountain.

We could hear the end of the tunnel before we ever saw it. Outside, the wind was howling like a hungry monster clawing with white paws, trying to thrust its head into the tunnel; while a half dozen men darted like little fish. Though the shovelers worked methodically, the biting wind seemed to blow in two more shovelfuls for every one they dumped outside.

Kilroy came limping up to us with Sean and Shrimp. *"Ready, boys?"*

Uncle Foxfire glanced out of the tunnel. *"It day or night outside?"*

Kilroy consulted a watch as he picked up one of the coils of rope from the snow. *"Day,"* he grunted.

I scratched my cheek. "You could have fooled me. I wonder what I'll look like without ears."

"You lose track of time in the tunnels." Uncle Foxfire drank in lungfuls of cold, fresh air as if it were wine.

"All right, boys, pay attention." Kilroy knelt awkwardly, having trouble bending his bad leg, and began to scoop the snow together into the shape of the summit. *"You're taking up two kegs of powder as a precaution. But one keg will do if it's placed right. Here's the tunnel."* He poked a quick hole to mark the spot. *"This is north."* He indicated the direction. *"This is where you need to go. Set off the charge here, and the snow will spill down harmlessly away from the camp. And,"* he said, dusting the snow from his finger, *"away from the men setting off the charges."*

252

"*He's so thoughtful.*" Sean handed us little tins of matches.

For once, Kilroy ignored him. Taking out a compass, he instructed Uncle Foxfire on its use until Uncle Foxfire nodded his head. "*Okay, I understand.*"

We strapped kegs of powder to our backs, and then Sean uncoiled a length of rope and began to wrap it around Uncle Foxfire's waist. As he did so, Doggy handed me the sack of markers.

Sean caught a glimpse of the frozen rags. "*Frankly, I prefer my dinners a little more cooked.*"

I gave a tug at the sack strap. "*Trail markers.*"

Even Kilroy had to admit that it was a good idea. "*And that trail's going to lead you all the way back to San Francisco, John.*"

"*That's all I want,*" I said as I knotted the rope around my waist.

Bright Star led Father over then. "Don't try to be a hero," he said to me. "Come back."

"We'll go to San Francisco together," I promised— and was surprised when he embraced me as well.

"Good luck," Dandy said, bowing his head; and the others copied him. It took me a moment to realize they were bowing to me as well as to Uncle Foxfire.

Sean had brought two pickaxes as well, and he handed one to each of us. "*Just the thing for the intrepid tamer of mountains.*"

I suppose Kilroy felt compelled to say something encouraging. *"It's a brave thing you're doing. Give me men to match my mountains."*

I wasn't sure he had even considered us humans; but I didn't say anything.

"Thank you," Uncle Foxfire said politely. Lifting one foot up high, he took a comic, exaggerated step outside. Three steps and he had vanished into the swirling snow.

It was my turn. I had thought that I was used to the cold, but the wind made it even colder and whipped the snowflakes into my cheeks like tiny needles. I gasped, and the wind seemed to snatch the very air from my lungs. Every breath after that almost hurt—as if the cold air had invisible blades that cut at my lungs. Keeping one hand on my pickax and the other on the rope, I leaned forward into the wind and tried to follow Uncle Foxfire.

Suddenly I heard a shout from behind us. *"What in blazes are you doing?"* Kilroy demanded.

Because I turned around, the rope grew taut. Uncle Foxfire stopped when he felt me tug at our lifeline. Behind us, a shadow plunged out of the glowing mouth of the tunnel.

"Excuse me. May I borrow that?" Sean asked, and deftly lifted a pickax from one of the work crew that had been trying to keep the tunnel mouth clear.

Kilroy took a step out into the snow. *"Come back here, you fool!"*

"Now, Da, you wouldn't deny me a little stroll, would you?" Sean floundered toward us.

Kilroy took another stride after him. *"I order you to come back."*

"Am I not serving the great, grand destiny of this country as well?" Sean taunted his father as he defiantly continued. *"Why don't you stop me with your whip?"*

With a roar, Kilroy charged after Sean. When he stumbled, he fell head-first into the snow.

Laughing, Sean linked arms with me. *"Hurry, before the old bull catches up."*

There was a wild look in his eyes, like the look he had on the evening we had gone hunting for the moon in the tunnels. In his crazy, lonely way, he was more my kind than any of the T'ang men on the tunnel; and that realization touched off the laughter inside me too.

Uncle Foxfire looked from him to me and back again. *"You sure?"* he asked.

Sean dragged me urgently up the slope. *"An avalanche'll fall on my head just as surely as on yours."*

"You understand risk?" Uncle Foxfire inquired carefully as he kept pace beside us.

Danger would never stop Sean from doing something. *"I can read a compass. Can you?"* he asked, and deftly lifted the compass from Uncle Foxfire's hand.

He squeezed my arm, and at his silent signal the two of us began to hurry, slipping and sliding up through the snow. As we pulled ahead of Uncle Foxfire, I felt as if we were in our own private world as we had been back in the tunnels. *"Your father will make you pay for this,"* I warned him.

"Hang for a sheep as hang for a dog." Sean winked. *"Though I'll miss our jaunts together, I'll see you off the mountain and free of that devil."*

At that moment, I felt closer to him than to any brother. Behind us, we could hear Uncle Foxfire panting as he caught up with us.

Soon Kilroy's hoarse bellowing was lost in the howling of the wind. When the mouth of the tunnel had shrunk to the size of a firefly, we stopped. *"Let me break the trail,"* Sean said. We redistributed the rope, tying it about each of our waists. Sean was to take the lead while Uncle Foxfire now brought up the rear. I gave him the bag of markers.

When we were ready, Sean began to forge on ahead, tilting forward against the force of the wind with his face almost touching the glass of the compass. Then a regular gale whipped the snow all around, and he became no more than a shadow. His tracks were already half filled. I could only stagger after him. From the tugging at my waist, I knew Uncle Foxfire was following. Every ten meters, when he paused to thrust in a stake, he would have to slow down and I would feel a jerk from behind.

Poor Sean. The point man had to take most of the force of the wind; and he had to try to beat the snow down with his body.

It was impossible to tell how far we had gone, but I thought we had traveled perhaps a kilometer when the rope at my waist tightened so suddenly that I thought I was being cut in two.

Then my feet went flying out from underneath me and I landed on the snow. I felt myself sliding across the surface. In front of me, I heard a thud and a crash.

At first I clawed with my gloves for some grip on the smooth snow. Then, in desperation, I rolled onto my back. Gripping my pickax in both gloves, I rolled back onto my side and thrust the pickax down hard into the snow. As it bit deep, I held on.

For a moment, I just clung to my pickax. The only thing I could figure out was that there was some hole in the snow that otherwise covered the camp. There, the snow had formed only a thin crust. Since it was on the cliff side of the camp, the hole might go down for some distance.

Sean must be hanging in some crevasse just up ahead. Uncle Foxfire crawled into view, pickax in one hand. He must have taken off his keg of powder, but I couldn't see even that short distance in this snow.

He grabbed my shoulder with his free hand, and though he was shouting into my ear, I could barely hear him over the wind. "Sean must have fallen into some crevasse. Hold on."

I could only nod dumbly, because the tightening rope made it hard for me to breathe.

Picking up his pickax, he stabbed it into the snow behind me so that the shaft angled up. Holding on to the rope, he yelled, "Let go."

I started to slide again, but this time Uncle Foxfire guided the taut rope around the shaft of his pickax.

The next moment he was fumbling at the knots around my waist. "Why did I have to tie it so tight?" Frustration finally made him take off his glove and work with numb fingers at the knot. Suddenly a shift in the wind caught the glove that he had clenched between his teeth. The next moment it went sailing into the air. I made a snatch at it, but it disappeared quickly in the swirling snow.

Uncle Foxfire finally untied my knots, and I was free. He and I tied the rope around the shaft of his pickax. It jerked and rocked back and forth as if it had come alive and wanted to fly away in the wind.

Jamming his ungloved hand inside his coat, Uncle Foxfire helped me shed my keg of powder; and then we cautiously followed the rope into the whirling snow.

Sean had lost his pickax and was holding on to his rope for dear life while he dangled in the air. I glanced down, but I couldn't see any bottom; and the bits of snow that crumbled from the edge seemed to take forever to land.

He was so happy to see us that he was even willing to try to joke. *"I bet I'm the biggest fish you ever caught."*

"I think we've landed too big a one," Uncle Foxfire panted to me as we began to haul in the rope.

The rope must have been old and frayed, or maybe there was a sharp rocky edge hidden by the snow; but suddenly we heard a sharp noise as several strands snapped.

"No." Sean desperately tried to dig his fingertips into the snow. "I'll hold the rope," Uncle Foxfire grunted. "You get him."

I threw myself toward the hole just as the rope broke. I grabbed at Sean's gloved hands. His cap fell off, and in a second it was lost within the swirling whiteness of the hole.

Slowly I felt myself being dragged backward. Sean's fingers curled tightly around mine. When he was out of the hole, he rolled onto his back, gasping like a fish that had just been dragged out of the water.

Uncle Foxfire crawled between us. *"You okay?"* He had to shout to make himself heard over the wind.

"I think my ankle's twisted," Sean yelled back.

"Can you make it back?" Uncle Foxfire asked.

"I can crawl, using your markers." Sean winced at the pain from his leg. *"But I hate to give my father that satisfaction."*

Uncle Foxfire began untying the rope from his waist. *"May not say so, but he be happy to see you."*

Sean began to pat his pockets and then twisted, groping frantically through the snow. *"I lost the compass."*

Uncle Foxfire nudged him back down the slope. *"We manage."*

"I'm . . . I'm sorry. I wasn't of much use." Sean began to drag himself away. *"I never am."*

"You're a good friend," I told him.

"I'll have the water boiling when you get back," he promised.

We watched him crawl away until he was lost within

the snow. "I hope he makes it," I said.

"It's not that far," Uncle Foxfire reassured me.

However, as the whiteness closed around him, I was not so sure that any of us would make it back.

CHAPTER | XXV

We hadn't gone more than fifty meters up the slope when I began puffing again. Uncle Foxfire was still breathing easily.

"You must have lungs of leather." I panted.

Uncle Foxfire looked over his shoulder. "Try to breathe through your nose rather than your mouth. The colder the air you breathe, the more phlegm your lungs make and the harder it gets to breathe."

I nodded dumbly and tried to do what he said. However, the wind was blowing steadily down the slope, lashing us with sharp-edged snowflakes. And the cold was a living thing, snatching the warmth from my body. I could feel it nipping at my ears and nose and hands.

The snow was so deep that it began to fall into my boots. In no time, my chilled feet felt as stiff as wood. And the white slope just seemed to get steeper and steeper.

In order to get enough air, I had to breathe through my mouth again. Up ahead, though, Uncle Foxfire kept moving on relentlessly like some small locomotive. I had to admire his spirit and his courage. Perhaps he was the stuff of legends after all.

In just a little while, my legs were so cold and tired that they wouldn't support me and I sank to my knees in the snow. "Let's stop for a rest." I wheezed.

The rope jerked to a halt, and Uncle Foxfire came back to me and squatted down. "How are your ears? Numb?"

I put my frozen fingers to my ears. "They ache a little."

He jammed my hat farther down on my head. "How about your hands?"

I wriggled them experimentally. "They're okay. But they feel cold."

Uncle Foxfire wrapped his arms around himself and tucked his hands into his armpits. "Then do this. Your hands'll warm up if you keep on going."

Suddenly the keg was an impossible weight to lift, so I remained kneeling. "I need to rest some more."

He tugged at the rope. "You'll never get warm staying still. If you stop for long, you'll die."

Afraid, I tried to rise; but my legs felt like icicles and the keg of powder threw off my balance so I wound up flopping back down. "I can't."

He changed tactics as he put a hand under my elbow. "Just concentrate on one step at a time."

I couldn't resist him as he lifted me back on my feet. "One step," I said.

"Right." He pivoted and began to stump along. "One step at a time," he repeated, and took another step himself. "One step at a time," he coaxed. "Come on. You can do it, boy."

As the rope rose up taut again, I felt ashamed. After all, it had been my idea to come out here. I raised one weary leg and brought it down ahead of me. This time, though, I made sure to copy him. I had my arms wrapped around myself and I bent my head slightly so that my hat took the brunt of the wind, rather than my face.

"That's it, boy," I heard him encourage me from above.

Though the brim of my hat flapped in my face, I saw him like a black shadow within the swirling snow. I took another step, ignoring how stiff and tired my legs were. And then I took a third step. The ropes that held the keg felt as if they would slice through my arms, but I took another step up the slope. Slipping another stake from the sack, I thrust it into the snow. I wasn't the most elegant picture of a mountain climber, but the camp wouldn't care if I just did my job.

We pushed on; but after a hundred meters my legs began to feel like wood, and it hurt to drag in every breath. The ropes holding the keg to my back cut into my arms. As a result, I began to flounder in the snow. Just like a fish. Wearily my mind went back to that warm day by the Dragon's Gate where it had all started. And I thought of all those poor fish that had never made it there. No one blamed them.

After another two hundred meters, I stopped. "I just can't do it."

The rope pulled him up short, and he turned clumsily. "Yes, you can," he shouted back to me. "Think of what Tiny or Squeaky would say if they could see you now."

"You can try to shame me. You can try to frighten me. But nothing's going to work. I'm exhausted." And I dropped to my stomach in the soft snow.

"Get up." He yanked at the rope.

"No." I lay where I was.

"Get up!" He tugged at the rope and wound up hauling me a meter through the snow.

I was beginning to feel annoyed with him. He might be superhuman, but I was mere flesh and blood. "Go away," I said.

For a moment, the snowfall thinned out so I could

see his face again. "We're almost near the cloud layer. Once we're through that, we'll be above the snow."

I looked up toward where he was pointing. Another hundred meters on, I saw a ceiling of dark gray that stretched across the sky. "It looks like we could just walk through that right into Heaven."

"We're not done down here yet." This time when he yanked at the rope, I got up, filled with new hope.

We hadn't taken more than a dozen steps when the snow began to fall heavier than ever. I went on as long as I could, reaching into my sack until I found it was empty. I was sure we should have hit the sunlight by now. I figured we had gotten lost and were wandering around the slopes. Discouraged, I felt that my whole body was as heavy as lead, and my lungs ached as they tried to pull in the cold air. Numbed and frozen, I began to feel as if it didn't matter if I lived or died—it was just a question of when I was going to be able to rest.

"No more," I said, dropping to my knees.

He turned sideways. "Try."

But I was beyond hope. "I just can't live up to my father. I can't live up to you. I'm no hero."

He came back to me and leaned down. Snow had transformed his eyelashes into white wires. "There's no magic. It's what's inside you."

"I just want to lie down." Wearily I got down on all fours.

He stared down at me for a moment and then said, "All right." He bit his remaining glove and jerked it off with a motion of his wrist. Then he was undoing the rope around his waist.

My jaw dropped open. "What . . . what are you doing?"

The rope slapped at the surface of the snow as he untied the knot. "You wanted to be on your own. Well, here you are." When he dropped the rope, it lay like an old snakeskin.

"You can't be that heartless," I panted.

"Just watch me." Uncle Foxfire jammed his hand back into his glove.

"You can't." I felt myself filled with a rage that surged up from my knees. "What about Mother?"

Uncle Foxfire backed up the slope. "You're nothing but a spoiled, selfish brat. She's sick of you and so am I. Or she wouldn't have shipped you over here."

I was so mad that I was determined not to die, just to spite him. Grabbing up the rope, I started after him. "Hold up."

He pivoted. "I knew you'd be too stubborn to die." He had only been pretending to reject me so that the resulting anger would drive me on.

"You're as bad as Kilroy," I grumbled, as I tied the rope around his waist.

"You can think what you like if that's what it takes to keep you alive," he said. When we were tied together again, we started on.

At times I lost him in the mist and snow. There was only the persistent tug of the rope to remind me that I was not alone. Suddenly we stumbled out above the clouds, and it was like stepping into another world.

I blinked at the unaccustomed brightness and stumbled along like a mole as we climbed onto a shoulder of the mountain just beneath its summit. I stopped in my tracks as the truth slowly dawned on me. "I wouldn't have made it without you."

When the rope pulled him up short, Uncle Foxfire turned around. "You're not done yet." Uncle Foxfire pointed behind us. "We still have to go back through that."

Below, the gray clouds stretched on endlessly like a dark, angry sea. "It's hard to believe anyone could survive that."

"It's just a question of little steps." He faced forward again. Above us, the snow hung on the peak like some heavy mane.

As the sun filled my body and limbs with warmth and I began to thaw, I felt contrite. "You really are a hero."

He was uneasy at being praised, maybe much more comfortable discussing ideas than his own personal deeds. "Forget it." Uncle Foxfire struggled through the snow again as the wind whipped up little sprites of snow to dance about us mockingly. "Don't make a big thing out of what I do——or what I did. Or you'll sound like the clan. The very same people in Three Willows who praise me now used to mock me for walking in the clouds. Even Cassia likes to forget that part of the past."

"And now you are." I chuckled and pointed at a stray wisp of cloud blowing by. "Literally."

"And now I am," he agreed. It was comforting to know that I wasn't alone in that savage but lovely wilderness. I think it was comforting to him as well.

It was strange, but behind his legend was a truly brave and modest man. It was a perspective that had been hard won; and, as we walked, I wondered what else I had been wrong about.

Had my anger caused me to forget his dream because of the situation down below? "Whatever has happened here to me and my father hasn't changed the truth about home, has it?"

"No," he said. "The British are still pumping their opium into the Kingdom, and the vultures are gathering to tear the carcass apart." He added, with a sideways glance, "But maybe I'm just walking in the clouds."

I thought about Stumpy's mother and Stony back in Three Willows, and I wondered just how many more men and women—and even children—had become addicted to opium since I had left. "No, you're not walking in the clouds either when you talk about the Great Work." I realized then that I had to separate my uncle's dream from the life we actually led down below. "We know how to end the injustices at home, and something should be done to end the injustices here; but I don't know how."

When he didn't answer right away, I thought that I had offended him in some way. Then we reached a tumble of rocks—from small ones the size of my fist to boulders bigger than a house—all of them piled up as if they were bits left over from the creation of the mountains. Snow lay piled in the spaces between the rocks, and there were patches of ice. Uncle Foxfire started to shuffle across.

He chose his words with care almost equal to the way he walked. "So you don't think I was lying?"

I kept my arms wrapped around myself to hold in the newfound warmth. "I was hurt and angry when I said what I did. There really is a lot to be learned here. You just picked the wrong schoolroom; but you couldn't know it at the time."

He disappeared around the rocks. "What have I accomplished, though?"

The rope grew tauter as the distance increased between him and me, so I hurried to follow. "It's like you said on the slope: It's small steps. You must know a lot now about laying tracks and making tunnels."

"Centimeter by centimeter." He chuckled from around the rocks. "And the more I learn, the more I realize I need to know—like how to build a *locomotive* and *railroad cars*. And once you've got your *railroad*, how do you run it?"

"You don't have to do it all yourself, though. Maybe you can make out a list of things you think we need to understand," I suggested. "Then I'll either get translations of the books or try to get lessons from someone."

I thought he was standing a little straighter as he gazed at a shallow bay of stone formed by the sides of the mountain. "You would?"

"Yes," I said.

He gave my shoulder a grateful squeeze as we stood captivated by the scene. In the center of the bay was a pond that spread out like a gleaming sheet of white glass tinted with blue streaks. The ice stretched outward to a mound of snow some four meters high. Something had sliced through the snow pack, so I could see the many layers of snow, each a different shade of bluish white.

"There must be a waterfall here in the spring." He pointed toward the wall. Opposite the mound was a cleft. The rocks there were worn down by some stream. Snow-covered icicles thrust up from the base of the waterfall, covering the bed of the stream; I could not quite make out their shape.

As I stared at that strange but beautiful landscape, I felt as if some magic had transported me to the moon; and it was just Uncle Foxfire and I.

He was the first to break free of the alien scenery's spell. Shuffling gingerly to the edge, he tested the surface of the pond. Since the ice seemed solid enough, he launched himself upon the pond.

As I followed him onto the ice, I said, "After you take Father home, I can stay in San Francisco and do research. I should have plenty of time to study while I wait for Mother to smooth things over in the Middle Kingdom."

The sun bounced off the surface, making it seem as if we shuffled over a pool of cold, blinding light. "I'm staying," he grunted. "We'll find some friend who's going home and have him watch over your father."

I was shocked for a moment. I thought that after all he had been through, he would finally retire overseas. "But you can leave too."

His fingers gripped the keg's ropes in an effort to ease the pull. "Bright Star's sharp, but I don't know if he's up to getting the crew out of these mountains."

I had to narrow my eyes to see as we crossed the ice. "Even though they turned their backs on you?"

He winked at me. "That doesn't mean I can turn my back on them."

It was also the reason that he hadn't turned his back on me, either. I found myself looking forward to becoming better acquainted with my real uncle. "Then we can coordinate the research easier."

Uncle's spirits had picked up; with a little skip he skated a few meters across the ice. "I think the task will take more than two."

His mood was infectious; and I slid a foot forward and I began to skim over the frozen surface even with the keg of powder on my back. "Then we'll recruit as many people as the task takes. We could even set up committees to study other things we need—like modern ships." As my body drifted along, my mind began juggling all the possibilities. "But to figure out ships, we'll have to understand their engines."

As energetic now as a small boy, he turned to face me as he glided backward. "And how to make steel. And a dozen other things we probably haven't even thought of."

I thought of poor Sean. I hoped he had gotten back all right. "Like using a compass." With a kick, I tried to skate after him. "There's no end to the Great Work, is there?"

As he sailed on, he spread his arms as much to suggest the scope of the vision as for balance. "Back home, there's the story of the old man who moved a mountain one spoonful at a time," he said.

Beneath us, the ice mirrored the surroundings over which we seemed to fly as effortlessly as gulls. "The task is bigger than any mountain."

His hands slapped against his sides. "It won't happen in my lifetime, but maybe in yours."

In his own quiet way, he was making me the heir to all his dreams. "It'll be an age of miracles," I declared, floating after him.

When we had reached the base of the waterfall, we saw that the snow-covered icicles swept from the bed of the stream like huge, strange flowers and climbed the cliff as if it were a trellis.

"It's like some sorcerer's garden." Sheltered by the curving walls from the relentless winds, Uncle Foxfire turned slowly as he sought a route to the top of the cliff.

I hardly dared to take a breath for fear of breaking the icicles. Here and there, the wind had rubbed off the coating of snow to reveal glasslike stems and petals that captured the golden light of the sun, so they seemed to glow with a life of their own. I couldn't help thinking of my birth father. "A garden of diamonds," I said, and I had a strange feeling as if there were someone else gazing through my eyes.

"Eh?" Uncle Foxfire turned to me.

"Something that my birth father had wanted to see," I explained.

"Did he? I'm sorry that he didn't get to see it." Uncle Foxfire's breath rose in white puffs like the steam from one of the fire wagons. "He was the bravest man I ever knew."

For some reason, the snow had dropped off one whole patch, and the sunlight filled the ice flowers now with miniature rainbows. I was almost tempted to pluck one. Instead, I did my best to memorize the scene so I could describe it to Father.

Uncle Foxfire started to climb, the powder keg bobbing on his back as he made his way among the garden of icicles. "Do you still blame me for his death?"

My eyes looked for a handhold among the shining

shapes as I started after him. "No," I panted, "he came here because he needed to hope."

My words seemed to inspire him with even more energy. "And because he believed the future is here," he was saying, when a delicate spire above us broke with a tinkling sound.

CHAPTER | XXVI

Shards of ice fell down on my head and shoulders. Alarmed, I looked up in time to see Uncle Foxfire falling backward.

I had a second to brace myself for the tug at my waist and Uncle Foxfire stopped, swinging instead to the right. There was a sickening crack and he gave a pained cry.

His face straining with pain, he still managed to claw for holds among the ice flowers. "I'm okay," he gasped. He clung to the rocks, among broken icicles, with one leg twisted at an ugly angle.

I descended until I was next to him on the cliff face. A break in the bone had been made worse by sharp icicles cutting up his leg. "You can't be hurt," I protested. "You've got the luck."

"Maybe I'm passing it on to you," he grunted.

Somehow we managed to get him back down to the

base of the waterfall. I got the keg from his back and then brought him over to a spot where two rocks gave some shelter.

"I'll start a fire." I began untying the rope from my waist.

He winced as he felt his leg. "You go on. Once you've set off the avalanche, you can always come back and set things up."

I tied a length of rope as a tourniquet around his leg. "I don't know how to set off the avalanche."

He began to scoop handfuls of snow into the shape of the summit. "Remember what Kilroy showed us. Take a rough reading from the sun, because any landmarks below are covered up by the clouds. Set the charge here." He pointed to the spot and then cut a long length of fuse. "One of this length should give you more than enough time to get away."

I pocketed the fuse reluctantly. "I don't want to leave you."

Uncle Foxfire seemed a little surprised and even touched. "Someone's got to do the job."

I felt as if someone had suddenly dumped a hundred kilos of lead upon my back. "We'll go back. Let some-one else do it."

Almost shyly, he put his hand on my shoulder. "Look

at the snow. It's ready to come down any moment. The job can't wait."

I looked at him for a moment; and I could see a faith that I felt was misplaced. I tried a half dozen times to tell him that; but in the end I just nodded my head. "I'll be back as soon as I can."

"I won't go anywhere," he promised.

I started back up the cliff. There were drops of his blood like bright crimson bugs on the flower petals. It was a reminder to take my time. I made it safely past the crumbling stone that had caused Uncle Foxfire's fall. The next terrace was smaller than the last. The diminutive pond was almost hidden by snow except for a curving sliver as bright as a diamond smile.

Here the spray had been caught in a kind of frozen lace to which the snow clung, fleshing out the strands to make sections that hung like spiderwebs between the flowers. As I made my way through the ice, I couldn't help thinking that this was a strange, beautiful place to die.

I couldn't help grinning. It was probably not the death the clan had expected for me. If you had asked most of them, they would have bet on an executioner's sword.

Finally I topped the summit and there was nothing between me and heaven but empty blue sky. The wind whipped veils of snow up into the air like ghosts whirling and dancing around me. My clothes flapped loudly and the thin air seemed to burn my lungs. Beneath me, the clouds looked like a dirty sea whose waves crashed about huge castles. Far away and higher up, I could see storm clouds—like black-hulled warships on the attack.

Then, shading my eyes, I squinted up at the sun and took a bearing. Facing in the right direction, I started to high-step through the snow carefully, hardly daring to breathe. The last thing I wanted to do was to fall into a hole like Sean.

When I was near the right spot, I shed the keg of powder. Behind me the snow stretched like a sheet of white cloth, and my footsteps looked like a ragged row of stitches. But I couldn't make out any sign of the lakes or of Uncle Foxfire. It was as if they had never existed. Now there was just me and the Tiger.

Getting out the fuse, I got everything ready and then reached for the matches. Whether because of the wind or my own nervousness, the first one wouldn't light. Neither would the second.

Until now, I had never thought of asking my father or mother for anything. Help me, I begged silently as I tried to strike the next match. Gratefully I watched it flare into life; and I used my free hand to protect the fragile flame until it rose tall and strong.

Carefully I lowered it to the fuse. The fire caught and sputtered. My first impulse was to run, but I cupped my hands around the fuse tip until I was sure it would go on burning. Then I turned and began to high-step back along my tracks. I was among the ice flowers halfway down the cliff when the rock shook and I heard a loud roar. The snow above me heaved, and bushels of it spilled down around me.

Suddenly the noise of the explosion was drowned out by an even louder sound—a huge roar as if from a giant throat—as if the Tiger itself was full of a great rage. I had done it. I had started the avalanche. For a moment, the Tiger even seemed to want to shake me off, and I started to slide down the cliff face, desperately trying to catch at rocks or icicles. Cold, glassy petals broke under my weight, cutting through my gloves; but the sound of their shattering was still hidden in the roaring of the Tiger.

I had one moment to wonder if I was going to impale myself on an icicle; and then I had landed, breathless and bruised but still alive. I tested each of my limbs, but though they ached, nothing was broken. There was snow swirling all around again, raised by the avalanche.

Cupping my hands around my mouth, I shouted, "I did it!"

My voice only echoed in the little bay of stone. From below there was no answer.

Feeling suddenly uneasy, I rose and limped to the cliff. While I had been gone, the storm clouds had swept in so that the lower pond was hidden now. They seemed to be rising up the sides of the mountain like a great, gray flood. Once I was in the clouds, I found it was snowing, so I took even longer to descend than I had to go up.

When I felt my feet planted firmly on the rocks at the base of the lower waterfall, I called to Uncle Foxfire again, but still there was no response.

Stumbling, I searched through the whirling snowfall along the cliff face until I found the rocks where I had left him. Drops of blood led away from the keg of powder. There was a trough in the snow as if he had dragged himself away. "Uncle Foxfire," I called in alarm.

When there was still no response, I began to hunt around; but the snow began to fall thicker and heavier, quickly covering up the blood and even his tracks. In no time I was once again lost in a swirling, white world. I stumbled around blindly, searching for him, and found myself once again by the garden of ice flowers, though the snow was quickly obscuring their shapes.

I realized that I had been lucky to wind up back at that point. I could have gotten myself lost on the mountain with no idea where to go.

I finally figured that he had gone down on his own; or perhaps someone else had even come up this far, found him and taken him back. I fought back a sense of panic at being deserted.

I shuffled cautiously across the snow-covered pond until I was at the slope. As I made my way down, I couldn't make out the marker stakes. I could only blunder on, hoping that I was heading toward the camp and not away from it.

I might have gone a hundred meters or five hundred—I couldn't tell—when I realized that there was no way that Uncle Foxfire could have made it to camp, even with help. He had realized it. He had also seen the storm clouds closing in and had known that I wouldn't have left him. Instead, he had crawled away so that I would not have to stay.

He had kept his promise.

As I staggered on, I could feel the moisture in the corners of my eyes; but the tears froze on my cheeks.

When I thought I had gone halfway back, the wind

grew even stronger, whipping up the snow. The snow-flakes reflected the light like miniature mirrors, and I was surrounded by a world of blinding white. I no longer could tell up from down or west from east.

Still I kept moving, while the wind hissed at my ears and whipped at my face. It was strange, but slowly the air seemed to warm up though the wind and snowfall were just as strong as ever. Furiously, I knew it wasn't the mountain that was warming up. It was my own body that was beginning to cool off. I found myself laughing deliriously. The cold had finally seeped so deep into my bones that they had turned permanently to ice. I could never leave the mountains anymore.

I sat down in the snow and was surprised to feel how soft and warm it felt now. It would be good to rest, and I lay down, feeling happy for the first time in months. I was just about to close my eyes when rocks tumbled down all around me.

Out of my head, I sat up angrily. *"Didn't we do enough for you?"* I yelled. *"Can't you let me sleep now?"*

"Who's there?" someone shouted in the distance.

"Me," I shouted irritably. My groping hand found an icy lump and I pitched it in the direction of the speaker.

A light winked in the white world like a little star.

Gradually it grew nearer, and I could hear excited voices. I was curling up when I saw the first man. They had formed a human chain, Americans and T'ang, to reach me.

Dully, I realized that I had wandered past the camp and picked the garbage heap for my bed. "It's Otter," one of the T'ang people said.

I tried to blink my frozen eyelids when I saw him. "Is Uncle Foxfire here?"

The man said nothing. He just kept coming closer as more men joined the chain.

"*If he isn't here, my uncle needs help,*" I mumbled through stiff lips.

However, the man just stretched out his hand silently toward me.

Annoyed, I stared at the rag-covered palm. "*Can't you understand? We have to find my uncle.*" My legs felt stiff as wood as I tried to get up. When I fell back down, I wondered if they were frostbit and had to be cut off like Doggy's fingers.

"*What's wrong with you?*" I shouted, and finally realized that I was speaking English.

One of the Americans shrugged his shoulders as he held hands with the others. Even though he was dressed in a checkered wool coat, he was shivering. "*Who's that?*"

"*My uncle,*" I insisted, and turned to the T'ang man,

almost panicking when the T'ang words wouldn't come right away. "Uncle Foxfire," I demanded. "Is he here?"

The man broke from the others and shuffled toward me. "Shh, of course he is. He's waiting right inside."

"Good," I said, and finally closed my eyes.

I woke in the darkness and listened for a while to the oddest sound. I realized there was a fire crackling away in the stove and the cabin was actually warm.

"Uncle Foxfire?" I asked.

Father was right there. "No, he didn't come back."

I struggled to sit up. "We've got to go look for him."

Dozens of hands forced me back down. "Easy, easy," Father soothed. "We've got search parties out looking for him right now. If you get yourself lost too, it'll only make things harder."

That seemed to make sense, so I lay where I was. "There's a fire."

"The storm ended about two days ago. The supply wagons have come in," Bright Star explained.

Curly gave me the thumbs up. "The avalanche did the trick. We're safe."

Next to my head, a draft made the paper cutouts flutter against the wall. "Father, why are you here?" I mumbled sleepily.

"I wanted to make sure you were all right." He grinned.

I heard a splashing sound, and Noodles held out a bowl to me. "Would you like some broth?"

But I was already asleep.

It didn't occur to me until I was halfway into my dream that I wasn't in my old drafty bunk by the door. The rainbow cutouts on the wall meant I was in Uncle Foxfire's bed nearest the stove.

CHAPTER | XXVII

For the next few days while I was healing, I had my back slapped so many times that I was afraid the lash scars would reopen. It wasn't just the crew. It was Brush and just about everyone else.

Father didn't say much, though, except that he was glad I had come back alive. We all assumed that he was mourning his brother-in-law and longtime friend; and so we left him alone. One day he suggested packing up Foxfire's belongings to ship home.

Since I was still sleeping in my uncle's bunk, it was easy to get his basket. Curious, I raised the lid. Despite his mansion and gardens back at home, the small basket said far more about the man.

There were his round-handled scissors for cutting and a small pouch of some shiny, colored pebbles that looked as if they had been polished by water—perhaps a souvenir of his days in the goldfield. Next to it was a red tassel of silk thread with an intricate knot tied at the top. It was looped around a solitary chopstick intricately carved from ivory. There were dozens of other little mementos that probably had meant much to him but now were just junk to anyone else.

"Bring the basket over here," Father said. I supposed he had heard me poking around.

Picking up the basket, I tried to rise, but my limbs felt stiff when I got up. Packy got up to help, but I shook my head.

When I had set the basket down before Father, I lifted the lid. Leaning over the basket, he sniffed at it. "It smells like him. It's almost a shame to open it."

I remembered what Uncle Foxfire had said about the avalanche victims. "What if we can't find his bones in the spring?"

"His ghost will stay here," Father said. "But don't feel bad. He liked it here." His fingers groped through his friend's mementos, while he smiled slightly as if he recognized their shapes. Suddenly the smile froze.

"What's wrong?" I asked.

"I hadn't realized he'd kept it." He lifted out a bullet from a western gun. The metal was old and dull, and the sides of the small cylinder were scarred.

I craned my neck forward. "Why keep that old thing?"

He cradled it in his palm for a moment before he held it out to me. "I think it's the bullet that killed your father. He was always sorry about it, you know."

I wouldn't take it, though. Instead, I dove into the basket, hoping there would not be any more morbid surprises. "Was Uncle Foxfire ever . . . well . . . lonely?"

Father put the bullet back in the basket and shut the lid. Next to Mother, he probably understood my uncle best. In fact, over the last twelve years, they had spent more time together than with their families. "He was a world changer. World changers usually are. If he were comfortable, why would he want to change things?"

"We should write to Mother and his wife," I suggested reluctantly.

Father nodded. "We should let them know what happened; and maybe prepare your mother for when I come home."

"I'll heat some water." Packy leaped toward the stove to get a pot.

"So the storm broke, like Bright Star told me?" I asked. He seemed to have an almost endless supply of fuel and food.

"No. Bright Star said it to keep you calm. It's one of

your perks. The other crews chipped in," Packy said, and went outside to get some snow.

I realized then that some of the cabins must be going cold so I could stay warm. Mother had never let me want for anything back home; but she had never given me as precious a gift as this: warmth in the dead of winter and in the middle of a blizzard.

While I got out Father's inkwell, brushes, paper and ink sticks, Packy fussed over the water until it was luke-warm. Gratefully, I poured the water into the inkwell, which was a thick slab of stone whose bottom slanted toward a depression at one end. "Uncle Foxfire said guesting here had given him a double set of eyes."

Packy permitted himself a slight, ironic smile. "Once you start guesting, you'll be a guest all your life— whether here or back home."

Rubbing the perfumed ink stick against the side released the scent into the warm air. Smelling it, I could almost smell home, or, I corrected myself, what I had thought of as home. Maybe it was already too late for me. I had already become a guest.

Once the ink was thick and black, I picked up a brush. "We can start."

"Dear Cassia," Father began. "First of all, the good news. You won't ever have to worry about me looking at another woman." It was like Father to try to make a joke.

"All right," I said, when I was ready for the next line.

"You should be proud of Otter," Father went on. "He saved the camp, so he'll return home the conquering hero."

I set the brush down. "No, Uncle Foxfire was the brave one."

Father's chin sank to his chest as he pondered that. "You went too, boy."

Suddenly it was as if someone had torn the corners of my eyes. The tears started pouring down my cheeks. "I only went because I didn't know the risk. He left so he could keep his word."

Father did not even hesitate. "No, your uncle went because he thought of you as the future."

The tears just wouldn't stop; but since Father couldn't see, I didn't feel ashamed. "If I'm the future, then we're all in trouble."

Father closed his eyes as if he were suddenly tired. "Tell your mother that we'll be returning as soon as she says it's safe for you to go home."

I didn't write anything, though. I just kept staring at the paper.

Father gave me enough time to write down his previous thoughts and then said, "Ask her if she wants anything."

He grinned. "It's easier to find it in San Francisco than in Canton sometimes."

By now, the ink had dried on the tip of the brush. I dipped it in the inkwell again and then straightened the tip to a fine point by brushing it against the side of the well. Uncle Foxfire had kept his promise even at the cost of his own life. I could do nothing less.

"Father," I asked, "could you find a friend in San Francisco to escort you home?"

"I know a lot of guests. One of them's bound to be going back." Father turned toward me. "But you hate it here."

My fingers nervously squeezed the wooden stem of the brush. The feeling had been growing and growing inside me. I was still afraid of the mountain, but I had survived its worst. "I'd like to find Uncle Foxfire's bones and ship them home." As I said it, I knew it was the right thing to do.

"This may be your last chance to leave," Father warned.

"The three of us are leaving this mountain," I countered.

It took Father a couple of tries to recover his voice. "And if I needed your help?"

"I'd go," I said. "Do you need me?"

"Yes," he snapped. "I do."

I rotated the wooden stem between my fingers. "Really?"

He hesitated and then said more thoughtfully, "No. I can manage. But it's not fair. All my life I made sacrifices for your uncle, and you want me to make another one."

Poor Father. All these years he had lived in Uncle's shadow. "Why did you give up so much?" I asked.

"Because he was right." He sighed.

"And I think I'm doing the right thing," I said gently. I remembered how disappointed I had been when he had first refused to help me come here. I wondered if he felt just as disappointed that I was now going to stay.

"You're growing up," he said huskily. "Very well. Find your uncle and then come home."

Despite everything, I had to laugh. "You've got the hard part. You have to explain everything to Mother face-to-face."

"And I can't even see so I can duck," he said, and rubbed his head as if he were already feeling Mother's hand.

CHAPTER | XXVIII

When the storm had broken and the wagon trains could make it up to camp, Father tried once again to convince me to leave. But it just didn't seem right somehow.

Kilroy examined me warily when I went to tell him of my decision. *"The deal is only for now. If you don't leave immediately, you forfeit the privilege. You sabe?"*

"You'd be a lot safer if you came with me," Sean said, as he leaned on his crutch.

"Where are you going?" I asked.

"Me ankle's been so slow to heal that me da's gotten me a transfer to the headquarters. I'll be below the snow line." At least Kilroy cared about his son that much.

Kilroy glanced at me self-consciously—as if embarrassed that anyone would know he had a tender spot—and then growled, *"You'll be someone else's problem then."*

I was tempted briefly; but how could I find Uncle Foxfire if I was based down there? *"No, I want to stay with my uncle's crew."*

There was a spark of respect in Kilroy's eyes. *"So be it,"* he declared.

Sean looked at me in disappointment. "Think. Change mind," he urged in the T'ang language.

"I have to find my uncle's body to ship home," I explained.

With Sean, though, there was no such thing as a simple explanation. "Put up marker. Marble. Carvings. Look nice." He shaped a square object with his hands.

I tried to ignore Kilroy, who was glancing suspiciously between Sean and me. I didn't want to resort to English in front of him. "If I don't, his spirit can't go home."

"That superstition," Sean said with immense self-assurance. "You superstitious?"

I felt almost as if he were weighing me on some scale. "I don't know," I admitted. "What if the superstitions really are true?"

Sean looked at me as if he, too, sensed the wide gulf

between us. Until then, it had seemed that there had been nothing that a common language and understanding could not bridge.

"You make mistake," he insisted.

It's funny how you remember someone who's died. You play over their conversations many times in your head, looking for nuances and shadings of feelings. All this time, I had felt a new notion tickling at the back of my mind; and I remembered that my uncle himself had been curious about the difference in working conditions between us and the westerners. Finding the answers to his questions was almost as important as finding his bones. Even if I could never tell him, I would still have the satisfaction of completing one of his tasks.

"You're probably right," I agreed. "But in the meantime, you could do a favor for me when you're in the headquarters."

"What?" Sean asked.

"I'd like to know the difference between the average T'ang man's wages and hours and a westerner's," I said, and waited for Sean to refuse.

Though he looked puzzled, he agreed. "I try. Maybe I can. Maybe I can't. It may take long time."

"*Speak English,*" Kilroy growled.

Sean turned to his father. "*If the lad changed his mind,*

you'd let him transfer down below, wouldn't you?" he asked.

"*I could do that,"* Kilroy agreed without hesitating.

I stared at Sean, unsure of what to say to him and uncomfortable of that fact. "*Good luck,"* I said to Sean.

He looked just as uneasy. "*And you."*

I saw Father off; he rode away on a wagon, looking like a small, frail bundle. And for a moment, I almost thought I should escort him down to the city; but then how would I get back to find Uncle?

So I stayed; and when I was well enough, I went back to work. And when I could, I searched for Uncle Foxfire; and I was pleased when the crew volunteered to help. It made up for the fact that Kilroy wouldn't give us any official time to look because we were still behind schedule. In fact, he was downright surly about it, as if he thought I was asking for an unusual favor. As a result, the crew had to use their Sundays to search, but we found nothing in the snow.

In desperation, the westerners began using a new type of explosive, blasting oil or nitroglycerine, on our tunnel and another stubborn one. Though it worked better than black powder, sometimes not all of it went off, but remained smeared on one of the rocks. Of course, it was impossible to see this in the dim light.

Curly lost two toes when his pickax struck a rock that still had some residual oil on it. I was cut by flying chips and my cheek would bear the mark for the rest of my life. At that, we were the lucky ones. More than one T'ang man was blown up.

When the spring thaw came and we could see the sky above the cabins once again, we still hadn't completed the tunnel. Much to my frustration, Kilroy said we would still have to hunt on our own free time. By then the movements of the snow or the spring runoff or even wild animals could have scattered Uncle's remains all over the slope.

It made me feel sad, and there were even times when I felt frantic that I couldn't keep my promise. I worried that his ghost would have to stay in this wilderness. He would be a guest in death as he had been in life.

Sometimes a teamster or survey crew would find the remains of someone, and they would bring him back. From the shreds of clothing or other clues, though, I always knew it wasn't Uncle Foxfire.

However, there were a lot of victims from that winter whom they did not find. We weren't even sure how many, because there had been other camps toiling in the snow.

Spring passed into summer. I had begun to memorize

the mountain slopes. There was still about a meter of snow in the higher parts of the mountains, though it had melted at the lower elevation.

By now our camp had some two thousand T'ang men, besides the hundreds of westerners. There were so many men that they couldn't build enough cabins for them all, but set up tents. The tunnel itself was finally nearing completion. Crews at the point swore that they could hear the other crew hammering from the other side. With the tunnel nearly finished, the bosses drove us even harder, forcing us to work longer and longer hours as the days themselves grew longer. Of course, daylight meant little inside the tunnel; but there was plenty to do outside now. In some spots, paths had to be cut along the cliff side from the last tunnel. In others, the slope had to be graded. Sometimes the bosses kept us there long after the sun had set. As long as there was enough twilight to see your hand, we worked.

Naturally, the resentment kept building in camp. Finally, one day in early summer when we had been let off work, we found Packy reading in the cabin. As we trooped inside, he set his newspaper down. "It's about time," he grumbled. "I've kept your supper warming so long, it's gotten as hard as your heads."

"Blame Kilroy," Dandy said, and put his hands behind him, in the small of his back. "It's already night outside. You can see the stars."

I was dying for something to read. "Was that a new San Francisco newspaper you were reading?"

"An old one. But you got that." Packy nodded to an envelope. "It was inside the cabin."

I picked it up. "Who's it from?"

Packy poured water from the great kettle into a bucket so we could begin washing. "I don't know. Someone slipped it under the door."

The letter was from Sean, and it said:

> *Miss the talk and miss the chow. Here's the information*
> *you wanted. I asked a teamster to bring this to you.*

It was a surprise to learn what the western crews earned. Each westerner earned thirty-five dollars a month while we earned only thirty; and the railroad paid for their food as well while we had to pay out of our own pockets. Moreover, it was official company policy that no one should work in the tunnels for more than eight western hours at a time—a policy that was applied to westerners but not T'ang crews.

When I read it to the crew, Dandy did some figuring.

"When you deduct the charges for food, we make a third as much."

Honker was waiting patiently on his bunk for his turn to wash. Though it was hot now, he wore his scarf against the dust. "It kind of sticks like a bone in your throat, doesn't it?" he asked. By now, I could understand even his scarf-muffled words. "I mean, we do all the dirty work."

Curly glanced at me and then said, "And all the dangerous jobs. Like when they want to stop an avalanche."

"When we were at Cape Horn," a wispy little voice said, "Kilroy didn't even try to ask his western crews." The voice sounded raspy, as if it had not been used in a long time. We all turned to see; it was Shaky. His head nodded up and down constantly as he spoke the only words I had ever heard from him. "He came to my crew. We were all young and fresh off the boat. What did we know?" He looked around the cabin. "We wound up dangling over a cliff in a basket, swaying on a rope while we hammered away with a chisel, with only the basket bottoms between us and a fall into forever. And sometimes after we packed the holes and lit the fuses, the fuses were too short or the crew took too long to haul us up. We were lucky if there was enough to bury. Even when the rest of my crew was dead, he kept ordering me to go over. Remember. Someone please remember."

We stared in astonishment as Shaky lapsed into his usual silence; but he was lost now in his own terrifying memories, and the nodding of his head changed into a gentle rocking of his whole torso.

With a sigh, Bright Star started to strip. "The westerners' history books will write about what a big hero Kilroy was."

"And us?" Dandy asked.

As the headman, Bright Star got to wash first. When he rose from the bucket, his face was scarlet from the hot water. "They're their history books. And the T'ang historians won't care a thread what happens in this barbaric land."

"So no one will know about Shaky or Squeaky or Foxfire?" Curly had stripped off his shirt, exposing skin that was bronze-red around his neck and wrists and hands.

"And you're underpaid and overworked to boot." Bright Star looked up from his washing. "Foxfire complained; and look what it got him."

What did it get him? An ungrateful nephew who thought he didn't complain enough—and yet a nephew whom he loved enough to sacrifice his own life for. So I asked myself what my uncle would have done, and I

realized he would not have have just sat on this information. He would have let everyone know.

"At least he didn't stay quiet. If you keep silent, then
you lose by default. Even if it won't go into the history
books, we can let the other crews know what a rotten
deal we've got." I got out my writing things. Back home,
important news was put on a placard and posted in some
prominent place. "I'll write out the information in T'ang
words on a placard and post it where people can read
it—maybe near a tea barrel. The more folk who know,
the better."

Smiling tolerantly, Bright Star dried his hands on a
clean rag. "Shrimp will tear it down."

"Then I'll write as many as I can." Determined, I
counted the sheets of paper. "I only have six sheets.
Could I buy more from you?"

At first, I thought he was going to find some other
fault with my scheme; but some sudden impulse seemed
to seize him, and he headed for his bunk. "I think I have
a dozen sheets."

I laughed. "My hand will get worn out after the first
dozen."

Bright Star opened his box. "Then I'll just have to
help you do it. That way we can circulate them among
the crews as well. What was that information again?"

Apparently some of my uncle's unselfish spirit had spread to him.

"Wait." With a hop, Curly pulled himself up to his bunk. Ever the gambler, he said, "Let's increase those odds. I think I have another ten sheets."

Honker's scarf dropped away from his mouth as he began to rummage around in his basket. "I'd like to see Shrimp wear himself out running around trying to tear down all the placards."

Dandy spread his arms. "And those who can't write can post the placards."

Packy turned to his bottomless trunk. "You can use rocks as hammers, but you'll need nails."

As I wrote, I couldn't help wishing that Uncle could be there to see this moment. It wasn't just work binding the crew together now, but an idea.

After about an hour, we had used up all the paper and even some boards; but the next morning we had the satisfaction of hearing the crews talk about our placards. It was all you heard on the way to work. And it was still on everyone's tongue when we returned in the twilight to our cabins.

Feeling rose so high that Shrimp spoke to Kilroy. Kilroy wasn't a fool. He could see the resentful looks that we shot at him; and even if he didn't know what the obscene gestures meant, he could guess their significance.

He must have spoken to his bosses, because a week later I had another note from Sean:

> *Still miss the talk and the chow. What did you do up there? Strobridge is burning up the telegraph wires to San Francisco.*

A few days after that, Shrimp went around the camp grandly proclaiming that the westerners would offer us each five dollars more each month.

"But," as Bright Star pointed out, "that still doesn't bring us up to the salary of the westerners, because we still have to pay for our own food."

"I'd settle for having the westerners honor their own policy," Curly grumbled. "Four hours in the tunnels instead of six, or even seven." He meant T'ang hours, of course, which were twice a western hour.

If anything, the small pay raise only increased the indignation of the camp. Feeling built in the camp until one Saturday afternoon. We were outside grading the slope on one of those days when the heat just bounced off the rocks and drinking tea never satisfied your thirst. It just changed the dust coating your throat into mud.

Doggy was singing a tune somehow, despite all the

dust. By now, the months of practice had made his voice true and strong, so it was as much a pleasure as his moon guitar had been. He had even started to talk about a career in the theater after he was done here.

He had begun a song about a woman at home wondering about her husband overseas. The melody alone was enough to make the tears flow in any guest, but the lyrics were so sad and poignant that it was impossible not to cry. "At night I dream you're holding me," he sang in a sweet, lilting voice.

I had rolled my sleeves up while I worked. Now I jerked one down on my forearm so I could use it to wipe my eyes. I couldn't help wondering if the Lion Rock lady wept for my uncle.

"But when I wake, I can't find you," he went on.

"Quit that caterwauling. Save your breath for digging," Kilroy said mechanically.

It was no worse than a hundred things he had said before; however, tempers were running as high as the heat; and it did not help any that we now knew just how underpaid we were.

So, slowly lowering his shovel, Doggy lifted his head and went on with the next line. "Come home like the wind from the sea." His voice grew clearer and sharper. "Come home, come home to me."

"I'll teach you to listen." Despite the heat, Kilroy wore a knee-length duster coat. He pulled it back now to display the coiled whip hanging from his belt.

To my surprise, Bright Star set his own shovel blade against the gravel. *"He sing. Time go fast-fast."*

Kilroy was growing irritated. *"If you worked, time would go by even faster."*

Bright Star rested his hands on the shovel handle. *"Our shift over long time ago."*

Some could understand enough English to follow what was happening. Others could at least copy Bright Star's example. You could hear metallic clinks as shovel blades and pickaxes were dropped on the ground.

"I can make someone else headman." Kilroy started to look around.

Honker jerked his scarf down from his mouth. *"No."* And the rest of us echoed him. Narrowing his eyes, Kilroy backed up a few strides so he could keep all of us in front of him.

Over the last few months, I had often asked myself if I could achieve what neither my father nor Uncle Foxfire had done: win an argument with Kilroy. Taking a deep breath, I knew I had to try.

Attempting to keep from trembling, I lifted my pickax. At first, Kilroy smiled smugly, thinking that I was going to go back to work. However, when I set it on my shoulder and started toward the path leading to the camp, he looked stunned.

However, astonishment quickly gave way to anger. *"Where are you going?"* he demanded.

As I faced my monster, my heart felt like some animal racing around inside my rib cage. My uncle had been brave just to question his orders. *"The shift's over."*

When he stepped directly in front of me, I almost turned and ran. *"Stop,"* he ordered as if speaking to a dog, his hand hovering by his whip.

All the scars on my back began to itch; but I managed to keep from shaking. Instead, I made myself stare straight up at him—like a human instead of an animal. *"What are you going to do? Whip every one of us? Then who'll build your precious railroad when we're too hurt to work?"*

A muscle on his cheek twitched, and I expected to feel the lash. He looked at me angrily—but I think a little guiltily too.

Then I heard the sound of footsteps on the gravel. *"That right,"* Bright Star said from behind me.

One by one the rest of the crew joined me. Perhaps, I thought, if they had backed up my uncle as they were doing for me at that moment, Father would never have been blinded; and many T'ang men would have been spared injury and even death.

"This is for you, Father," I whispered, and raised my foot. It seemed forever to take that first step away from Kilroy, and then the next and the third. It was the longest three meters of my life. All the while I could feel the ferocious intensity of his gaze; but something—amazement or guilt or even fear—stayed his whip hand. Finally I heard the crew's boots following me. I felt warm inside and sad at the same time. I just wished Uncle Foxfire could have been here. He would have been so proud.

"Come on." I beckoned to Keg Mouth's crew who were next to us. "The shift's over."

A boy looked up. He had allowed the hair to grow on the crown and sides of his head, so it took me a moment to recognize Brush. "Kilroy hasn't told us to quit, though," he said and raised a foot to point at him.

"We're on T'ang time, not on western time." I felt so giddy that I could have laughed.

Brush hesitated and then grinned. "It'd be nice to have supper before dark." He swung his shovel up to his shoulder but glanced at Keg Mouth for approval.

"Come on," I called to Keg Mouth. "Are you on T'ang time or western time? My crew will have bathed and eaten while you're still sweating up here."

Keg Mouth put on a mock scowl. "And where would

the justice be in that?" Raising his pickax, he let the shaft slide through his hand until the head rested on his fist. "I'm on T'ang time too."

Laughing like schoolboys on a holiday, the rest of his crew shouldered their tools as well. As they fell in with my crew, they called to the others.

Kilroy just stood there shouting helplessly as little streams of men flowed down the mountainsides to merge into a regular river of men that poured right into camp.

CHAPTER | XXIX

E ven after we had bathed and eaten, we were too
excited about what we had done to go to sleep.
There was a festival atmosphere everywhere in
the camp. We had time to rest our backs, write letters,
visit one another, play some dominos. Soon the headmen
were palavering about a possible strike.

Since the next day was a Sunday anyway, we got to eat
a leisurely breakfast. On Sundays, the western butchers
killed fresh chickens and pigs. Instead of salted and pickled foods, we could have real roast meat, even barbecue.

With the air already filled with the smells of the different feasts, the conversation naturally turned to food.
Each member of the crew had an elaborate menu planned
for his welcome-home banquet—as if he had reflected
upon the topic and embellished it for years. The dishes
ranged from the exotic to favorite but ordinary fare.

"And once I'm done eating," Curly insisted as he shoveled another mouthful of rice into his mouth, "I'm going to build a house three stories high—just like the ones in San Francisco."

Bright Star looked up from the board on which he was writing the notes of last evening's strike meeting. Later, it would be posted in the middle of the camp, where everyone could read it or have it read to him. "And it'll be a beacon for every bandit in the district."

"So invest in the arts," Doggy urged. "When I go home, I'm going to build a theater and put on plays." Doggy's face shone as he pictured it in his own mind. "Produced by Doggy. Written by Doggy. Starring . . . ?" He raised an eyebrow toward the rest of the crew.

Bright Star consulted a scrap of paper. "Let me guess. Doggy?" He began writing again. "You'll be mooching off us in a month."

As the others ate, each chatted about his own plans—and in each Bright Star managed to find a flaw. I never heard a more misplaced name, since he was the gloomiest fellow; but then he was already in his forties.

"Me—I'm going to invest in something steady when I go home," Noodles announced as he ate. "Everyone needs to eat. I'll open a restaurant. I already have the name picked out." He shaped the sign with his hands. "Fat Is Happy."

We all waited for Bright Star to find something wrong with the scheme; but he simply hummed a tune as he went on writing.

It was Curly who was the first to give in. "Well, what's wrong with Noodles's scheme?"

"Nothing."

"Nothing?" Even Noodles was startled.

Bright Star jabbed his brush toward Noodles. "We're just going to hold all our reunions at your restaurant. And naturally since you're such a good fellow, it'll be 'all you can eat.'"

"I'll go broke for sure." Noodles gave a mock groan.

"We've heard from everyone but Otter," Honker said through his scarf.

As the others urged me to speak, I set down my empty bowl. "My uncle had a dream of making the Middle Kingdom strong. But now I know that it can't be strong until we are. What we're doing here today is the first step."

Bright Star crossed his legs. "Back home, when a man passes the government exams, he calls everyone else who passed his classmate. And it doesn't matter if that other fellow is ten years younger or fifty years older. He's a classmate."

"We've certainly gone through some hard schooling."

Curly grinned at the rest of the crew.

"We shouldn't work," I said, "until we get decent wages and working conditions."

"Well, I say let's spread the lessons, classmates," Dandy urged, and we divided the camp into sections, with each of us assigned to one.

While Bright Star went off to a meeting with the other headmen, we circulated through the camp, joining the various groups who were discussing the strike. As it happened, the first group I wound up with included Keg Mouth's crew.

"We got away with today because Strobridge and his hoodlums weren't around," Brush said. "But they'd be up here if we struck."

Among the group, I saw men nodding their heads as if they, too, were afraid of being whipped and beaten.

"If we can stay united, they're the ones who will be helpless," I told Brush. "They can't injure too many workers, because that will put them behind schedule as surely as a strike."

"That's right," someone else said.

Encouraged, I went on. "And what if they did try to beat us? How many of them are there? And how many of us? Their arms would wear out before they could finish."

Brush cheered up. "Or we'd take their pickax handles away and show them how a proper drubbing's done."

It didn't take much more talking to screw up their courage. By the time I left, they were shouting, "Strike! Strike!"

With arguments like that, the crew and I bolstered the others. By Sunday evening, the strike was official. We wanted the westerners to hold the workday to four T'ang hours or eight western ones in the tunnel, five T'ang hours or ten western ones in the open. We wanted five dollars a month more (which still wouldn't bring us up to the westerners' subsidized wages, but it would help). And we wanted the right to not be whipped and beaten, and to leave if we wanted to.

On Monday when no one went to work, Strobridge's hoodlums swaggered into camp, raking their pickax handles over log walls or poking at canvas tent sides as they ordered us to come out. Out of the cabins and tents surged the crews to form an army, three thousand strong.

Strobridge's hoodlums tried to bluster and threaten; but no one left the camp. I thought the westerners might next try to take a couple of men and make examples of them as Kilroy had of me; but I think for the first time they realized that there were three thousand of us and only a few dozen of them. Cursing and swearing, they skulked away.

The next assault came from Shrimp. He went everywhere, pleading, threatening, whining; but the crews just laughed at him. As he stormed away in a rage, he happened to catch sight of me as I visited Keg Mouth's crew. "I know you had a hand in this. I should have kicked you off the mountain the moment I laid eyes on you. You make as much trouble as your uncle did."

"Really?" I couldn't help smiling in surprise.

"You needn't be so pleased," he snapped. "It wasn't meant as a compliment."

"But that's the way you should take it." Keg Mouth chuckled.

I gave Shrimp a mock bow. "In fact, it's something to be proud of." But when I looked up again, he was already gone. The rest of that day, I basked in the warm glow his words had given me.

Later the westerners themselves came to the edge of our camp to harangue our headmen, but they didn't try to come inside. When even that failed, a delegation of bosses led by Strobridge sat down to negotiate with our strike committee.

In the meantime we had dispatched men to carry word to the other camps, to the some twelve thousand

T'ang men in camps across the mountains and down in the desert. To our disappointment, though, the other camps lacked the spark or the nerve that drove our camp. The difference, I thought, was that they hadn't had a Foxfire inspiring them.

The next five days were heady times. During the first week of a revolution, everything seems possible. Finally, though, the big boss, Crocker himself, got worried and showed up.

That night, I had a dream. I was back at the pond where I had left Uncle Foxfire, except that it was spring and everything had thawed. He was standing near the waterfall in a patch of wildflowers so thick that they hid his ankles. When I shouted to him, he smiled and beckoned for me to join him.

The air, however, became as thick as glue. Each step was a struggle. By the time I traveled a few meters, I was panting and sweating. All this time, Uncle Foxfire had continued to encourage me with waves of his hand.

I tried to reach him. I tried until my lungs burned like fire and my arms and legs became numb. Suddenly my whole body began to tingle until my skin started to itch and my bones to ache.

"What's happening?" I tried to ask Uncle Foxfire, but even shaping the words was now too much of an effort.

Uncle Foxfire went on smiling and waving unconcernedly.

When I stumbled, the fall seemed to take forever. The rocks beneath me suddenly became as sharp as fangs, and I waited for the awful pain. However, when I thudded against the slope, I felt nothing.

I tried to move my legs and felt myself thump against something with a loud crack. When I glanced to the side, I saw that I had broken a boulder in half. Hovering above the fragments was a long, green thing like a vine.

Then I realized the green, vinelike thing was a tail. My eyes followed the tail to a long, green body with paws. I arched my back to see more and found—much to my shock—that the tail belonged to me.

I checked again. No, the tail and paws were mine. I surged easily up the slope now, but Uncle Foxfire was gone. Leaning over the pond, I looked at my reflection upon the calm water. When I saw the green snout and great eyes and long teeth, I reared back in surprise.

At the same time, the reflection of the creature also curved upward.

"I'm a dragon," I said in awe and wonder. I spread out my wings. "I'm a dragon," I cried louder, and my voice echoed around the stony bay. "I'm a dragon—and I'm free."

And with a kick of my legs and a flap of my wings,

I rose into the air in a leap without end.

I don't remember any more of the dream; but I was sorry when I had to wake up the next morning. As I lay there, I thought that Uncle Foxfire had sent me that dream to make me feel better. I had passed through my own Dragon's Gate. I'd saved the camp. I thanked him for sending that message to me; but it didn't make me feel any happier. I still had to find his bones.

When I finally sat up, Noodles was complaining about breakfast, which was only last night's cold rice and lukewarm tea. "I can't help it." Packy defended himself. "Crocker's cut off our food."

"We paid for it already," Noodles protested.

"But it has to come on his railroad." Packy shrugged.

Each of us considered that in silence. Noodles got his half bowl of rice. "How far away is San Francisco anyway?"

Bright Star poured himself a cup of tea. "It's a long, long way. And home is even farther away."

Doggy gloomily helped himself to tea and slurped it noisily. "And it's not like we could stroll out of the mountains either. We need the westerners' help."

"We don't have any food without them," Packy said. "So you'd starve to death long before you left the mountains."

"They need us more than we need them," I argued, "and they want us alive so they can't afford to let us starve."

While the rest of us tried to encourage the other crews, Bright Star left to discuss the latest developments with the other headmen.

In my assigned area of the camp, I found that everyone was afraid. I can't say that I blamed them. We were a long, long way from our own kind and safety, and Crocker had found our weak point. Discouraged, I returned to the cabin to find the others had met the same reaction.

Shrimp himself came by to gloat. "You see what your talk's done? You've done nothing but single yourselves out for every hard, dirty job on this railroad."

But I had sensed a strength that could sweep across oceans and achieve all of Father and Uncle's dreams, if I could learn how to sustain it. "Bring on the work. I'm ready."

"And so are his classmates," Doggy said.

"That's right," Dandy growled.

Shrimp opened and closed his mouth several times, as if he could not decide what to say. Loyalty and trust were concepts that he just did not comprehend. "Bah, you idiots belong together," he muttered, and stalked away.

When Bright Star returned from the meeting of the

headmen, we could already tell from his angry expression that the news wasn't good. "I argued and hollered, but the others are scared."

Curly waved off a fly. "So when do we go back to work?"

"Tomorrow morning." Bright Star held up a package. "But I managed to trade for some food."

Since the strike seemed over and there was nothing else to be done, I got up. "May I have mine now? I'm going to look for Uncle Foxfire."

Bright Star handed the package to Packy. "I don't know if it's such a good idea to go out looking today. There are westerners about."

I got my coat. "What are they going to do? Whip me? They've already done their worst to me—short of hanging me. And Kilroy would never lose a worker if he could help it. Besides, they don't want to antagonize the camp just when they have the strike broken."

"Some of the demon crews from the *Union Pacific* might make their own plans," Bright Star warned. "I heard they set an explosive trap for one of the advance T'ang crews. They killed a couple of boys." The *Union Pacific* was the rival railroad laying tracks on the other side of the mountains.

I'd heard the same rumors about that incident. "It's

said they didn't try it again after the T'ang crews set up explosive traps for them. And it was far away from here. I'll be fine." I walked over to Packy. "So what about some supper?"

Packy began to open the package. "Ah, pork. I'll slice it up with some dried vegetables and put it on top of some rice. I can bring it up to you."

Doggy swung his legs out of his bunk. "While you're at it, bring my share up there too."

When the rest of the crew joined in, I looked at them gratefully. "I appreciate it, classmates." Not everyone would have risked the wrath of the westerners.

Doggy hovered over Bright Star. "What about you, headman?"

Bright Star took the lantern from where it hung on the wall. "Of course, I'm going. You children would get yourselves lost between here and the next ocean."

We hunted in all the likely spots again and some of the unlikely ones too. By prearrangement with Packy, we met by the pond where I had left Uncle Foxfire.

We had our supper up there as dusk fell. All around us, the mountain ranges loomed like the waves of some endless black sea that had frozen in place, and we were just little insects floating on a leaf. For a moment, it all seemed so hopeless.

Then, as I looked down the slope into the darkness, I saw a light wink in the distance. It shone with bright promise, like a star that had fallen from the sky. As I watched, another light sprang to life. And then a third, and then another. I realized they were lighting lanterns in the camp.

The lights spread across the slope until the side of the mountain burned like a fiery patch. And then in the distance I saw a dot of light wink into existence. I figured that it must be another camp. It was so small that it didn't seem possible that it could represent thousands of men. My eyes followed the dark mountain range as it stretched to the horizon. And still farther away in the distance, I saw another speck of light.

That's all we are, I thought to myself, just fireflies trying to stay alive in the dark. Like Father. Like Mother. Like Sean. Like Uncle. It made me aware of just how fragile and precious each life was. And how we had to do everything in our power to protect it.

The others had gathered a short distance away to discuss something in low voices. In the twilight, they looked almost like shadows; and then Bright Star struck a match. "You know, Otter," he said, "we may never find your uncle's remains." Honker moved the dangling ends of his scarf away from the lantern before he raised the glass chimney to expose the lantern's wick.

"I know. Thank you for helping me look for him." The moment had arrived when I would have to come to a decision. And I thought back to that time—it seemed ages ago—when I had first asked to come to America. Even back then, Uncle had been warning me to live my own life.

Suddenly I saw a rocket whiz into the air and explode like a giant flower. Down below, from the western side of the camp, I began hearing popping noises. "What's happening? Are the westerners shooting?"

Bright Star shook out the match after he had lit the wick and lowered the glass chimney to protect the tiny flame. "It's the Fourth of *July*. Today is the day *America* declared its independence. They always shoot off fireworks and guns."

We watched as more rocket flowers boomed into life in the night sky, the flashes brightly lighting up the crew's faces for a moment. They were smiling as happily as children.

I felt just as young as they. "Kilroy and Strobridge must be going crazy at all the black powder being wasted." I laughed.

Streamers of light flashed into life in the middle of smoky veils. "What will you do if you can't find your uncle?" Bright Star asked.

Behind us, I could hear the rushing sound of the waterfall, and finally I thought I began to understand the real message of last night's dream: This was my true gate, not the climb up the mountain. Uncle Foxfire had despised public opinion and hadn't wanted it to trap me in the Middle Kingdom. He would want even less for me to chain myself here for the very same reason.

I remembered his advice when I had failed my first test of courage: I could learn to change things or go on being changed by events. That was the real point of coming to America. He would want me to become like him and not remain like the others—even if it meant he had to stay here forever. "My uncle wouldn't want me to waste my life up here."

The fireworks forgotten, Bright Star and the others stared at me. You would have thought I had confessed to dining on Uncle Foxfire. If it had been their uncle, they would have felt the same sacred obligation to find him that I had—even though the task was virtually impossible.

Uncle Foxfire had been right: You can't help what other people make of you. "I tried," I told them, "and that's all he would have asked of me."

For once, Doggy was speechless. It took Bright Star a while before he could voice their thoughts. "But he'll never be able to go home," he protested. "You said so yourself."

Poor Uncle. First he had given up his life. Now he would have to give up his chance of going home. Pivoting on my heel, I took one last look. The water seemed as black as ink except where it foamed among the rocks as it fell. It was lovely in its own harsh way—like my uncle. "There are worse places to be." The words came hard, but I said them.

Then, as the others continued to stand in stunned silence, I started back down the slope toward camp. There were other things I could do to honor Uncle Foxfire's memory—like carrying on the Great Work. As I strolled down toward the fireworks, I knew that he would want me to go on.

CHAPTER | XXX

May 10, 1869.
Promontory Point, Utah.

I n the late summer of 1867, we finally finished the tunnel; but I took little satisfaction in driving a hole straight through the heart of the Tiger. Two years later, in the spring, we had taken the railroad into the deserts of the place the westerners call *Utah*; and I had filled up several notebooks with observations, plans and ideas.

I didn't look up when I heard the cheering begin. Doggy and Honker were on a wagon, standing on tiptoe and trying to get a better peek. "We're too far away," Doggy complained. "I can't see a thing."

Instead, I began to reread Father's last letter. I recognized Uncle Blacky's scholarly hand; I suppose Father had dictated it to him. I read quickly the gossipy part about how the Lion Rock lady had become quite the professional widow. She wore nothing but the white of mourning—always of the finest silk—and never missed a chance to remind everyone that Uncle Foxfire had died saving everyone's life. The local magistrate had even started a subscription to build a memorial gate eventually as a testament to her virtue. Everyone was convinced that she herself had hatched the idea and that the magistrate would take a hefty cut out of the building funds.

"Your mother," Father wrote, "spoils me so much that I never have a moment's peace. Now that she's bribed all the Manchus to forget what happened, won't you help your poor father by coming home and assuming your fair share of her attention?

"The Manchus are taxing everything in sight, so they're in even worse odor than usual. There's even a cynical little song—done to the tune of 'How Blessed We Are'—making the rounds of the village that says that perhaps more Manchus should meet with 'accidents.' I even caught your mother singing it the other day. You'll find yourself quite the hero when you return. Make it soon."

Folding up the letter and putting it away, I walked over to a bare patch of dirt among the weeds. From the volume of cheering, I figured that the westerners must have driven the final spike.

"They say the spike's pure gold," Curly said from his perch on another wagon.

"It's not fair." Sean was bursting with indignation. I turned to see him wearing a frock coat and derby. He still had a limp because he had never quite recovered from his fall. *"You've got as much right to be there as anyone."*

I began dragging my heel through the dirt. *"They can have their little ceremony. We know the truth."*

He rubbed his nose, which was peeling from the desert sun. *"After our little jaunt on the mountain, Mr. Strobridge took an interest in me. Now he says he wants to help me go to school so I can become an engineer."*

I was glad for Sean. I hopped into the air and began drawing my heel along once again. *"Do you want to?"*

He had to talk louder because I was farther away. *"We did build quite a railroad."*

I gave a hop and backed up in a different direction. *"We did."*

"And what will you be doing? Is it home for you?" Sean started toward me.

I raised a hand for him to stop. *"Not yet. My uncle had high hopes for this country. I'd like to see if he was right."*

Sean scratched his head in puzzlement. *"What're you doing?"*

"Climb up on a wagon if you're curious." I pointed.

Sean clambered awkwardly into the back of the wagon. The others turned and stared. "Well, well," Packy said.

I gave a leap so that I wouldn't cross over anything that I had done. The rest of the crew began climbing on the piles of wooden ties. Sean held out to me a hand that was brown from the sun and as tough as leather, though it wasn't quite as brown as mine. He had been stationed at the headquarters, but he hadn't been inside much. I never asked him how he had gotten that information on the contracts.

When he had hauled me up beside him, I noticed that my friend was a head taller and twenty kilos heavier than before. This close to him, I also saw that he had begun to sprout a beard. We had both grown up building a path for the firewagon.

Ever curious, Sean pointed at words I had written with my heel in the dirt. *"Those are Chinese words, aren't they?"*

"Yes," I said, and faced the dark-colored hills. Beyond them were the mountains where Uncle Foxfire was.

"But what do they say?" Sean persisted.

I said, *"I won't forget."* It was a statement. It was a promise.

AFTERWORD

This novel was begun over twenty years ago, at the same time as my novel *Dragonwings*; but it has taken this long for it to find its proper form.

Though the novel is a work of fiction, I did not make up the working conditions and dangers the workers faced. It is a matter of record that avalanches swept away crews; and there are no accurate statistics on how many Chinese died in other ways. However, it is estimated that twelve hundred Chinese—or 10 percent of the Chinese work force—perished building the railroad. In any event, ten tons of bones were finally shipped back to China. There are no figures on injuries.

I need to emphasize that the strike was real. Almost all the newspapers of the time ignored the strike; or if they mentioned it at all, they acknowledged only the monetary demands. One correspondent even made fun of the Chinese workers' desire for an eight-hour working day in the tunnels. However, on July 1, 1867, the Sacramento *Union* stated that among other conditions, the strikers wanted "to deny the right of the overseers of the company to either whip or to restrain them from leaving the railroad when they desire to seek other employment."

This novel could not have been finished without the help of many people over two decades. First of all, I want to thank the long-suffering librarians of the Bancroft, San Francisco Public, and Sutro libraries. Next I want to acknowledge Candy Clark for providing me with maps and information about the Sierras so I could see parts of it for myself. Marilou Sorensen went beyond the bounds of kindness when she took me to Promontory Point though she was recovering from pneumonia; and the rangers at the Golden Spike National Historic Site could not have been more cooperative or helpful. Moreover, I would be remiss if I did not express my gratitude to Dr. Earl Bruce of the Reno Historical Museum for sharing his labors at the microfilm reader.

The following are some of the works that I have consulted:

Newspapers from the period, including the Stockton *Independent*, the Sacramento *Union* and the San Francisco *Daily Chronicle* and *Daily Alta California*.

Beebe, Lucius. *The Central Pacific and the Southern Pacific Railroads.* Berkeley, Cal.: Howell-North, 1963.

Best, Gerald. *Snowplow.* Berkeley, Cal.: Howell-North, 1966.

Chinn, Thomas, H. Mark Lai, and Philip Choy, eds. *A History of the Chinese in California.* San Francisco: Chinese Historical Society, 1969.

Chiu, Ping. *Chinese Labor in California.* Madison, Wis.: University of Wisconsin, 1963.

Griswold, W. S. *A Work of Giants.* New York: McGraw-Hill, 1962.

Kraus, George. *High Road to Promontory.* New York: Castle Books, 1969.

McCague, James. *Moguls and Iron Men.* New York: Harper, 1964.

Mayer, Lynne Rhodes, and Kenneth E. Vose. *Makin' Tracks.* New York: Praeger, 1975.

Nordhoff, Charles. *C.P.R.R.* Kimball, Col.: Outbooks, 1976, reprint of 1882 edition.

Reinhardt, Richard. *Out West on the Overland Train.*
Secaucus, N.J.: Castle, 1967.

Riegel, Robert Edgar. *The Story of the Western Railroads.*
Lincoln, Neb.: University of Nebraska Press, 1964.

Signor, John R. *Donner Pass.* San Marino, Cal.: Golden
West Books, 1985.

Stewart, George R. *Donner Pass.* Menlo Park, N.J.: Lane
Books, 1964.

Utley, Robert, and Francis Ketterson, Jr. *Golden Spike.*
Washington: National Park Service, 1969.

Williams, John Hoyt. *A Great and Shining Road.* New
York: Times Books, 1988.

Yenne, Bill. *The History of the Southern Pacific.* New York:
Bonanza Books, 1985.

Two-time Newbery Honor author

LAURENCE YEP

delivers an extraordinary new novel in the acclaimed
Golden Mountain Chronicles saga

The Traitor

In 1885, tension is spreading like wildfire between
the American miners and their Chinese rivals in
the small mining town of Rock Springs in the
Wyoming Territory. As the groups plunge toward a
bloody confrontation, two young outcasts—one white,
one Chinese American—forge an unexpected friendship. While others may call them traitors, their bond
continues to grow until a terrible day when the boys
must use everything they have learned together to save
themselves and their families.

Based on actual events, *The Traitor* is a powerful,
haunting, and ultimately hopeful story about one of the
worst race riots in American history and a unique friendship that brings together two worlds.

■ HarperCollins *Children's Books*
www.harperchildrens.com